WALTZING ON THE DANUBE

WALTZING ON THE DANUBE

MIRANDA MACLEOD

Apple Blossom Press
Boston, MA

Waltzing on the Danube

Copyright © 2016 Miranda MacLeod

All rights reserved. No part of this publication may be reproduced, distributed, or transmitted in any form or by any means, including photocopying, recording, or other electronic or mechanical methods, without the prior written permission of the publisher or author, except in the case of brief quotations embodied in critical reviews and certain other noncommercial uses permitted by copyright law.

Find out more: www.mirandamacleod.com
Contact the author: miranda@mirandamacleod.com

ISBN-13: 978-1547121281

This is a work of fiction. Any resemblance of characters to actual persons, living or dead, is purely coincidental.

Apple Blossom Press
PO Box 547
Bolton MA 01740

ABOUT THE AUTHOR

Originally from southern California, Miranda now lives in New England and writes heartfelt romances and romantic comedies featuring witty and charmingly flawed women that you'll want to marry. Or just grab a coffee with, if that's more your thing. She spent way too many years in graduate school, worked in professional theater and film, and held temp jobs in just about every office building in downtown Boston. It's no wonder she finds writing a reliable gig by comparison.

ALSO BY MIRANDA MACLEOD

Stand Alone Novels:

Telling Lies Online

Holly & Ivy (cowritten with T.B. Markinson)

Love's Encore Trilogy:

A Road Through Mountains

Your Name in Lights

Fifty Percent Illusion

Love's Encore Omnibus Collection

Americans Abroad Series (stand alone romances set across the globe):

Waltzing on the Danube

Holme for the Holidays

Stockholm Syndrome

Letters to Cupid

London Holiday

Check mirandamacleod.com for more about these titles, and for other books coming soon!

WALTZING ON THE DANUBE

ONE

"AND LAST BUT NOT LEAST, your private terrace." The porter whisked the curtains back as he spoke, drenching Eleanor's stateroom in sunlight. The massive French doors afforded her a floor-to-ceiling view not only of her secluded balcony, but of the Budapest skyline and sparkling Danube River that lay just steps beyond. "Will there be anything else, miss?"

"Nothing comes to mind." She uncrossed her slender arms and held out one hand, discreetly slipping a crisply folded ten euro note into the porter's palm as she gave it a firm shake.

"Enjoy your time aboard the *Danube Queen*, Ms. Fielding." He tucked the tip into his pocket with a deft, practiced motion. "If you require anything while aboard, your personal concierge is just a phone call away, night or day."

Eleanor bobbed her head in curt acknowledgment

as the porter retreated from her suite, then swiveled on her heels to take in the details of her surroundings, from the gleaming wood veneer of the paneled walls to the sleek lines of the Scandinavian furniture. Despite the soothing orderliness of her quarters, she remained hollow inside. The coming fortnight held little interest for her, an inconvenient interruption to her routine that provoked more anxiety than joy.

The cell phone in her pocket vibrated and Eleanor tensed, her heart racing as a shot of adrenaline burned through her veins. *Jesus, Eleanor. It's just the phone.* She drew a steadying breath as she reached into her pocket, irritated with her body's overreaction. Why did the most mundane things have to cause her to react like someone had just pulled the fire alarm?

"Hey, Big Sis! How's the ship?"

"It appears seaworthy." Eleanor struggled to maintain the disaffected tone that Miriam deserved. She'd sworn she would never forgive her for forcing her on this trip, but she couldn't help feeling a rush of affection at the sound of her sister's voice. "I doubt it will sink, unfortunately."

"*Stop being bitchy, Elle. You know you're going to have fun! How's the room?*"

Eleanor cradled the phone against her shoulder as she removed her shoes, scowling as one loafer landed on its side. "It's...hold on a second." She bent to arrange them perfectly perpendicular to the wall, toes pointing neatly to the center of the room. Satisfied with the result, she straightened up and shuffled across the sitting room, her feet sinking into the deep, woolly carpet. "It's fine."

"Fine? It's their most luxurious suite! For twenty thousand euros, I hope it's better than fine."

"It's top-notch, Mimi. Sylvia would've loved it." A chill settled over her at the memory of her faithless ex.

"Sylvia? Huh! Send me a picture and I'll post it to my wall. She can see it there and weep."

"Oh, Mimi. Why haven't you unfriended my ex-girlfriend yet? It's been over a year!"

"Keep your friends close and your enemies closer, Elle."

Eleanor snorted at her sister's melodramatic flair. "Enemies is a bit much." Sure, things had ended badly, but it wasn't all Sylvia's fault. Eleanor knew that when she was a nervous wreck it made her a difficult person to love. Which is why the last place she wanted to spend her first vacation in over a year was searching for love on a singles cruise.

"Did you get the gift basket?"

Eleanor glanced at the chic glass coffee table in the center of the room, spying the overflowing basket of fruit that graced its top. A half smile teased her lips. "Sure did! There's enough fruit there that I won't have to leave the room for breakfast the whole first week."

"Elle!"

She chuckled at her sister's frustration. "What? The less interaction I have with other passengers, the better."

"That's hardly the point of this trip, remember? Two hundred and fifty single women, Elle. And you haven't been on a date in an eternity. It wouldn't kill you to at least look around a little. Maybe smile at someone for once, and see what happens."

"We'll see. Look, I've gotta go. If you want me to make it to the meet and greet on time, I need to get ready."

"So you're gonna go?"

Eleanor rolled her eyes at the triumph in her sister's voice. "Settle down. I haven't decided yet." She ended the call before Miriam could argue.

She tucked the phone into her pocket and opened the bedroom door. The suite's sleeping quarters were even smaller than what she was used to in her Manhattan apartment, but it seemed spacious for a ship. Built-in nightstands topped with shining chrome lamps flanked either side of a large bed. A mirrored closet door stood closed along one wall, and Eleanor knew from the porter's spiel that her sparse wardrobe had already been unpacked and arranged inside it in anticipation of her arrival. It was a convenience, but the VIP treatment was mostly wasted on her. While she could afford a luxurious lifestyle as a matter of course, she rarely bothered with it except when trying to impress a girl. Miriam had chosen the Empire suite on her behalf, apparently aware that for her matchmaking plan to pay off, Eleanor would need all the help she could get.

Another mirrored door, this one opened wide, led to a well-appointed *ensuite* bathroom. Here, too, all was perfectly in order and sufficient for her needs. She might go so far as to call it nice, if she were to allow a moment of positivity to scrub some of the grit from her dour mood. But she was not so inclined. She wouldn't give Miriam that victory, at least not before sulking a little longer first. Uttering a tired sigh, she let her body sink into the feathery softness of the Egyptian cotton duvet.

The bed was festooned with an absurd number of pillows, all in shades of aqua and gold. The color scheme evoked memories of the Caribbean, where she'd spent her last vacation. That trip had been no more of her choosing than this one was. Sylvia had insisted. Eleanor had been content enough to go along with the idea after only minimal coaxing. Sylvia had had that effect on her, much to Eleanor's chagrin.

It was irrational how often she'd acquiesced to please that woman, but at the time she'd thought she was in love. Or something approximating it, anyway. *Some weak imitation of love*. According to Sylvia's parting words to her, that was all her damaged psyche would ever be capable of. Eleanor squeezed her eyes shut, trying to block out the pain of the memory but failing. Behind it were similar accusations from lovers long since past. It was a common thread running through her life that Eleanor could never get a handle on how to change.

She'd tried with Sylvia. God, how she'd tried. Eleanor would have been content to stay close to home most of the time. Sylvia had loved to travel the world, though she'd usually lacked the funds to go on her own. So Eleanor had paid—gladly, even. She'd found a certain thrill in treating her girlfriend to all the finer things in life that she seemed to enjoy so much. In retrospect Eleanor suspected that the plumpness of her bank account had been at least as attractive a quality to Sylvia as was her svelte, athletic frame. It hadn't been the first time a woman had stuck around for that reason until, inevitably, something better came along. That was another pattern that had become more obvious over the years.

I really should have seen it coming.

She'd expected the relationship to end eventually. They always did. She just hadn't realized it would happen so soon. For one thing, if she'd had an inkling of how close they'd been to their expiration date, she would never have booked this ridiculous cruise. Well, she hadn't booked this exact cruise, though that *would* have been ironic. Eleanor gave a mirthless chuckle at the thought of taking her ex on a cruise with two hundred and fifty single lesbians. It would have been like letting a toddler loose in a toy store. But Sylvia hadn't needed any help in finding someone new. Her wandering eye had done the job all on its own.

Eleanor rose from the bed and smoothed the wrinkles from the duvet, shaking her head. She really *should* have seen it coming. What good was being a genius at risk analysis if she could so easily be blindsided by something as obvious as a cheating girlfriend? Sylvia had left her for a flight attendant, for heaven's sake. *How cliché is that?* Eleanor gave the mattress top a final, fierce whack with the palm of her hand. A year later, it wasn't losing the girlfriend that bothered her so much as it was her lack of ability to predict it. She created forecasting models for a living. With what she'd learned about failed relationships over the years, she should have been able to build a model to predict their demise in her sleep.

The cruise company had been understanding about the whole thing, to a point. They'd credited the cost of the tickets toward a future cruise, and given her ample time to rebook. But as the deadline approached, Eleanor hadn't suffered any increase in her desire to travel, so she'd given the credit to Miriam to book a trip for herself and her husband Mark. Of course, Miriam had had a different idea. Meddling little sisters always knew how to throw a wrench in the works.

Eleanor trudged back to the sitting room of her suite, rummaging in the satchel she'd set near the door. She pulled out a folder and fanned through the pages her sister had printed for her. Six cities, fourteen days, and at least a hundred ways to die of awkwardness and social humiliation. *Thanks, Sis!*

Who even knew they offered river cruises catering to lesbian singles? Eleanor certainly wouldn't have guessed prior to this that anyone could have been cruel enough to devise such a torture. *There really should be laws against it.* Well, not laws against lesbian cruises, per se. To each their own, and all that. But laws against sisters who went behind your back and booked non-refundable tickets, and then applied ninja-level guilt tactics until their older sisters were forced to give in? She'd back legislation to rectify that injustice in a heartbeat.

Eleanor's last hope for reprieve had been that her boss would deny her vacation request. It was the type of thing he'd usually do without a second thought. But that, too, had been snatched away when the new head of HR decided that it was absolutely vital for employees to use their backlog of vacation days. For work-life balance. *Or some bullshit like that.*

So, here she was, stuck on a boat full to bursting with single women desperate to find true love. Poor saps. Did they have no comprehension of the odds? Didn't they know what a long shot it was? Maybe she'd stay in her room for the next few weeks and build that forecasting model, after all. Present it to them at the end of the cruise, a foolproof tool to assess how and when their new relationships would wither and die. It would make a thoughtful parting gift, much more useful than a fruit basket.

She kicked open the French door, wincing as her bare toe connected with its solid frame. There were two bistro chairs and a small table on the balcony, and

Eleanor grabbed the scrolled back of one of the chairs and dragged it far enough out to sit. She propped her bare feet up on the railing, not the most dignified pose, but she reveled in the feeling of defiance it gave her. This was her vacation, after all, and she would do as she pleased. No one could force her to go to a single one of the horrible events listed in that folder if she didn't want to.

And yet…

Eleanor cursed the churning in her gut as she eyed the folder. She pressed her lids shut and could picture page after page of full-color grids telling her where to be and what to do at every minute. The vision calmed her agitation. She thrived on schedules, craved the orderliness of them. It was one of the many quirks she'd developed for keeping the anxiety that plagued her at bay. The knowledge that the calendar on her phone was completely blank until late July was enough to make her weep. True, she'd rather eat a live squid than do a single thing on the cruise itinerary, but was it so much worse than drifting aimlessly on her own for fourteen days with no schedule at all? She shuddered at either prospect.

Snatching the folder from the table, she swiped the cover open to the first page and read. *Day One: Meet and Greet.* The schedule instructed her to report to the observation deck at three o'clock. Her eyes darted to her watch, hoping it was already past time, but she encountered no such luck. Characteristically ahead of schedule, she still had a full thirty minutes to make her way upstairs. Should she go and subject herself to a sea of wolfish women trolling for a holiday hookup? Her brain informed her that staying in her suite was a much better idea, but her body betrayed her. The involuntary tingle that coursed through her loins hinted that certain parts of her were of a different opinion on the matter.

What was it Miriam had said? *It couldn't hurt to look.* Perhaps she was right. After failing too many times, Eleanor wasn't interested in a relationship, but she wasn't a nun, either—though as an actuarial accountant, people did sometimes confuse her for one. Eleanor knew all the stereotypes that came with her chosen profession, that she was a frigid, humorless pencil pusher. She couldn't argue with humorless, but she took offense at the word frigid. She enjoyed sex as much as anyone, and it *had* been a long time. A casual fling wasn't entirely without merit. In the unlikely event that Eleanor found a willing partner, a two-week trip wasn't quite enough time for her usual foibles to drive someone new insane.

She stared at the schedule again and curled her upper lip in distaste. *Fine. I'll go—but only to prove once and for all what a mistake it is.* Stopping at the front door, she slipped her shoes on one by one, first the left and then the right, as she always did. For whatever inexplicable reason, it made her feel safe. Then she cursed herself for needing to do it, as if somehow the ritual of putting on shoes could influence anything. This self-loathing over it was hardly something new, though it never succeeded in changing her behavior. With a shake of her head, she jammed the folder into her satchel and, hoisting it to her shoulder, strode out the door and down the hall.

The observation deck was empty when she had arrived, though Eleanor wasn't surprised. She was terribly early. She always was. She spied a deck chair off to one side that seemed like a reasonable choice, partially hidden from view behind the rigging for a lifeboat. She sat down and slipped on a pair of sunglasses, valuing them less for their ability to shield her from the sun's rays than from the gaze of her fellow passengers.

You're always hiding. That's was another thing Sylvia had said to her the day she'd left, in addition to accusing her of using her nervous habits to shield herself from loving or being loved. It rang true. Falling in love was a risk that couldn't be calculated or controlled. In other words, it was precisely the type of risk that Eleanor couldn't take. It was against her nature to try.

Yet here she sat, waiting for—what? Not love. Lust, perhaps. Companionship, maybe. More likely, she'd just do something awkward and make a fool of herself before slinking away to her room. She exuded self-assurance in a boardroom, but was at her worst in forced social settings such as this. She balled her fists.

She'd have to remember to kill Miriam when she got home for putting her through this. She willed her muscles to unclench, then closed her eyes and practiced deep, cleansing breaths as she awaited the coming hordes.

TWO

"OH, SHIT!" Jeanie grimaced as she spotted the time on a clock by the dock. She needed to be on the observation deck for the meet and greet in fifteen minutes and she hadn't even made it on board the ship yet. The *Danube Queen*'s berthing location had changed since she'd printed her boarding documents and it had taken her an extra half an hour to find the new location. Jeanie was no stranger to running late, but she couldn't help but wonder why things couldn't have gone smoothly for once. Was it really necessary to kick off this once-in-a-lifetime vacation in full panic mode?

"Oh, shit, shit, shit!" The wheels of her massive suitcase rattled and bumped along the steel grate of the gangway as she ran. "Excuse me! Excuse me!" she shouted to a crew member who stared quizzically at her as she raced to the bottom of the deserted ramp.

The fact that he was in the middle of packing up the registration table drove home the point that she must be the last passenger to arrive. "Janine Brooks," she panted, wincing as her suitcase skidded to an abrupt stop against her bare calf. "Checking in for the cruise?" She shoved a wad of papers into his hand with the hope that her ticket and passport were hidden somewhere within.

The crew member nodded and consulted his clipboard, checking it against her crumpled documents. "Miss Brooks, yes. You'll be on D deck, cabin twelve."

"Please, call me Jeanie." Her broad grin sparkled. "D deck. So, is that a good deck to be on? I've never been on a ship like this before. Or any ship, for that matter!"

The man smiled in return. "It's water level. That's the deck with all the single cabins."

"Well, that's me! Single as can be. Though maybe not for long if I'm lucky, right?" She gave him a saucy wink. "Now, how do I find where I'm going?"

"Take the lift down one level," he responded with a nod in its general direction. "The cabin doors are numbered. You'll find a sink in your room, and there are shared toilets and baths at each end of the hall."

"Thank you so much. You've been extremely helpful. What's your name?"

"It's Rolfe, Miss Brooks."

"Now, Rolfe—just call me Jeanie, remember?" she

teased. "It's been a pleasure to meet you. I'm sure we'll see each other again."

His final best wishes for the cruise were barely audible over the din of her suitcase wheel, which had lost its fight to stay intact during the final sprint down the ramp. It jangled around at a precarious angle as she headed along the hall in search of the elevator—or 'lift' as it was apparently called in these parts. She squinted at a sign in the distance with a symbol that she was fairly certain marked her destination. She'd spent the entire flight from New York pouring over a European travel guide to prepare for her voyage, doing her best to memorize the meanings of enough signs and vocabulary to get her through her first trip abroad.

Then she'd slid the book into the seat pocket in front of her before drifting off to sleep, and, much to her regret considering the thing had cost her fifty bucks, left it behind when she disembarked. Along with chronic lateness, absent mindedness was far from unusual behavior for her. She always had the best of intentions, if not the best follow through. But as the door in front of her slid open to reveal the hoped-for elevator, she was able to shrug off her earlier missteps. Luckily for her, things usually turned out for the best, despite her blunders.

She stepped out of the lift and into a narrow, windowless hall, her rolling behemoth of a bag rubbing black marks along the stark-white walls, which were barely far enough apart to accommodate a human of average proportion. Packing light had not been an option. A two-week trip to Europe on its own would have been cause for a sizable wardrobe, but combined with a ship full of eligible singles, Jeanie's packing preparations had taken on the focused intensity of training for an Olympic sport. She was a queer woman who'd been born and raised in a hamlet in upstate New York so small that a trip to Poughkeepsie qualified as an adventure in the big city. She knew better than to squander a golden opportunity for finding love. She was on the hunt, and dressing to kill was her weapon of choice.

Her bag clattered to a stop in front of a door marked with the number twelve. She took the key that Rolfe had handed her and twisted it in the lock. The door swung open to reveal a shadowy space lit by a sliver of a window high up on the opposite wall. She smacked her palm against the switch until an overhead fixture spluttered to life, bathing the room in flickering neon. She blinked as she took in the cabin, then blinked again. For the first time since embarking on this journey, her perpetual optimism flagged.

To begin with, they'd assigned her a room with no bed. The tiny space in front of her was equipped with only a narrow bench. Stepping over the threshold and giving her bag a gentle tug, she discovered a potentially larger problem, which a forceful yank of her suitcase handle confirmed: the door was too tiny to allow her suitcase to pass. The sinking feeling inside her belly intensified. What was she supposed to do for two weeks in a room with no bed and all her earthly possessions stranded in the hall? She would have to complain to someone about this, and she dreaded the prospect. She lacked the forceful personality for confrontation, mostly relying on honey rather than vinegar to get her way.

The staccato echo of approaching footsteps prompted Jeanie to look up, embers of hope flickering at the sight of an approaching crew member. He looked like a pleasant man, and if she was nice to him, perhaps he could fix her problem before she had to ruffle too many feathers.

"Is everything alright, miss?" The man surveyed her and her bag quizzically.

"I'm afraid it's not," she said, her engaging smile crooked with embarrassment. She gestured toward her luggage. "It won't fit through the door. And that's only half the problem. Somehow they've forgotten to give me a bed."

The crew member's eyebrows shot up. "No bed? Let me take a look." He peered over Jeanie's shoulder and began to laugh. "Let me guess. You're American?"

"Yes, why?" Jeanie tilted her head, unable to figure out why that could possibly matter in her current crisis. What did her nationality have to do with having no place to sleep, no way to unpack, and exactly two minutes to make it up four floors to the observation deck to meet a few hundred potential loves of her life? She was beginning to suspect that he didn't take her seriously!

"You Americans always react this way the first time you see a single bed."

Her eyebrows knitted together as she took a closer look into the room. "A single bed? Where?" She stared again until the crew member gestured in the direction of the narrow bench. Jeanie's eyelids sprung open wide. *Surely not.* "You mean, I'm supposed to sleep on *that*?"

The man nodded. "I assure you, the size is very common. And see the drawers built in underneath? That's for storing your clothing."

Jeanie sighed. "I'm not sure how I'll get them there. No way is this bag going to fit through the door." She gave the crew member her most pitiful look, adding a dramatic tug on its handle for good measure.

"That *is* a problem. Perhaps you could unpack it and I can store it someplace else for the duration of the trip? But you'll need to do it right away, I'm afraid. Blocking the passageway is against regulations."

In a matter of seconds, Jeanie unzipped each compartment and tossed her belongings by the armload into her tiny cell. "There we go!" She surveyed the resulting heap with a sense of accomplishment. "Thank you so much...I'm sorry, what was your name?"

"Thomas."

"Thank you, Thomas." She pulled the door to the room shut with a reverberating click. "Now, which way to the observation deck?"

Thomas stared uncomfortably at the obstacle blocking their path, pointing down the pathway on its opposite side. Without a second thought, Jeanie hiked up the hem of her skirt and stretched one long leg high up and over the offending bag, teetering momentarily at its top before dragging her other leg successfully over and onto the floor on the correct side. "You're a determined woman!" He regarded her with a mixture of awe and surprise.

"As my Nanna used to say, Thomas," she called back gleefully as she scurried down the hall, "you ain't seen the half of it!"

Pinching pennies, supplementing her teaching income with after-school tutoring and summer jobs—now *that* was determination. And all for this. Not just the singles cruise, though that was a welcome perk. Jeanie's hometown wasn't quite so far removed from civilization that she didn't know she could meet single women of like-minded inclinations closer to home. Finding someone special on this trip would be the icing on the cake, for sure, but that wasn't why she'd traveled all this way. No, she'd come seeking redemption. Or at least to make herself feel better about the past she'd left behind.

For as long as she could remember, she'd dreamed of becoming the curator of a museum. Instead of going to community college like most of her high school friends, she'd gotten into the art history program at Vassar, where she consistently placed at the top of her class. But she was a scholarship student and her family couldn't afford things like study abroad programs. Her parents owned a hardware store where they didn't exactly cultivate the social connections to get a prestigious internship. Most of those were unpaid, anyway, so even when she'd landed one she couldn't make ends meet. Even so, Jeanie had kept at it as long as she could, enrolling in a graduate program for museum studies at the City College of New York, even though her parents thought she should come home and teach.

By the time end of the first year of graduate school, she still had never so much as stepped foot in Europe. That knowledge humiliated her, and she knew that her fellow students regarded her as a little country mouse in the big city. When the fellowship she'd been counting on to afford doing research abroad was awarded to some trust fund screw-up instead, her cheerful optimism was crushed under the weight of reality. She was trying to make it in a world where she would never belong. When the history teacher at her old high school retired, she'd ended up quitting her graduate program just a few credits short of completion to return home to take the job. That had been ten years ago. The least she could do was get a few stamps in her passport before the reunion rolled around.

She gave the elevator button a sharp jab, annoyed at herself for dredging up old memories. She was on the trip of a lifetime, and about to meet scores of sexy single women. She had no reason to complain. The bell dinged and a woman in her eighties stepped out of the elevator and started down the hall. Jeanie stared after her in surprise. A singles cruise at her age? *You go, Granny!* Jeanie laughed. That little old lady had her beat in the determination department if she was still looking for love this far into her golden years.

Jeanie lifted her head high as she strode toward the observation deck and gave the door a push. Her smile froze, however, as she stepped out onto the sun-drenched, and extremely empty, deck. Jeanie looked around and gulped, her pulse beating a chaotic rhythm in her ears. She had to be running much later than she'd thought, and had missed the meet and greet entirely. What other explanation could there be? There wasn't another soul in sight.

Correction: there was precisely one. Jeanie saw her on the second sweep, a solitary figure with a pair of sunglasses covering her eyes. She was partially hidden behind a life boat rig, slumped slightly in her chair in such a way that Jeanie wondered if she was asleep. Jeanie studied the woman closely. She had a slender, muscular build. The somewhat ghostly pallor of her skin suggested that the woman got her exercise at a gym and spent the rest of her time behind a desk.

Jeanie recognized Eleanor's ensemble of black palazzo pants and muted print tunic as belonging to an easy-care travel collection recently touted by several of her favorite celebrity lifestyle bloggers. She'd considered buying a few pieces herself, right up to the point where she glimpsed the price and realized she could buy a week's worth of clothing for the cost of one no-iron skirt. Whatever this woman did for work, she was obviously very successful at it.

Perhaps most important: this woman was definitely no more than a few years older than herself. Jeanie breathed a sigh of relief. After seeing the elderly woman in the elevator, she'd started to worry about exactly who the other women on this cruise would be. But the presence of such an attractive woman reassured her that she'd had no reason to be concerned.

She cleared her throat loudly as she approached, and the woman stirred and stretched fitfully, then looked up with such a comical expression of surprise that Jeanie stifled a giggle with only marginal success. The woman's expression shifted to a scowl at the sound, but in doing so it first passed through a state of such exquisiteness that Jeanie's heart lurched into her throat. She tried to call out a greeting to the woman, but choked on the words in a fit of coughing instead.

She finally managed to whisper a single word —*"Mercy!"*—and was glad the stranger was too far away to hear her. She couldn't tear her eyes away, or even move a muscle as the lovely vision lifted her lithesome body from where it rested. The woman wound her way slowly through the sea of empty deck chairs that separated them. Jeanie's heart ricocheted against her sternum and she prayed she wouldn't pass out.

THREE

ELEANOR'S THOUGHTS had been consumed with work as she'd settled into the deck chair to wait. She'd turned over a particularly enticing project to one of her colleagues just before the trip, and the details of it still filled her brain. But soon her mind had grown fuzzy and she'd drifted into a light sleep, falling victim to the combined effects of jet lag and the warm July sun.

Suddenly she found herself running around the deck, clutching fistfuls of color-coded spreadsheets in her hands while being chased by hundreds of screaming women. Eleanor stretched her arms in front of her to fend them off, until she awoke in confusion, heart racing and lungs tightening, to find that she was alone. No, strike that. During the time she'd been asleep one other woman had joined her on the deck. From first glance, Eleanor's already rapid pulse ticked into the red zone. *Calm down! A pretty face is no reason for alarm.* She struggled to control her ragged breaths. This was no place to start to panic.

The stranger stood several feet away, her wavy blond tresses blowing in the breeze. She wore a white cotton skirt with colorful embroidery at the hem, and a matching blouse that exposed the tops of her sun-kissed shoulders. It was the type of vaguely tropical outfit that people felt compelled to buy when going on vacation. It was hardly special in itself, but the way the woman stood, back-lit by the sun's rays, rendered the gauzy fabric nearly transparent. Eleanor's eyes swept along miles of shapely leg and she wondered if this might not be the most fascinating bit of sightseeing she would partake in during her trip.

She swallowed roughly as her body buzzed like someone had flipped the switch of an electromagnet in her nether-regions. Hadn't she just been lamenting her lack of a sex life? Perhaps the answer to that problem was standing right in front of her. *Perhaps you should stop being such an idiot,* snapped the part of her brain that was not currently in thrall to the flood of hormones coursing through her veins. Still groggy and disoriented, she heard the stranger laugh and felt the muscles in her face contort in a fit of pique. If there was one thing Eleanor could not tolerate, it was being laughed at. Perhaps this woman was not as intriguing as she had first appeared.

Eleanor rose and strode to the middle of the deck where the stranger stood. "Who are you?" Eleanor immediately regretted the unintended brusqueness of her tone as a cloud of uncertainty darkened the stranger's face, and she began to sputter and cough. Being discovered mid-nap had provoked an anxious awareness in Eleanor of her own vulnerability, which triggered her body's overdeveloped sense of fight or flight. Her knee-jerk reaction in such cases was always to go on the offensive. It was a tactic that worked well enough for her in the office where she spent most of her time, but when it came to more delicate human interactions, she sometimes needed reminding that not every situation was a zero-sum competition, or a gladiator battle to the death. "I'm Eleanor," she added more gently, taking a delayed stab at civility.

"I'm...uh, Jeanie?" The woman managed to cough the words out, but without conviction.

Eleanor stared, dumbfounded. *Did she just say she's a genie?* Eleanor felt her insides heat up like a furnace as she took in the woman's shapely body. *Is she going to grant me a wish?* Eleanor wondered what the policy was on inviting a genie back to your place to get better acquainted. Was that an acceptable wish?

What the hell is wrong with me? Obviously, she couldn't have said she was a genie. Eleanor wondered if she was still asleep, because this interaction was making about as much sense as the spreadsheet dream she'd just had. "I'm sorry, could you repeat that?" she managed to say, more than half convinced that she was going soft in the head.

"Janine? Jeanie for short. Jeanie Louise Brooks." The woman stuck out her hand in greeting.

"Eleanor Fielding." Eleanor grasped the outstretched hand, her senses returning to her at the familiar, businesslike gesture. The ritual calmed her enough that she might even be able to remember the stranger's name. "Did you say Louise Brooks?"

"I know what you're thinking. Haven't I heard that name somewhere before?" The woman gave a self-deprecating shrug. "Mom's a huge fan of silent films. With a last name like Brooks, she couldn't resist." Jeanie giggled nervously, tossing her head to one side so that her golden hair flew. "I didn't like it when I was younger, but when I first came out to my mom, she said she could hardly hold it against me since she'd named me after the most notorious bisexual of the flapper era, so at least I got some practical benefit out of being saddled with the name."

"Oh?" Eleanor squinted in confusion, feeling hopelessly out of her element at the woman's steady stream of chatter. She could barely keep up. "Are you bisexual?" Eleanor's heart, which had only just managed to return to a normal speed and rhythm, lurched in embarrassment and sent a rush of blood to her cheeks. She'd realized the second *after* the words were out of her mouth just how inappropriate they were. It was simply the first thing that had popped into her head, and her brain was still muddled enough to have let it slip out. *I'm such a disaster!*

"No, not me." Jeanie took the question in stride, smiling as pleasantly as if Eleanor had asked the time of day. "Nothing against people who are, or anything. I just never saw the appeal. How about you?"

"How about me?" Eleanor repeated dumbly. "Am I bisexual, you mean? No, not me, either. Like you said, I never saw the appeal." This was possibly the most bizarre conversation with a stranger that she'd ever experienced in her life.

Jeanie laughed. "I feel like we've made it through a lightning round of speed dating, don't you?"

"Well, Louise, tell me your stance on sex toys and it might qualify as a first date," Eleanor quipped, proud of herself for her display of humor.

"It's Jeanie, actually. And I have an entire bag of them back in my cabin."

Eleanor gaped.

"Oh." Jeanie bit her lower lip as her cheeks flushed scarlet. "That wasn't a serious question, was it?"

"No. But your answer was…informative." She felt her body tense with arousal as her mind drifted over the possibilities of what was in that bag. She struggled to rein in her imagination. Why was she so easily captivated by this odd woman, anyway? She didn't usually go for the carefree bohemian type, no matter how pretty they were. Way too unpredictable. *There will be lots of other women on this cruise,* she reminded herself. *No need to get attached to the first one I meet!* She glanced at the woman's legs and felt a stab of regret. There were bound to be better matches yet to come, but they would almost certainly not come with legs like these.

"I wonder when the others will arrive," Eleanor said, then wished she hadn't. Saying the words out loud flooded her with the realization of how many other introductions she had yet to suffer through, and her lungs tightened like she was about to drown. *I'm barely surviving the first encounter. I'll never make it!*

"The others haven't arrived yet?" Jeanie seemed surprised. "I assumed I was running so late that the meet and greet was over and everyone else had already left."

"Running late?" Eleanor's eyes widened in alarm. "I arrived half an hour early." *I couldn't have slept that long, could I?* Her heart was pounding wildly again, suddenly unsure. She'd been exhausted, but could she really have remained passed out in the middle of a crowd? *Anything could have happened to me!* Her breathing became shallow, and she nearly jumped out of her own skin in panic when Jeanie grabbed her arm.

"It's only a few minutes past three," Jeanie informed her after reading the time off Eleanor's wristwatch. She let go of Eleanor's arm. "Sorry. I wouldn't normally have grabbed you like that, but you sort of froze with the watch halfway to your face."

"Oh. Right. Sorry," Eleanor mumbled, mortified. *I'm making a complete fool of myself.* "Well, then I guess everyone else is just running even later than you were."

"That would be a first!"

A woman who's perpetually late? Eleanor cocked an eyebrow as she considered this revelation. *Definitely not my type.* "Statistically it's much more likely they switched the location of the event than that every other person on board is running late, you know," she lectured, forgetting that she was the one to have suggested the possibility in the first place. "We should probably try to find out."

Jeanie nodded amiably, apparently willing to overlook Eleanor's scolding tone. They walked side by side across the deck and into the semi-darkness of the ship. Eleanor took off her sunglasses and blinked, momentarily blinded. She was still trying to get her bearings when Jeanie grabbed her elbow, and the electromagnetic hum inside her started up once more, completely beyond her control.

"Oh, there's Rolfe! He'll know what's going on." Jeanie gave Eleanor's arm a tug, dragging her along as she raced after the crew member. "Rolfe!"

The man stopped and turned, an expectant look on his face. "Oh, Miss Jeanie! How can I help?"

"Do you know him?" Eleanor asked in a half whisper as they approached.

"That's Rolfe." Jeanie said it as though it should be obvious. "He was the one who was checking everyone in for the cruise."

Eleanor squinted at the man's face until she thought he might seem vaguely familiar. "Oh, right."

Apparently Jeanie possessed an uncanny memory for names and faces. It was an ability that Eleanor had never been able to cultivate. It wasn't that she didn't care, but she knew that's how it came across sometimes. She envied the ease with which this woman seemed to make friends.

Jeanie smiled sweetly at the man. "Rolfe, we were out on the observation deck for the meet and greet, but no one was there."

"It's been moved to the lounge on C deck," the man replied. "Easier on the knees without all the stairs."

"Oh, okay." Jeanie turned to look at Eleanor. "Would you like to head down and see what we missed?"

"I suppose so," Eleanor replied with a practiced shrug, though she wasn't certain why the cruise line was concerned with their knees. As Jeanie strode ahead, Eleanor's eyes were drawn to the shadowy crease in her skirt where the woman's long legs met and a rather naughty explanation for saving her knee-strength popped into her mind. She snorted softly, half convinced that her nap in the sun had fried her brain beyond repair. She wasn't feeling like herself at all.

As they rode the elevator to C deck, an awkward silence settled between them. Eleanor conjured up images of the hundreds of single women who even now were packed into the lounge. Her heart fluttered and flapped, less from excitement and more with the desperation of a bird trying to escape its cage. She sympathized with her heart's desire to flee, one hundred percent. She would do just about anything to get out of this situation right now!

The elevator door opened with a ding. "I don't...I don't think...," she stammered as a murmur of voices from the lounge reached her ears and she felt the now-familiar blind panic begin to descend.

"Come on, this way!" Jeanie grabbed her by the hand, sprinting the last few steps and leaving Eleanor no chance of escape.

You wouldn't normally grab me, huh? I don't think I believe you! Eleanor's fingers tingled at her touch for at least the third time since they'd met. Her new acquaintance was very much the hands-on type, which was equal parts worrying and alluring. Being touched could be a nice thing, under the right circumstances, though Eleanor usually preferred some warning, and a little privacy, first.

They came to a full stop in front of the entrance to the lounge and stared into the crowded room in confusion. It was as packed as Eleanor had foreseen, but not with sexy ladies. No, before them instead was a room chock-full of gray haired *old ladies*, and bespectacled old gentlemen, too.

"What the hell?" Eleanor muttered in shock.

"Umm." Jeanie's face froze in confusion, then melted in relief. "There's Thomas! He'll know what's going on."

"Thomas? What, do you know everyone on this ship?" Her overwhelming confusion made her words sound sharper than she'd meant and she winced at how Jeanie would react.

"Not everyone," Jeanie said dryly, seemingly without taking offense. "Not the two hundred senior citizens in lounge C, for starters." Jeanie strode toward the man she'd identified as Thomas as Eleanor raced to catch up. "But I was chatting with Thomas earlier while he helped me with my bags, so I imagine he can help now."

Chatting with a porter over luggage? *Who does that?* Eleanor's forehead wrinkled in bewilderment. The fact that someone as friendly as Jeanie existed brought her own social failings into stark contrast.

"Thomas, do you know anything about the lesbian singles cruise?" Jeanie asked when they'd reached the smiling porter.

"Yes, of course!" he responded with an eager nod.

"Oh," Jeanie patted the sleeve of the man's uniform, letting out a happy sigh. "That's wonderful news!"

"Yes, my cousin said it was fantastic."

"Oh, how nice! So you have a single cousin who's a les—"

"I'm sorry," Eleanor interrupted, sensing that this conversation would go off course quickly with Jeanie at the helm. "*Was* fantastic?"

"Yes, she was raving about it a few weeks ago when I saw her in Vienna."

"But that cruise starts today," Eleanor corrected with a scowl.

"No," Thomas corrected. "It was last month."

"There's obviously some sort of mistake." Eleanor reached into her bag and pulled out the schedule, waving the paper in front of Thomas' face. "This is what we're talking about. See, right here. It says the meet and greet is at three o'clock on July the sixth. It's printed right there. Seven-six."

"Yes, I see. Seven-six. The seventh of June."

"So, she was on last month's cruise?" Jeanie smiled nervously.

Adrenaline crackled through Eleanor's body as she realized the potential magnitude of the mistake. It made her insides feel crinkly and before she could stop herself, she snapped. "Honestly, Jeanie, just how much demand do you think there is for lesbian singles cruises?" Eleanor shot her an incredulous look. "You booked the wrong month. You've mixed up the European way of writing dates with the American way."

"Well, so have you," Jeanie pointed out.

"I most certainly have not." Irrational annoyance at the accusation made Eleanor's insides prickle. When it came to numbers, Eleanor didn't make mistakes. "My sister did. I would never do something so foolish."

"Oh. I see."

Her voice was quiet, but something in the underlying tone made Eleanor realize she'd said the wrong thing. *Why can't I stop myself from sounding insulting when I don't mean it?* Her stomach clenched and she turned to Thomas, hoping she could find a way to salvage the situation. "So, if this isn't the lesbian singles cruise, would you happen to know what it is?"

"Yes, of course. It's senior swingers."

"Swingers?" Eleanor was sure her face had turned a sickly green. *Key parties and trading partners? At their age?*

"I think he means swing *dancer*s, Eleanor."

Eleanor's eyes narrowed at the smug expression on her new acquaintance's face. The woman had clearly read her thoughts. "I knew that," she snapped.

Jeanie studied her for a moment, blinking slowly and not buying Eleanor's assertion one iota, but she didn't press the issue.

"Sorry, yes, swing dancers. Sometimes my English gets confused. They'll have lessons and dancing every day during the cruise. You can join them, no problem."

The forlorn expression Jeanie had worn ever since the news that she had booked the wrong cruise suddenly brightened with a broad grin. "Really? That would be okay?"

"Of course! You just need to upgrade and you can attend all the classes you want."

"Upgrade." Jeanie's smile faded and her brow creased. "It costs extra?"

Eleanor took in the woman's crestfallen expression

with dismay. *Janie... Jenny?... is much too pretty to look so sad!* Her back stiffened indignantly and she gave the steward a stern look. "Now look here, Timothy."

"Thomas," Jeanie corrected.

"Whatever. The way I see it, the cruise company is as much to blame for this error as either one of us. You should know better than to use European dates on an American website without making it more clear. It's misleading."

"Well, I—"

"You're really lucky we don't sue." Eleanor bit the inside of her cheeks to keep from smiling as Thomas' face blanched. She would never dream of following through on her threat, but she knew Americans enjoyed an international reputation for their love of litigation, and she was more than willing to use that to her advantage. "But I think, as a sign of goodwill, the company can make it up to us by offering a free upgrade."

"I... I can check, ma'am. What is your name and room number?"

"Eleanor Fielding. I'm in the Empire suite."

At the mention of her room, the steward turned white as a sheet. "Yes, Ms. Fielding. Of course. We would be happy to add the classes to your ticket immediately. No additional charge."

"And my friend." It was not a question.

"Yes, ma'am. It would be my pleasure to accommodate you both." He glanced back and forth between the women nervously. "If you'll excuse me, I have duties to attend to now, but I'll have the schedule sent to you this evening."

Eleanor nodded and turned to Jeanie, who was staring at her as if awestruck.

"That was... spectacular."

Eleanor blushed, the woman's admiration giving her a thrill.

"Swing dancing!" Jeanie exclaimed, her eyes wide.

"Yes, swing dancing." Eleanor shuddered. She hadn't given much thought to concepts like hell since she quit going to temple shortly after her Bat Mitzvah, but she was pretty certain, if pressed to describe the details of that particular location, dancing would be one of its most prominent features. "Just our bad luck, I guess."

"Bad luck? It's marvelous!" Jeanie bobbed up and down on her toes with the enthusiasm of a small child on a sugar high. "Two full weeks of dance lessons! Haven't you always wanted to learn?"

"No."

"Oh, come on." Jeanie smacked her palm playfully against Eleanor's shoulder. "You'll enjoy it once we get started!"

For the fourth time that afternoon, a shock of pleasure surged through her at the feel of Jeanie's hand against her bare skin, but this time it was sorely at odds with the revulsion she felt at this particular proposition. "Absolutely not. I don't dance."

"But what else will you do?"

"Whatever I like!" Eleanor's mind flashed back to the ship's library and the tennis courts that she'd stared at longingly earlier in the day. "Maybe I'll stay in my room and read the whole time."

"What?" Jeanie appeared taken aback.

"It's not like I haven't seen all of these cities a dozen times before. I could make a whole list of things to do now that I'm free of any obligation to that ridiculous singles cruise. With the possible exception of dancing, I can't think of anything I'd find less enjoyable than spending two weeks fending off a gaggle of desperate lesbians."

"Oh." The last remnants of a smile faded from Jeanie's face. "I…"

Eleanor's chest tightened as she realized too late how terrible that must have sounded. The way she'd described her previous travels made her sound spoiled, and obviously Jeanie didn't share her cynicism about the romantic prospects of this cruise. *Why can't I ever say the right thing?* She quickly attempted to smooth things over. "Look Janet, take the dance classes if you want to. Just because we are, quite literally, the only two eligible women on this cruise doesn't mean we're obligated to spend any time together," she ended her rambling with an awkward laugh.

Jeanie drew in a slow breath, squaring her shoulders determinedly and becoming imposingly tall. "No. Of course not."

Eleanor gulped, realizing how thoroughly what she'd said out loud deviated from how it had sounded in her head. "I just—"

"No, you're absolutely right. I should go now, but have a lovely cruise—doing whatever it is you decide you'd rather do. And my name is Jeanie," she added through gritted teeth.

Eleanor's face fell as Jeanie turned to walk away. Usually she enjoyed being told she was right, but she took no pleasure in it now. It wasn't the first time her innate clumsiness in social interactions had come across as gruff, or even hostile. In fact, given her initial attraction to the woman, it was amazing the easy rapport between them had lasted as long as it had. *Well, it's over now, and it's all my fault.* The sting of tears pricked the corners of her eyes. As Jeanie entered the elevator, a pool of sunshine from a nearby window showcased her remarkable legs in much the same way as on the observation deck before, but Eleanor felt much too glum to enjoy the view.

Eleanor dragged the back of her hand across her eyes, refusing to cry. *Jeanie Brooks is a compulsively late chatterbox who loves to dance.* Eleanor reminded herself of this unpleasant truth as she tried to shake off the nagging sense of guilt and sadness that weighed her down. *We would make the worst match in history!* Even a meaningless holiday fling was too crazy to contemplate. She didn't need to build a forecasting model to know that the risks far outweighed the rewards when it came to that woman and her quirky charm...and infectious grin...and friendly disposition...and smoking-hot body.

She stared at the elevator doors where Jeanie had disappeared moments before, and for the first time in quite a long while, Eleanor questioned whether her analysis could be leading her astray.

FOUR

JEANIE STEPPED from the gangway and directly into the rush of morning commuters bustling along the busy sidewalk. Her body hummed with excitement at the prospect of spending her first full day in Europe. She glanced behind her at the ship, then squinted into the distance at the towering bronze figure of Liberty atop the stony, tree-covered face of Gellert Hill on the opposite side of the river. Holding its giant palm leaf, the statue looked exactly like the pictures she'd seen in countless tour books; a fact that, strangely, made it harder rather than easier for her to believe that she was really there. The details seemed too perfect to be anything but the product of her own imagination.

She closed her eyes, letting the alien yet strangely melodic tones of the Hungarian language wash over her from the chatter of the passing crowd. She breathed deeply, seeking out the uniquely identifying scent of the city. She'd assumed there would be one, perhaps a subtle perfume of exotic spices that would immediately signal that she was no longer in upstate New York. But it turned out that the smells of Budapest were indistinguishable from American air: the standard blend of car exhaust, a hint of vegetation mouldering in the summer heat, and just a whiff of coffee from a stand on the corner. She let out her breath, disappointed but reassured that this was probably not a dream after all. In her dreams, the city smelled of cinnamon and paprika, and the Danube water sparkled in sapphire hues, as opposed to its actual muddy brown.

And in my dreams, I had no end of beautiful women to keep me from feeling so alone. Jeanie sighed, thinking of the curmudgeonly companion who was her only choice for this cruise. Not that she could even be considered as such, since they most certainly wouldn't be spending any more time together. And she'd had such high hopes for them, too!

Even when she'd thought she'd have a ship filled with options, something about Eleanor had caught her eye. She was attractive, of course. With her fine, chiseled features and her cropped mahogany locks tousled sexily by the breeze, Eleanor had seemed like a dream. There was even the chance for something more long term, which even Jeanie had barely dared to hope for, but it seemed to be true. She'd pegged Eleanor as a fellow New Yorker as soon as she'd spoken. Manhattan, probably, judging by her clothes. But beyond any of that, it was her self-assured presence and take charge attitude that really got Jeanie's juices flowing.

In the midst of a crisis, like when Eleanor was demanding the ticket upgrade on her behalf, she was the type of woman who exuded pure confidence. The type of woman Jeanie never quite managed to be, who could speak her mind and stand up for herself without resorting to playing the damsel in distress. And sure, she'd been a little bit bumbling, too, which Jeanie thought was kind of cute. But it had all been spoiled when Jeanie realized what Eleanor really thought of her. Then it became clear that she was just another rich, city-dwelling snob who had nothing but disdain for what she considered to be an unsophisticated, small-town girl. The disappointment had been palpable. *She didn't even bother to remember my name!*

Loathe as she was to admit it, Jeanie had to consider the possibility that she'd let her expectations for this entire trip get out of hand. After years of subscribing to travel blogs and hoping in vain, the opportunity to book this cruise had come out of the blue. She'd jumped at the chance with hardly a thought, then watched in thrilled disbelief as every detail fell into place. She should have known her luck was too good to last, but her eternal optimism had blinded her as usual.

Correcting a mistake on the previous year's tax returns had yielded an unexpected refund that paid for her ticket. *That's right, another number mistake—wouldn't Eleanor just cringe to learn that!* And when the only cruise that fit into her schedule—the one that departed just after classes let out for the summer and allowed her to get home with time to prepare lessons before the new semester began—just happened to be a lesbian singles cruise? At that moment, Jeanie had suspected that she might be the luckiest woman alive. *Little did I know!*

Jeanie launched herself into the sea of pedestrians heading in the direction of Chain Bridge. She cast a backward glance at the ship, catching sight of half a dozen couples toddling up the gangway arm in arm, looking adorably in love even after decades together. She sighed, heart heavy, at the thought that, despite her earlier expectations, this was destined to be a solo trip for her after all. Just when she'd thought it would never end, her winning streak had fizzled and died.

There'd been a few warning signs that it was waning. Leaving that expensive tour book on the plane. Showing up at the wrong berth and the resulting mad dash to make it to the ship on time. The complications involving her miniature cabin and gargantuan luggage. But Jeanie had dismissed them all as nothing more than the usual travel hiccups, inconveniences that could happen to anyone, and had walked on to that deserted observation deck the previous afternoon still believing in her unstoppable good fortune. *I couldn't have been more wrong,* Jeanie thought sourly.

Jeanie reached the intersection and spotted a sign pointing out directions to the Hungarian Parliament. She hadn't set an itinerary for the day, preferring to wander freely and keep herself open to whatever experiences came her way. The parliament building was as good a place as any to start her adventure. When the light changed she bounced giddily between the stripes of the crosswalk, following the arrow. As she walked, she struggled to convert the distance on the sign into miles, hoping she was correct in thinking it was just a few blocks away and not on the opposite end of town. *No doubt Eleanor would consider this more proof that I'm just an ignorant country bumpkin who doesn't know a kilometer from a tea kettle.*

Jeanie scowled, uncertain why she couldn't shake that infuriating woman from her thoughts. The haughtiness Eleanor had displayed when they'd realized their mutual mistake over the cruise dates left Jeanie feeling about three inches tall. *Or seven and a half centimeters—see, I'm smarter than you think!* It was like college all over again, another sophisticated city dweller looking down her nose and wondering how some townie had slipped past the gates into their exclusive club. A surprisingly large number of them had been eager enough to take her to bed, but not to take her home to meet their families. *Snobs!*

The road curved gently ahead of her as the majestic dome and spires of the parliament building came into view. Jeanie gasped at the site, all other thoughts pushed aside as she stared in admiration. She'd done an independent study on the Gothic revival movement in American architecture, but nothing she'd seen in the States compared to this. She felt a tingle in her spine as it struck her once more that all of this was real. She was finally living her dream!

I wonder if Eleanor's back in her room reading a book right now, she thought scornfully, but with just a shade of sadness, too. For just a split second, before Eleanor's true personality had been revealed, she'd daydreamed that the two of them might explore the wonders of Budapest arm-in-arm. *No way was that going to happen!* She shook off her disappointment. Even if she hadn't turned out to be an all-around obnoxious person, Eleanor would've made a terrible touring companion simply on the basis of her blasé attitude about the whole thing. Skipping sightseeing to read a book? Maybe it was possible for a person to visit amazing places so often that it started to feel commonplace, but Jeanie couldn't imagine ever becoming that way herself.

There was a line at the entrance to the parliament building and Jeanie could just make out two security guards inspecting bags. She swung the backpack from her shoulder and slid the zipper open as she approached the table. One of the security guards said something to her in Hungarian, to which she responded with an uncomprehending stare.

"Your bag, miss," the guard spoke again in stilted English. "You need to check."

"Check?" Jeanie frowned. "You mean I can't take it in?" She looked at her bag, perplexed. There was nothing about this on the signs, and she hated the idea of being parted with her things.

"Today, no. Government meeting, extra security," he tried his best to explain.

"Oh, I see." Reluctantly, Jeanie reached into her bag, pulling out her wallet by its wrist strap. "May I bring this, at least? It has my money and passport inside." She prayed he wouldn't say no and force her to beg. *Eleanor wouldn't ask permission. She would make demands!* Jeanie felt a fleeting regret that her shipmate wasn't nearby.

"Yes, little one is okay." The guard took her backpack and handed her a claim ticket, which Jeanie slid into her wallet. "Enjoy!"

Relieved, Jeanie took a wand for the audio tour from a nearby table and held it to her ear as she made her way slowly to the main hall. Her mouth dropped open at the sight of a gold staircase flanked on both sides with statues, and punctuated with exquisite stained glass windows every few steps. "Mercy!" she breathed, her go-to exclamation for when all other words escaped her.

She climbed the stairs to the main level and spent the next hour admiring more statues and windows than she'd believed could possibly be housed in one place. Even the carpet was a work of art. When at last she reached the grand stairway at the end of the tour, with its imposing granite columns and large frescoes, Jeanie felt almost numb from the experience of so much grandeur in one place. She was going to need to pace herself if she planned to make it through the next few weeks.

"You enjoy?" the security guard asked as Jeanie returned to the checkpoint.

She nodded with enthusiasm, having long since forgiven the guard for holding her backpack hostage. "Very much!" She slipped the strap from her wrist and rummaged around for the claim ticket, finally producing it and handing it to the guard. "It was amazing, like nothing I've ever seen before! But now I think I need something less stimulating. I never thought I'd say it, but I'm overwhelmed by so much art!"

"No more art?" The guard laughed, seeming to understand. "Maybe bath? Szechenyi, you know?"

Jeanie thought for a moment. "Oh, the Szechenyi thermal baths? Yes, I was planning to go there at some point. That's a wonderful idea! Are they close?"

"Ehh." The guard's forehead wrinkled as he searched for the words. After a few seconds he shrugged in defeat. "Too difficult explaining. You go Nyugati station. Get city map there."

"They have maps at the train station? That's probably a good idea. Is it very far?" The guard motioned like he was writing something on his palm, and Jeanie set down her backpack and wallet on the table and dug around until she found an old receipt and a pen. After a few moments of scribbling, the guard handed her a crude diagram of the path from the parliament building to the train station. Jeanie slung her backpack over her shoulder, thanked him, and headed out the exit toward the street marked on the map.

The sky, which had been clear and blue at the start of the day, had turned cloudy during her time indoors. She wouldn't be able to swim in the outdoor pools, but from what she knew about the Szechenyi baths, there were indoor options, too. After the solitude of her morning tour, Jeanie needed the energy of being around people. The fact that some of those people would be attractive women in swimsuits was a bonus. *Although, you know who would look really hot in a bikini...* Jeanie stopped herself mid-thought, chasing the image of Eleanor from her mind. *Enough! You'd barely remember her name by now if she weren't the only eligible woman on the ship!* The fact that she never forgot anyone's name didn't mean that Eleanor couldn't have been the exception to the rule.

It grew darker as she walked, and when she paused, squinting to make out the unfamiliar street names on the scrap of paper in her hand, a droplet of rain fell and the ink began to run. "Shit!" Jeanie looked up and spotted a sign with a train-shaped symbol in the distance. Stuffing the ruined paper into her pocket, she raced toward the sign in relief, managing to duck into the shelter of an underpass just as the clouds burst open and rain poured from the sky.

Jeanie stared at the solid sheet of rain and marveled at her good luck in reaching shelter in time. It wasn't until she turned her attention more closely to the underground walkway where she stood that a sense of trepidation overshadowed her. Despite the sudden bad weather, the pedestrian underpass was mostly deserted, and Jeanie could see graffiti covering the walls in the dim light. She swallowed uneasily, pulling out the now smeared map. She was certain she'd seen a sign for the station pointing this way, but it appeared that the security guard's map showed a different way. She'd taken a wrong turn.

She looked out into the still-pouring rain, then deeper into the dark passage. Squaring her shoulders, she turned toward the blackness and took a tentative step as her stomach clenched. As her eyes adjusted to the lack of light, the foreboding atmosphere of the underground space began to subside and it became just an ordinary, if somewhat grimy, corridor. Relaxing, Jeanie laughed to herself that she'd actually considered going back out into the rain. In the distance she could make out the brighter light of the outdoors. It appeared that the worst of the downpour was subsiding, which lifted her spirits even more.

But as she got closer to the light, shadowy figures filled the space one by one. Menacing. Her heart slammed against her ribcage as fear needled her insides. Her gaze darted in search of an escape, but the options were few, and the figures were approaching far too rapidly to outrun. Jeanie's mind raced, wondering what she should do, since sweet talking her attackers wasn't likely to work. She needed to be stronger than that. *What would Eleanor do?*

FIVE

EARLIER THAT SAME MORNING...

Eleanor set her book on the bistro table and closed her eyes. Her plan to read in seclusion on the terrace all day had seemed so enticing when she woke up, but now she found herself unable to focus on the page. Her eyes kept being drawn away by the bustling city that lay just beyond the balcony railing, and every time she looked down, all she saw was the shocked expression of Jeanie Brooks, judging her for how she was wasting the day away. *Jeanie Brooks.* She swore the name would haunt her until she died.

"If I don't want to go sightseeing, that's my own business, Ms. Brooks," she informed her book with a scowl. "It's my vacation, damn it!"

Except, thanks to the aforementioned Ms. Brooks, her stubborn determination to stay on board the ship suddenly felt childish. Budapest was one of the most beautiful cities in Europe. Skipping a day of sightseeing in it was just her way of sulking for being coerced into this trip, some vain attempt to punish her sister by depriving her of photos to share on social media. She stood with a sigh and grabbed her book, then wrenched the door open and stormed inside to prepare herself for a day of touring the town.

While Eleanor had been to Budapest before, as well as several other cities along the cruise route, it had always been for work. Sylvia had mostly dragged her to tropical places for vacation, from Tahiti to Saint Kitts. Most of Eleanor's time in Europe had consisted of long days meeting with clients, and returning alone in the evening for dinner in the restaurant of an unmemorable chain hotel. Beyond that, she'd never stepped foot in the cities at all except to get in and out of a cab at the airport. She might not have signed up for this trip voluntarily, but she was here now and there were a few things she'd like to see. *Might as well make the best of it.*

"But I'll be damned if I'm going to any of those dance classes," she muttered, shoving first her right foot, then her left, into her shoes. She froze, staring at her feet. She'd gotten the order wrong. Rationally, Eleanor knew there wasn't a particular order in which to put on a pair of shoes, but being rational had little to do with her dilemma. Failure to do so could lead to a panic attack. She'd been doing better in recent years and hadn't had a full-blown attack in quite some time, but it wasn't something she wanted to mess around with. Not when fixing it could be a matter of just changing her shoes.

Her brain had always been highly attuned to searching out patterns and organizing data. It was a skill that made her very good at her job, but sometimes very bad at getting through the day like a normal person. Eleanor had a natural aversion to anything unpredictable or out of control. The more chaotic the world felt to her, the more her anxiety increased. The more anxious she became, the more her brain tried to create order, even when there wasn't any. Like putting her shoes on the same way every time. It helped her to tame the uncontrollable.

There was no particular cause, and no easy cure. She'd worked with a therapist for years, achieving enough success that most of the time her anxiety and its accompanying compulsions were little more than a minor annoyance. Most people chalked her behavior up to a few funny habits and didn't guess the truth. Her family understood all too well since it was a trait many of them shared. Her lovers eventually became overwhelmed and left for greener pastures.

Some days she had more resolve to push back against these compulsive quirks, but today wasn't one of them. Sighing at her inability to let it go, she slipped the shoes off and put them on again, starting with the left this time, then the right, before grabbing her bag and stepping into the corridor. She kept her chin up and back straight, projecting confidence even as she berated herself the whole way, because that's just how she rolled.

At the top of the gangway, Eleanor pulled a tour book from her bag and studied the walking tours it offered. Several of the options covered interesting routes, but they started on the other side of the river. That made for too long of a trek. She knew most people would've just started the tour partway through at a more convenient location, but Eleanor wasn't most people. She needed to go in order. *Another of my weird obsessions.*

There was a garden tour that began at Chain Bridge. Eleanor didn't have a particular interest in gardening, but it was close and covered most of the major sites nearby, so she figured it would do. She walked the few blocks to that spot, oriented herself in the correct direction using the map, then traced her path according to the book's instructions.

She dutifully stopped to read about each shrub and flowering vine along the way, even though she didn't really care. It was the type of behavior that most of her previous traveling companions had found immensely annoying. Unless she'd paid for their ticket and they felt obligated to pretend it was fun. *Jeanie would be out of her mind with boredom.* Eleanor frowned. The woman hardly needed any other reasons not to like her after Eleanor had given her so many to choose from already. Still, she wondered why thoughts of

Jeanie kept popping into her head at the strangest times.

The first major stop on the tour was Saint Stephen's Basilica, one of the grandest churches in Hungary. She liked churches. Though not a member of the faith, Eleanor could still appreciate the buildings for their beauty and historical significance. For some reason, there were a lot fewer synagogues to choose from on tour maps, though Eleanor didn't mind. At churches, she never felt the need to explain her spotty attendance record at weekly services to anyone. Catholic friends who swore they had a corner on the guilt market had never met Eleanor's mother or sister, both of whom had elevated it to an art form.

She arrived just as the doors were opening for the first tour, purchased a ticket, and went in. The crowd was sparse, Eleanor being one of the few tourists up and moving at this early hour of morning. *I wonder if Jeanie's even out of bed yet.* An image of tousled blond locks on a crisp white pillowcase popped into her brain. One bare leg peeking out from beneath the covers and stretching for miles. She shook her head to clear it, knowing that this particular fantasy was heading somewhere not at all suitable for anyone's house of worship, no matter which religion you belonged to. *What has gotten into me?*

The familiar humming was already starting up inside her, as it seemed to do at the mere thought of that odd woman from the cruise. She wondered if anything could be done to stop it. While her brain was a model of disciplined logic, her body was not. Most of the time Eleanor's brain remained firmly in control, but she wasn't immune to momentary lapses of judgment, not when her body was especially motivated. It had been over a year since she'd been with anyone in that way, so her defenses were already low, and unfortunately for her, Jeanie Brooks seemed to be a powerful motivator indeed.

Why couldn't her body understand that, fantasies to the contrary, she couldn't have dreamed up a person less compatible with her if she'd tried? Aside from an instant physical attraction when they met on the deck —an attraction which Eleanor thought might be mutual but wasn't completely sure—they had nothing in common. *Which I shouldn't have to remind myself is not the best basis for a relationship.* She was also positive that Jeanie had been offended the day before by her complete lack of social grace, so even a casual friendship was probably out of the question. *That* was somewhat unfortunate.

Eleanor didn't have to be harboring romantic feelings toward the woman to have made an important realization. They were not just the only two lesbians on the ship, but the only two people under the age of seventy-five, period. If she wanted any spry company during the trip, Jeanie was really her only choice. It was a very good thing she didn't mind being alone, because unfortunately Eleanor knew she lacked the interpersonal skills to win Jeanie back after her initial gaffe. She had no doubt that Jeanie would know how to accomplish such a feat, but of course she had no motivation to share her secrets with the likes of Eleanor. It was a real catch-22.

Eleanor checked her guide book as she entered the basilica, locating the stained glass window labeled with the number one on her map. With no one to be annoyed, she once more indulged her need to stop at every point on the map in numerical order, and read every sign no matter how mundane. She couldn't help it. Despite all common sense, if she skipped over something, the feeling of a missed opportunity lingered for days. There was no doubt that her insistence would drive an impulsive person like Jeanie completely insane, as it had all the other women in her past. Yes, it was definitely better for everyone that Eleanor was on her own.

Rounding the corner beyond the main altar, she came to a small chapel with a glass case against one wall. It was too dark to see inside, but after slipping a few coins into a slot, a light came on to reveal a reliquary containing the mummified hand of Saint Stephen, draped in gold and rubies.

Eleanor shuddered and took a step back. Her admiration of the beauty and craftsmanship gave way to revulsion. *Why would anyone think it was a good idea to keep something so disgusting on display?* While the beauty of the church's architecture were impressive beyond creed or culture, other things, like shriveled up body parts, were somewhat less transcendent.

I need to get out of here! Eleanor hurriedly checked her map for the exit as her pulse throbbed. There were a few more numbered stops on the tour, but she'd had about enough of churches for now. She prayed she could keep her OCD at bay long enough to make her escape before a panic attack ensued. *I should have stayed on the ship.*

As Eleanor stepped outside, a gust of wind whipped at her back and she was surprised to see that the sky had grown dark with clouds. Rummaging in her bag, she pulled out an umbrella. Though she longed for the quiet of her room, the unfinished tour beckoned. She'd committed to taking the tour, and anxiety was already slithering in her belly from skipping the last three stops in the basilica. She checked her book. Next stop: Freedom Square, complete with a Soviet monument and a life-sized statue of Ronald Reagan. Eleanor gave a loud snort. That was the *last* thing she was interested in seeing. But like it or not, she was better off just following the map.

The square itself was stately, filled with flowers and plants. The statue of Reagan was exactly as corny as she'd pictured it being, amusing her. She pulled out her phone to snap a selfie as she stood beside it. Eleanor wasn't typically one for taking selfies, but what else were you supposed to do when faced with a life-sized bronze Reagan? Besides, selfies were necessary when traveling alone, and Miriam would get a real kick out of posting the image to her wall.

A few blocks behind Reagan was the dome of the parliament building. Eleanor assumed that was her next stop, but a glance at the tour book suggested a different way to walk, by way of the train station. Knowing it was useless to argue with her obsessive brain at this point, she turned away from the dome and headed toward Nyugati Square. A raindrop plopped onto the top of her scalp, and she cringed as it ran down her forehead in a cold, wet line. She opened her umbrella with a snap and quickened her pace as the rain began to fall in earnest.

By the time she reached the edge of the square, the rain was falling in heavy sheets and Eleanor scurried the last several yards to the shelter of a pedestrian underpass. She blinked as her eyes adjusted to the dim light, then closed her dripping umbrella and tightened her grip as if it were a club. The underpass was isolated and filled with graffiti, exactly the type of place you should never go by yourself. As she took a step inside, she could see several shadows at the far end. She wasn't alone after all.

At that moment, Eleanor heard a woman's muffled cry and saw the group of shadowy forms descending on a smaller lone figure. Raising the umbrella above her head, she charged the length of the underpass, letting out a loud "Hey!" as she ran. The figures stopped, one doubled over, and then they all ran. They left behind what appeared to be a woman, seemingly unharmed, though Eleanor thought they may have made off with her bag.

"Are you okay?" she called out as she approached.

"I...I think so," was the timid reply.

Eleanor slowed her steps and lowered the umbrella to her side, then stopped completely in her tracks as she realized, unlikely as it seemed, that she knew that voice. Actually, considering to whom the voice belonged, it wasn't as surprising as it seemed. Who else would wander blindly by herself into a deserted tunnel filled with dangerous ruffians?

"Jeanie?" Her voice echoed off the walls, making the shadowy figure jump. Eleanor squinted at the trembling figure, trying to make out her face. "Jeanie Brooks, is that you?"

SIX

JEANIE SHUT her eyes tight and held her breath as the three men approached. They spoke in a language she didn't understand, but the way one of them tugged at the strap of her backpack made it clear that he intended for her to hand it over. *Think, Jeanie! What would Eleanor do?* She gulped, tightening her grip on the strap. At that moment, a whooping sound from deep within the corridor startled her and her would-be attackers alike. In a flash, her knee connected with her attacker's groin and he doubled over with a grunt. Her hands flew open in alarm at what she'd done, and all the men ran, taking her backpack with them. Jeanie stared in disbelief as the figure of her rescuer emerged from the shadows, like an avenging angel wielding what appeared to be a sword. "Mercy!" she squeaked.

"Are you okay?" a strong but unexpectedly feminine voice called out.

"I…I think so," Jeanie replied, feeling confused. *What is a woman doing here…with a sword?*

"Jeanie?"

Jeanie jumped. *The avenging angel knows my name?*

"Jeanie Brooks, is that you?"

"Yes, it's me!" Jeanie called out, eyes wide with shock as the angel stepped from the shadows, dressed in a sensible tunic and leggings, clutching the handle of an umbrella in her sword hand and wearing a familiar scowl. *Eleanor?* "I thought you planned to stay on the ship," Jeanie remarked dumbly, her mind suddenly blank.

"I changed my mind." Eleanor drew alongside her, the scowl changing to concern at Jeanie's disheveled appearance. "Lucky for you. Are you sure you're okay?"

Jeanie nodded. She straightened her top, which had been pulled askew in her struggle. She could feel the rawness of her hands from where her backpack's canvas strap had chafed as it was pried from her grip, but otherwise she was unharmed.

"Was it my imagination, or did you kick one of those men in the balls?"

Jeanie gulped and nodded again, speechless as she recalled what she had done.

"What were you thinking?" Eleanor scolded.

That I needed to act more like you! Tears stung Jeanie's eyes. "I thought it might help."

"That's not what I meant. Why were you walking

all by yourself into a dark underpass? This is a big city, not Hartsdale or Schenectady, or wherever it is you're from."

Jeanie stiffened. "You walked down here all alone, too," she pointed out matter-of-factly.

"Yes, just in time to save *you*."

"Maybe, but that's not the reason you came down here. You came charging up all of maybe a fraction of a second after I screamed. You had to have been half way through the corridor before you even knew what was going on." She could tell by the look on Eleanor's face that she'd struck a nerve. This was a woman who clearly hated being told when she was wrong. *Which makes it surprisingly fun.*

"Well, that's some gratitude."

"I'm sorry. I am grateful." Jeanie found it hard to keep a grudge, and the memory of Eleanor swooping in to rescue her drove away most of her earlier annoyance. *She got you into the dance classes, too, don't forget.* Resigned to wiping the slate clean, she couldn't resist one final jab first. "I just don't see why when I come down here to escape the rain, it's foolish, but somehow it isn't for you, even when you did the exact same thing."

"I wasn't escaping the rain, I was following a tour map," Eleanor corrected her, as if somehow that made her choices make more sense. "I didn't need to escape the rain because *I* planned ahead and brought an umbrella."

Jeanie cocked her eyebrow as she stared at the object that dripped in Eleanor's hand, looking nothing like a sword anymore. Her self-assurance was impressive as ever, but Jeanie wondered if the woman knew how misplaced it probably was when her only weapon was an umbrella. "Well, unless that thing comes equipped with poison in its tip, I really don't see how you were any less likely to get mugged than I was." Jeanie bit back a chuckle as Eleanor glared at her silently. *Another point for me!*

"Speaking of mugging, we should get you to a police station so you can report this. I assume they got everything: wallet, passport? You'll need to contact the embassy."

Overwhelmed by the onerous tasks ahead of her, Jeanie began to nod, then paused as something fluttered through her memory. "Wait, no. I don't remember putting it back in the bag." She grinned as the realization struck. "I left my wallet at the security desk in the parliament building, with my passport inside!"

Eleanor looked at her, dumbfounded. "So what was in the backpack?"

"Nothing!" Jeanie laughed. "All I had was a water bottle and a swimsuit. I was on my way to the thermal baths."

Eleanor studied her for a moment, a funny look on her face. "Do you have any idea what the odds are against that? I don't even know if I could calculate it."

Something that Jeanie might almost describe as admiration flitted across Eleanor's features. Admiration, or indigestion. Either interpretation was plausible.

"Honestly, things like that happen to me a lot." Jeanie shrugged. "Well, I guess I'd better head back to retrieve my stuff."

"I'll go with you. After what just happened, I think we'd both be better off not walking alone, don't you? Besides, I was just headed that way."

Jeanie began to walk back into the underpass as Eleanor took a step toward the outside. "Uh, Eleanor? Parliament's this way."

"Yes, but the map says to go this way."

"Just to be clear, this is the same map that told you to walk into a deserted underpass full of dangerous thugs?"

Eleanor glared at her again, and this time Jeanie couldn't help but laugh. A perverse part of her actually enjoyed confounding this woman, teasing her until her eyes narrowed into amber slits and her thin peach lips curled into a pout that was remarkably sexy beneath the annoyance. It wasn't that Jeanie was a rule breaker, but Eleanor wrote the book on following directions. Pushing her buttons made Eleanor flustered in the most enticing way.

"I'll have you know, I was following a walking tour. A tour which was interrupted quite suddenly by my having to rescue *you*. And one that I wouldn't mind finishing."

Jeanie smoothed the smile from her lips, remembering with a slight shiver her avenging angel charging out of the darkness to save her. "I'm sorry. Of course we can finish your walking tour."

Eleanor gave her a curt nod. She crooked her elbow toward Jeanie. "Shall we?"

Jeanie gave the elbow a bemused look as she slipped her arm through. As unlikely as it had seemed earlier in the day, she was setting off to explore the wonders of Budapest arm-in-arm with Eleanor Fielding, after all. The prospect left her conflicted. Eleanor was as stunning as a Botticelli, as intriguing as a thousand-piece puzzle, and as prickly as a cactus. Half an hour ago, Jeanie would've sworn she'd be happy never seeing Eleanor again, but now she thought she might not mind getting to know the woman a little better after all.

They emerged from the underpass just a few yards from the train station, where Eleanor paused to consult her guide book. After orienting herself to the map, the two women set off on a circuitous route back to the parliament building, seemingly stopping every three or four feet to look at some completely mundane piece of shrubbery that the tour book insisted they needed to see. By about the eighth such stop, Jeanie was bouncing on the balls of her feet, unable to reign in her agitation.

"Honestly, Eleanor," Jeanie said with a whine. "It's a rose bush on a median strip. What about this could possibly be worth stopping for?"

"It says here that this variety was specially cultivated for the millennial celebration in 1896."

"I see." Jeanie stared at the bush, unimpressed. "And are you an avid gardener, or something, that this is fascinating to you?"

Eleanor shook her head and Jeanie rolled her eyes. "Then why are we stopping? We could cut through that alley and be there in half a second."

"Because that's not how it is on the map." There was something in the way she said it that made Jeanie refrain from her initial snarky retort and remain silent so Eleanor could explain. "I get…anxious sometimes. Doing things in the right order, well, it helps." Her eyes were downcast, as if doubting that Jeanie would understand.

It felt to Jeanie like one of the puzzle pieces had fallen into place, perhaps even one of the corner ones that would make the rest of the picture easier to put together. She felt a sympathetic stirring at the woman's honest response, and at the pain that etched her face. She didn't know Eleanor well, but she knew enough to understand that admitting her struggle couldn't have been easy. The fact that Eleanor had confided in her sparked an unexpectedly tender response. "It's okay. Let's just stick to the map. Lead the way."

They continued their stroll, the dome of the parliament building slowly coming closer as they made their stops. When they arrived at their destination, Jeanie ran inside and emerged seconds later, waving her wallet triumphantly as she raced back down the steps.

"You found it!" Eleanor smiled, shaking her head with a look of disbelief. "You really do beat the odds, don't you." This time, her expression was undeniably one of admiration.

"I'll admit, I was a little worried." Jeanie glanced back up the steps where she had just been. "So, I guess this is where we part ways, huh? Thanks for walking with me."

Eleanor's brow wrinkled and Jeanie was surprised to see what might be interpreted as disappointment in her eyes. "Oh. I guess I—"

"I guess I assumed. I've already done the tour here and I don't want to throw off your list by having you skip a stop, so—"

"No! I mean, no, it's not part of the tour. I mean, the one I was doing ends here, but technically going into the parliament building would be the start of a new tour. And, well, I mean, I don't have to…"

"Oh." Jeanie's breath caught as she felt an unexpected fluttering inside her chest. "You don't?"

Eleanor shook her head. "After what happened back there by the train station, it would be safer for both of us—"

The fluttering in Jeanie's chest subsided and she

felt a little silly that she'd had that reaction at all to what was at most a friendly gesture. *Safety.* Two women traveling in a foreign city were safer together than alone. Eleanor was just being practical. It was nothing personal. "Yeah, that's what I was thinking, too. Safety first, that's my motto."

Eleanor gave her a sideways glance, as though she wasn't quite convinced of Jeanie's ability to live by such a motto, but she said nothing. They'd drifted away from the steps as they talked and now were standing at the corner among a crowd of pedestrians. When the light changed, they crossed along with them, then continued down to the cobblestone promenade along the river. After they'd walked several yards, Eleanor stopped. "Wait. Where are we going?"

Jeanie shrugged. "On an adventure." She wilted under Eleanor's withering stare and suppressed a groan as the other woman whipped out the tour book. "Oh, honestly. Put that thing away." Jeanie made a swipe for the book, but missed as Eleanor moved it from her reach. "You don't really want to go on another one of those awful tours, do you?" She swiped at the book again, this time catching it by its corner full force. Jeanie stared, horrified, as the book was suddenly lifted airborne, gliding in a graceful arc above their heads and across the width of the cobblestone walkway before landing with a splash atop the swiftly flowing waters of the Danube.

Eleanor watched, mouth agape, as the current

whisked her book away. She raced after it, leaving a stunned Jeanie in her wake. Eleanor was a surprisingly brisk runner, and by the time Jeanie caught up with her, her own breath was labored. But the river had moved faster than either of them, and the book was lost to its depths. Eleanor stood motionless, staring at the turbid water of the Danube.

"Oh, Eleanor. I'm so sorry." Jeanie panted painfully between words, but the stitch in her side was nothing compared to the white-hot embarrassment that threatened to burn her from the inside out. *I can't believe I threw her book in the river!* And just when they'd been getting along so well, too. Eleanor would never want to spend time with her after this, and the stinging sense of loss that accompanied that realization took Jeanie somewhat by surprise.

The toes of Eleanor's shoes were inches from the edge of the promenade, at the start of a line of dozens of other pairs of shoes. At first glance they looked real, and Jeanie racked her brain to figure out who had left them there, but she soon realized they were made of metal. *Some sort of art?* Her usual expertise on the subject failed her. The further art strayed from the Renaissance period, the less attention she paid to it. Unable to make sense of it, she dismissed it from her thoughts and turned her energy instead to something more important: making amends. If only she knew where to begin.

"Eleanor? Look, I—"

"I need to go." Without another word, Eleanor turned from the water's edge, moving with long, determined strides in the direction of the ship.

Jeanie watched helplessly as she disappeared from view, uncertain what to do. *Should I follow her?* An image of Eleanor's face, hollow and pale, flashed into her mind. Probably the last thing Eleanor wanted right now was to have Jeanie around. She seemed furious, and Jeanie reluctantly admitted she had every reason to be. Her insides tightened into a knot. One thing was clear, her clumsy blunder had inflicted much more damage on their budding friendship than Jeanie had initially realized, and she was far from certain that she had the skills to set it right.

SEVEN

ELEANOR PINCHED HER CHEEKS FIRMLY, searching her reflection in the bathroom mirror for any returning signs of life. The results weren't promising. Even after dabbing on some foundation beneath her puffy eyes and adding a coating of gloss to the thin lines of her mouth, she looked haggard. The emotions of the afternoon had taken their toll.

Her eyes squeezed shut and she could see the hard edge of gray cobblestones dropping off into swirling brown water beneath, and the seemingly endless line of iron shoes coated in rust. *So many shoes.* A shudder ran from her shoulders down the length of her back. Her lungs tightened like hands were squeezing them inside her chest. She'd realized instinctively what it was, where she was standing, even before reading the plaque at her feet. *To the memory of the victims shot into the Danube.*

She gasped as her cell phone rang, then her breathing returning to normal as she recognized the ring tone reserved for Miriam.

"Mimi? I'm so glad you called me back!"

"*Of course I did, Elle. I always call when you use the code.*"

They'd devised the codeword years ago, an ordinary word that could be left as a message or sent as a text to signal that something important was going on, good or bad, and needed to be discussed pronto. Eleanor had texted it to her as soon as she got back to the ship.

"Oh, Mimi, it was awful."

"*Awful? Ah, crap. I was hoping you were calling to tell me you'd already met someone and were planning to elope.*"

Eleanor laughed despite herself. "Seriously, Mimi? This is only my second day on the ship! Besides which, we're going to need to have a little talk when I get back about the difference between European and American calendars."

"*What? Why?*"

"Because you screwed up the dates, my dear. I swear, between you and Jeanie! The lesbian cruise you were so desperate for me to go on was *last* month. This month's cruise is for senior citizens who want to learn how to dance."

"*No! You didn't use the code to tell me you're coming home, did you?*"

"No, nothing like that. If anything, I guess I could use some relaxation more than I'd realized. I started to have a panic attack this afternoon. Not a full-blown one, so don't worry. I managed to keep it mostly under control. But still, it had me scared."

"*Oh, Elle! But you'd been doing so well. You haven't had one in over a year.*" Not since the one that finally drove Sylvia away, Eleanor silently amended her sister's words. "*What happened?*"

"It was that Holocaust memorial. Remember the one with the shoes that you wanted me to photograph for you? Well, I ran into it today. Quite literally."

Eleanor's mind raced back to that afternoon when she'd chased after her tour book and all of a sudden she'd been just inches from the shoes. *To the memory of the victims shot into the Danube.* The memorial hadn't specified that the victims were Jewish, but it didn't need to. In a Nazi-occupied country at the height of the war, who else would it be?

"*So, you went to see it on a tour?*"

"No, it was a stupid accident. Jeanie had knocked my book into the river and I chased after it—no idea why, since any fool would've known it was lost for good—and almost tripped over the first shoe before I realized where I was. There was so much hatred there, Mimi. I swear I could still feel it."

Eleanor's body shook while she described it. As a Jewish woman and a lesbian, she'd faced more than her fair share of bigotry before, but nothing in her life had prepared her for the visceral impact of standing in that spot. The magnitude of the atrocity that had once been enacted on that river bank had hit her like an icy wave where she'd stood. Her body had grown unbearably heavy, her knees threatening to buckle while her head spun. For one terrifying moment she truly believed she would follow in their footsteps, into the murky depths of the river.

"Remember Rabbi Schultz's wife, wasn't she Hungarian? I think she grew up in Budapest during the war."

"Yeah, I remember her. She used to make the best *hamantaschen* for Purim, and she'd let us kids have as many to eat as we could stuff in our mouths." She squeezed her eyes shut to keep back a fresh flow of tears. "I thought of her when I was standing there, Mimi. I thought of all of them—the ones we knew who survived, and the ones who didn't. And I just kept thinking that if I'd been alive then, it would've been me, too. I had to get away from there, and when I got back to the room, the panic hit me full force."

"Oh, Elle, honey. That sounds awful." The conversation fell silent for a moment. "So, who's Jeanie?"

"Sorry?"

"*Jeanie. You mentioned her twice.*"

"I...no, I didn't."

"*Yes, you did.*"

Crap. "She's just another passenger I met on the ship." *Whom I abandoned on the promenade when I ran off like a lunatic. What must she be thinking of me right now?*

"One of the senior citizens?"

"No. She's about my age, I guess. Maybe a few years younger."

"*I see. So she was supposed to be on the singles cruise, too, huh?*" The glee in Miriam's voice was unmistakable.

"You can stop right there. I know where you're going with this. Yes, she likes women. No, that does not mean we're going to be in a relationship, nor are we running off to get married."

"*I see. So you don't find her attractive?*"

"I…" Eleanor cringed at the hesitance in her voice.

"*Ha! I knew it. You totally do!*"

"She's attractive, okay? Nice hair, great legs—so what? She's unpredictable, and unreliable, and absolutely, one hundred percent, the opposite of me in every way."

"*So, what you're saying is, she's fun?*" Miriam teased.

"Shut up. I can be fun."

"*Mmm…hmm.*"

Sitting on the edge of her bed, Eleanor twisted the corner of the duvet around her fingers nervously as she remembered her behavior that afternoon. "The thing is Mimi, even if I were interested—and I'm not saying I am—she's not going to want to talk to me after today."

"*She was that freaked out by your OCD?*"

"Actually, no." Eleanor smiled faintly as she recalled their walk from the train station. "That was the weird thing. There was a point where she was teasing me—"

"*I like her already!*"

"She was teasing me about the walking tour I was following. You know me, I had to do each step of it in the correct order. It was this historical gardening thing—"

"A gardening tour? Elle, you grew up in Manhattan. Have you ever planted a single thing in your life?"

Eleanor snorted. "Not as I can recall. You do know that this is the one area in my life where logic doesn't play a role, right?"

"Oh, I know. So you insisted on stopping every fifteen feet to read the signs?"

"It's scary how well you know me. But the weird thing was, she seemed to get it."

"Really? That is weird. Do you think she has anxiety herself?"

"Jeanie?" Eleanor laughed. "I think that Jeanie Brooks lives on her own special planet where anxiety and worry don't exist. But she handled it really well. And it's not like she had any reason to pretend it bothered her less than it did." Not like Sylvia, who'd enjoyed riding in first class enough to hide her frustration, at least in the beginning.

"Wait, you know her last name, too? This is serious. You never remember people's names."

"Shut up." It was true, but not something she was proud of. She knew it made her seem rude, unlike Jeanie who could remember the name of every person she ever met like some sort of magical memory goddess.

"Fine. But you've never said why she won't want to talk to you again. If it's not the anxiety…"

"Mimi, it was so embarrassing." Eleanor's stomach clenched. "I just froze when I saw those shoes. Then I said I had to go, and I turned and ran. No explanation. She has to think I'm crazy."

"*So explain it to her.*"

"How do I explain something like that?"

"*Look, you like her. So all you do—*"

Eleanor stiffened. "Wait. I never said I liked her."

"*You like her. Maybe just as a friend, but you like her. So you just tell her the truth. She'll probably understand. I mean, she already suffered through that gardening tour and survived. That sounded way worse than the panic attack.*"

"But, Mimi, I don't even know where she is."

"*You're on a boat, Elle. On a river. So how many places could she be? It's almost dinner where you are, right? Go find her in the dining room. Everyone's gotta eat, and from what you described, she'll be the only one there without silver hair.*"

Eleanor sighed. "Okay. I guess it couldn't hurt. Thanks, Sis."

She hung up the call and stretched out on the bed, trying to summon the strength to go out and face the world. It was slow in coming. All she really wanted was to call the concierge and have a dinner tray delivered to her room. She could go to bed early and look for Jeanie in the morning. Or not at all. Despite the hour or two they'd spent touring together today, they were virtually strangers. Jeanie was probably just as happy to be rid of her company. Wouldn't it be easier to accept defeat now than try to make it right and fail anyway?

That's just the anxiety talking. Eleanor pushed herself up from the downy depths of her duvet with a whimper. *You know that's not how you operate anywhere else. Eleanor Fielding does not accept defeat!* She and Jeanie were different as night and day, but they'd gotten along, and Jeanie had shown her a great deal of consideration in indulging her idiosyncrasies. The least she could do was apologize for running off. Eleanor owed her that much. Jeanie would probably not want to spend any more time with her on the trip, a realization that left Eleanor feeling hollow inside, but at least she could explain and be brave enough to face the consequences.

But how? Telling someone you'd just met that you had a panic attack because the ghosts of your ancestors cried out for justice on the banks of the Danube sounded…totally nuts. Eleanor felt her cheeks tingle, mortified at how she'd allowed herself to lose control. She hated that her anxiety had the power to turn her into someone she barely recognized. It was humiliating.

On her way out the door, Eleanor caught a glimpse of her face in a mirror and laughed in spite of herself. She looked a hundred times better than she had, her cheeks once more exhibiting a peachy glow. At least she could thank the utter embarrassment that she felt in herself for putting some color back into her complexion.

She made her way reluctantly to the main dining room and peered through the glass doors. She squinted in confusion to find that, though the doors had opened for dinner a full five minutes before, the room was empty. Could the whole rest of the ship really be running late this time, or was she about to discover another snafu?

"Excuse me, but are you looking for your friend, Miss Jeanie?"

Eleanor spun around to see one of the crew members that Jeanie had spoken with on their first day. The nice one, not the one she'd threatened with a lawsuit. *His name is…*Nope. Eleanor couldn't remember. "Where is everyone?"

"The first dance class was today, and it's running behind schedule. They're down there," he added, pointing down the corridor.

"Thank you…Rolfe!" She added his name with a grin, feeling inordinately pleased with herself for recalling that detail.

She found the classroom and pushed the door open, freezing in her tracks at the sight of dozens of couples swirling to the recorded music of a jazz band. She was completely out of her element in this setting, the chaos of the movements making her jittery. Just as the song concluded, she spotted Jeanie on the opposite side of the room. She'd changed into a full-skirted polka dot dress that twirled out around her as her partner gave her a final spin with a surprising amount of energy for a gentleman who could have danced to this music when it was new. Eleanor watched, transfixed.

After a smattering of applause for the instructor, the dancers gathered up their things and headed to the door. Jeanie chatted amicably with a few of the other women as she approached where Eleanor stood. Her face clouded over as she caught sight of Eleanor, her jovial mood seeming to evaporate, and Eleanor's stomach clenched. Jeanie was anything but happy to see her, and Eleanor still had no idea what she was going to say in her own defense.

EIGHT

A FEW HOURS EARLIER...

"Oh, Mama, I feel like such an idiot." Jeanie lay across her narrow bed, elbows propped up on her single pillow, with her chin resting on folded hands. "Why am I always getting myself into situations like this? I'm too impulsive."

Her mother's sympathetic face looked back at her from the screen of her tablet. "You know I won't argue with you about that. Not after you just emptied your savings account and flew off to Budapest on a whim!"

"It wasn't a whim! I've been saving up for a trip to Europe for years."

"A trip, yes. But not this particular trip. You went from seeing the ad to booking the ticket in a matter of minutes! It's no wonder you mixed up the dates."

"Yes, but that wasn't the mistake I was talking about. We already discussed that one yesterday, and

I've gotten over it. I've decided this is still a very nice cruise, and I'm going to learn how to dance, too." Jeanie stuck out her tongue at her mother's doubting face. "Today's issue is why I can't stop myself from flinging other people's books into the Danube!"

"Oh, Jeanie." Her mother chuckled. "You've always had trouble maintaining your poise when there's a pretty girl involved."

Jeanie bristled. "How do you even know she's pretty? I never said she was."

"You didn't have to, sweetie. It was obvious as soon as you said that you tossed her book in the river."

"Fine. She's pretty." Jeanie rolled her eyes. Her mother could always be counted on to see right through her. "And confident. And gallant. And sometimes dorky, but in a cute way. But also rigid and arrogant. And if there were any other single women on this ship like there were supposed to be, I wouldn't be giving her a second thought right now."

"You're certain about that?"

"Yes! We have nothing in common, except the ability to reverse dates on a calendar, apparently. And she won't even admit that she did it, which is really annoying. Blamed her sister."

"Still, you like her enough that you're upset by the possibility of not seeing her again."

Jeanie sighed. "We were having a nice time before I ruined it." She shut her eyes tightly as she recalled the way the tour book had sailed through the air. "The thing is, Mama, I can't help doing stupid things sometimes. I get nervous. I ramble and say things I regret later. That's just me. If she's going to get angry every time I do, there's no use thinking we could get along for the next two weeks, let alone anything else."

"Goodness, you must really like her."

"What do you mean?" Jeanie frowned in confusion. "No, I don't. She's rigid and arrogant, remember? I'm sure I mentioned it. But it would have been nice to have a companion on the cruise. That's all."

"So why are you worried about getting along after the cruise?"

"I'm not! I…" Jeanie's earlier words played back through her mind. "Oh."

"So maybe she's more than just a convenience?"

"I…" Jeanie slumped against the pillow, burying her face. She let out a muffled scream. "No," she answered, looking at her mother on the screen. "It's just me being stupid again. Rationally, even if we patched things up enough to go sightseeing together again, that's all it would be."

"You're sure about that?" her mother asked, and Jeanie nodded. "You're not usually all that swayed by what's rational. But if that's really how you feel, and you do end up spending more time together, try to go easy on her."

"What do you mean?"

"What I mean, Jeanie Louise, is that you're a merciless flirt! You don't want to lead the poor woman on."

"I am not!"

"You are, sweetie. Women, men, straight, gay. You can't help yourself. You flirt with everyone."

Jeanie thought back to her recent encounters with the security guard and the men on the crew. She was always nice to people, and sometimes she'd butter them up a little so that she could get their help, but that wasn't really flirting, was it? She groaned. Her mother might have a point. "I don't mean any harm by it."

"I know that. But Eleanor doesn't. Try not to confuse her."

"I won't, not that it matters," Jeanie added with a sinking heart, remembering the cold, sunken look on Eleanor's face. "She's too angry to ever give me a second chance."

Once the video chat ended, Jeanie slid off the bed into a pile of clothing on the floor. Trying to fit her wardrobe into the built-in drawers had been an exercise in frustration, and Jeanie appreciated that leaving everything out allowed her to see all of her clothing options at a glance. What her system lacked in tidiness it made up for in convenience, at least as long as she remembered to lift her feet when she walked so she wouldn't trip. It worked for her. *Some* people would probably not approve.

Jeanie groaned and looked around the room,

desperate to get her mind off Eleanor. She knew she was putting too much energy into worrying about a casual acquaintance. *So what does that mean?* She found Eleanor interesting. And smart, and attractive, with an almost regal bearing that made Jeanie's knees go weak. She obviously had a successful career, and money, too, though that fact made Jeanie more nervous than excited. In Jeanie's experience, combining women and money was the fastest route to a broken heart. She'd thought she could manage a quick holiday fling, but if she was already talking to her mom about the future beyond this cruise, there was little chance that would succeed.

Besides, it didn't matter how long a list she might make of Eleanor's good qualities. The list of negatives would surely be at least as long. They were completely incompatible! That might not matter too much for a few weeks of fun, but it did for anything more serious. For once in her life, Jeanie was determined to be practical. She was finally touring Europe, maybe for the only time ever in her life. She couldn't let worrying about some non-existent future with a woman she'd just met get in the way of that! Especially a woman who most likely hated her.

Her eyes landed on the dance schedule that Thomas had delivered to her room the night before. *Thanks to Eleanor.* She pushed the thought away. Picking up the sheet, she saw that an introduction to swing dancing had just started a few minutes before in the ballroom upstairs. Eleanor had fought for her to gain access to the classes, so she might as well go. She stood and rummaged around for a pair of shoes, then headed out to join the class. In her mind, she could see Eleanor's face, eyebrows raised in alarm, as if about to lecture her on the fact that she was going to be late. *Yes, Eleanor, I know!* she grumbled to herself.

She stopped at the ship's snack bar to pick up a sandwich on her way. It made her even later to class, but it had to be done. By the time class was over, the snack bar would be closed, and Jeanie hadn't purchased a meal plan with her ticket. The dining room was expensive and she'd needed to save where she could, so a packaged sandwich and bag of chips would just have to do. It was just as well, since she'd be eating alone, anyway.

As she approached the glass doors to the ballroom, she heard big band music playing inside and could see couples dancing across the floor. She watched from the sidelines, moving her feet in place as she tried to pick up a few of the steps. When the music stopped, a gray-haired gentleman wearing pin-striped trousers and a matching vest approached her and held out his hand.

"Would you like to try it?"

Jeanie smiled and took his hand. "I'd be delighted! But I have no idea what I'm doing."

They danced the next song together, with Jeanie quickly picking up the basic moves. By the time it ended, Jeanie was laughing breathlessly.

"See?" her partner asked. "You did very well!"

"Only because I had such a good partner," she said, her cheeks flushing pink.

At the teacher's instruction, they traded partners several times until they came to a break. When the music stopped, Jeanie suddenly found herself surrounded by three of her former dance partners. Each held out a paper cup of water for her. Three women, probably their wives, glared in her direction as they filled their own cups with water. Jeanie felt a sinking feeling inside. *This is exactly what Mama warned me about!* She hadn't intended to, but she was almost certain she'd been flirting with all three. Their wives certainly seemed to think so.

Jeanie wondered if she could rectify the situation by calling out, "It's okay, ladies, I'm a lesbian!" in her loudest voice before the next round of dances. *What if one of them yelled back, "Me too!"* Jeanie snorted at the thought. *Wouldn't that be convenient?* Then she'd have a new tour companion and could put all thoughts of Eleanor right out of her head for good!

After the last dance ended, Jeanie made a point of approaching the three women who had given her such sour looks during the break. "I just wanted to thank you ladies for sharing your husbands with a beginner like me," she said with her most sincere smile. "It was so nice to be able to dance. My girlfriend couldn't make it," she improvised with a little fib, emphasizing the word 'girlfriend' and wondering if they'd understand the hint. Or were they firmly of the generation where all women were girlfriends, and announcing you were gay just meant you were particularly happy that day?

The women looked at her with surprise, their formerly frosty expressions warming by several degrees. "Oh, well that's quite all right, dear," one of the women said. "Isn't it nice that a young person like you is interested in these old dances."

Jeanie chatted with the ladies on her way to the door, relieved that in this case, she was able to put her natural charm to good use. She'd made enough enemies already for one cruise. As she grabbed up the brown sack that held her dinner, Jeanie caught sight of Eleanor by the door and froze, a cold lump forming in her stomach. *Speaking of enemies...* She had no idea what to say to her, and rather than making the situation worse, she pivoted and headed to the other exit, praying she hadn't yet been seen.

"Planning on a picnic?" Eleanor's voice sounded over her left shoulder.

Jeanie turned with a startled jump. "Oh. Eleanor." *Damn.*

Eleanor eyed the bag in Jeanie's hand. "I noticed you'd brought a lunch to class. I was about to head in for dinner," she began, her face unreadable. "I thought maybe we'd be at the same table, only I guess you have other plans."

"Oh, this." Jeanie glanced down at the sandwich

without enthusiasm. "I'm on an economy ticket. The meals cost extra, so I'm trying to save where I can."

"You should join me." Eleanor's face took on a startled expression, as if she'd been as surprised by her words as Jeanie was. "That is to say, my suite automatically included meals for two people. It doesn't make sense for it to just go to waste."

Jeanie regarded her with a cautious smile. "You're sure?" Her smile widened at Eleanor's nod, relief flooding her as she realized she must have been forgiven for her earlier mistake. "So you aren't mad at me?"

"Mad at you?" Eleanor's brow knitted in confusion. "Why?"

"Because I threw your book in the river."

A burst of laughter erupted from Eleanor's chest. "I was positive that you were mad at me!"

This time Jeanie was the one looking confused. "For what?"

"Running off and leaving you this afternoon. You must've thought I was a crazy person!"

"No!" Jeanie laughed at this unexpected turn of events. "I just assumed you'd had enough of me after that. It's not like I could blame you. I deserved it."

"I was never mad about the book, Jeanie," Eleanor assured her. "God, you should have seen the look on your face when it flew out of my hands! The shock was priceless. I knew all along that it was an accident."

"You did?" Jeanie frowned. "But then, why did you storm off so suddenly?"

"It's a long story," Eleanor said with a sigh. "Probably better to explain over dinner."

"Okay." Jeanie's forced herself to look away from Eleanor's warm amber eyes, and reminded herself that this wasn't a date. It was a friendly dinner. No, it was just pity, really, with no further friendship implied. Eleanor simply had an extra meal ticket and Jeanie was in need of one. It was charity. Usually she would bristle at charity, but as she walked beside Eleanor to the dining room, her pulse ticked up nervously just the same. She told herself she it was just that she was looking forward to a hot meal.

Once they were seated and the waiter had taken their orders, Eleanor began to explain. "So, earlier today. You know that memorial?"

"Memorial?" Jeanie's face wrinkled as she thought. "Oh, you mean that sculpture with the shoes?"

Eleanor nodded. "See, my family is Jewish and—"

"Oh, no!" Jeanie's jaw dropped as the significance hit her, a sudden flash of panic in her eyes. "Don't tell me. It's a Holocaust memorial. Now I feel like an insensitive idiot. I had no idea!"

"Yeah, if only one of us had had a tour book to provide useful information like that." Eleanor's deadpan expression shifted to a grin and Jeanie let out the breath she'd been holding. "Relax, I'm kidding. My sister had mentioned it to me before the trip, so I knew it existed. I just hadn't planned to nearly trip over it like I did." Her expression turned pensive. "Did you know, they used to shoot people there, right along that spot, and let the river carry them away. Men, women, even kids. Coming up on that spot without warning caught me off guard. Just the emotion of it, knowing how easily it could've been me." A tear glistened in Eleanor's eye. "Or us, I guess," she added as if it had just occurred to her. "People like you and me hardly fared much better back then. But it wasn't a good excuse for running off like I did."

"No, Eleanor. I understand." Jeanie regarded her for a moment, feeling as if she wanted to say more, but wasn't sure what. *Why does being around Eleanor seem to leave me so confused?* She opened her mouth to speak. "Wine?" was all she could think to say.

"What?"

"I think we need some wine. With dinner."

"God, yes."

Eleanor motioned to the waiter and Jeanie relaxed into her chair. *Finally, I found something we both can agree on.* The ice between them thawed, Jeanie once again felt the warmth of the connection between them that seemed to have appeared the moment they met. The longer they talked, the more Jeanie hoped to spend time together. But if meaningless sex was off the table, and a long-term relationship impossible, too, it left her wondering: *What else can this be?*

NINE

JEANIE DRUMMED her fingers against the ticket kiosk, waiting. She'd arrived more than twenty minutes before it opened—an eternity!—but it was the only way she knew to get there before Eleanor, who ran a perpetual fifteen minutes ahead of schedule. *If she shows up at all.* That part had been left vague as they parted after dinner, a casual mention of an excursion the next day, and a tentative agreement that such an idea might hold appeal, but without any firm commitment to a plan. Did a woman like Eleanor do anything without a plan?

Jeanie flashed back to the night before when, lying on her tiny bed, all she could think of was Eleanor. *Not in that way! Okay, maybe a little...* But mostly she'd thought about how much nicer the day had been during the parts they'd spent together. It had helped Jeanie make up her mind on one thing. There might not be any romantic potential between them, but the somewhat unconventional friendship they were forming was much preferable to spending two weeks alone. At least, Jeanie thought so. After a pleasant dinner together and more than a few glasses of wine, Eleanor had seemed to come around to a similar way of thinking. The question now was whether she would still feel the same this morning, or if Jeanie would be taking this excursion alone.

As Jeanie watched the ship's gangway with an eagle eye, a lone figure emerged from the ship, one that appeared to be well under the age of sixty and was sporting a new variation of her by-now-familiar travel wardrobe. *Definitely Eleanor.* Jeanie held her breath to see which way she would turn at the promenade. When she pivoted to face the kiosk and took a step in that direction, Jeanie let out a rush of breath with satisfaction. *She's coming this way!* As Eleanor approached, Jeanie faced the shuttered window of the booth and attempted to look nonchalant.

"Is it open yet?" Eleanor asked as she approached.

"Oh, hi, Eleanor!" Jeanie feigned surprise. "No, not yet. So, you decided on an excursion today, too?"

"Well, it sounded nice when you brought it up. Plus, I'm fresh out of tour books to plan anything on my own."

Though it was clear she was teasing, Jeanie felt the heat rise in her cheeks. "About that." She rummaged in her bag and pulled out a brown paper sack. "I stopped in a shop on my way back to the ship yesterday to pick up a new backpack, and while I was there, I spotted this." She handed the bag to Eleanor, who meticulously peeled away the bag to reveal a thick, glossy tour book inside. Jeanie knew that she could easily afford to get a new one for herself, but that wasn't the point. "They didn't have the exact same one as yours, but there are some nice maps and it covers most of the cities on the cruise."

"Jeanie, you didn't have to...thank you." Her face held the same exquisite expression as it had the first afternoon on the observation deck, the one that immediately set Jeanie's heart thumping. "You know I was only joking with you, though, right? I guess I should look through it and figure out where to go today."

"Oh, I've done that already!" Jeanie blurted out, suddenly anxious lest Eleanor decided not to spend the day with her after all. "I mean, that is...you know, if you don't..."

"You? Planned ahead?" Eleanor asked, rescuing her from an endless loop of spluttering. "This I've gotta see. What did you have in mind?"

"There's a day trip to the cave baths at Miskolc-Tapolca. I checked the schedule and a bus leaves for there in about twenty minutes. I read all about it last night in the tour book, and it sounded spectacular."

"Goodness. Looks like you've done all the research for me. Okay. Why not?"

Jeanie grinned. "Yeah? You're sure? I mean, if you

had other things planned and wanted to do something else..." *Shut up, Jeanie! Don't talk her out of it!*

"I'm sure whatever you chose will be fine. I trust your research. My only real plan was to hide on the ship and read for two weeks, remember?" Eleanor seemed more at ease than on the previous two days, and it made Jeanie smile to see her happy.

The ticket kiosk opened and Jeanie purchased two tickets to Tapolca, insisting on paying for Eleanor's fare as a final gesture of her regret over the tour book incident. They climbed aboard the coach and chose two spaces near the back. Jeanie slid in first, trying to ignore the sudden tingling she felt as Eleanor's thigh pressed against hers in the narrow seats. *Stop it, Jeanie! Friends, remember?* Jeanie hadn't forgotten the talk she'd had with her mother. If friends was as far as this could go, she'd need to keep an eye on her more flirtatious tendencies, and the more vivid parts of her imagination firmly in check.

Besides, the last thing Eleanor wants is a girlfriend. As the bus bumped along on its two-hour trek, Jeanie turned this fact over in her mind, and the more she did so, the more it struck her as odd. Eleanor had shown nothing but disdain for the idea of a boat full of lovesick lesbians, but why would someone book a cruise where the sole purpose is to meet single women if they're hell-bent on being alone? It didn't make any sense. And yet Eleanor had affirmed again this morning that her initial plan was to sit by herself for two weeks. *So why is she here at all?* It was another puzzle piece that didn't seem to fit. Finally, the mystery became too much for her.

"Eleanor, may I ask you something?"

Eleanor, who had been resting her head against the back of the seat with her eyes closed, opened them slowly, grunting her assent.

"Why did you come on this cruise? I mean, you don't care about sightseeing, and you had no interest in any of the singles stuff…"

Eleanor sat up straighter in her seat and turned to look at Jeanie. "I'd booked a different cruise, for me and my partner. But she's no longer with me, so—"

Jeanie gasped in dismay. "Oh, God. She's dead?" *First the Holocaust memorial and now this! How many other tragedies can I put my foot in it?*

Eleanor's eyebrows scrunched in confusion. "What? No, she's not dead. She left me. For a flight attendant. From Paris."

"Oh." Jeanie squirmed in her seat. The way Eleanor used the phrase 'no longer with me' just led her to assume the worst. "Oh, my."

Eleanor continued to study her quizzically. "She's thirty-eight, same age as me. Do you know what the odds are of someone dying at that age?"

"No," Jeanie mumbled. "Do you?"

"Of course I do. Or, how to calculate it, anyway. I could probably calculate the odds of someone cheating, too, if I tried." Eleanor laughed as Jeanie gave her a befuddled look. "I'm an actuary. It's a job requirement."

"You are?" She only vaguely knew what that meant, except that it was notoriously dull.

"I am. I'm an expert on risk. Health and life expectancy is just a small part of the industry, though —and I'm afraid no one in their right mind insures against cheating, as they'd lose their shirts. But it's not like I actually spend my day figuring out when people are likely to die, if that's what you were picturing. I work for a global insurance and risk management firm. We assess corporate risk."

"That sounds important." No wonder the woman was always so put-together, with a job like that. "And you're in Manhattan?"

Eleanor nodded. "But I work with offices in Budapest, Vienna, Amsterdam, Prague…all over Europe, really."

"Oh, how exciting!" Jeanie's enthusiasm was sincere. "Don't you ever just want to pack up and come work here?"

"Here?" Eleanor gave her a look as if she'd just suggested running off to join the circus. "Not really, though it's not for lack of offers. Several of my clients would offer me a position in a heartbeat, if they thought I'd take it. But I grew up in the city. Plus I work for a solid, reliable company." She thought a moment and shrugged. "I wouldn't mind being Head of Risk Management, someday, and the bastard who's in the position now is likely to be there until he dies. Which I've calculated to be another twenty to thirty years, unfortunately. But all things considered, it's much more secure to stay where I am."

Jeanie nodded her head, but in truth she was unable to comprehend how someone could have the chance to live and work abroad and not take it. There was no polite way to point it out, so she changed the subject. "But you never really explained how you ended up on this cruise. It's pretty obvious you didn't come here to meet someone."

"In my defense, can you blame me? I've just admitted I like things to be reliable. Can you think of anything with more unknowns than a relationship? I can't. It's nearly impossible to assess the risks. My sister, on the other hand, disagrees with my stance. So she booked the ticket and then persuaded me to go." Eleanor rolled her eyes, but the affection she had for her sister was clear. "Enough about me. How about you?"

"I'm a history teacher at my hometown high school. It's in a very small town, not too far from Poughkeepsie."

"Really?" Eleanor looked surprised. "Sorry, it's just that's kind of the middle of nowhere. I always assumed a place like that would be too closed-minded to live unless you were the type to marry the star quarterback and have a dozen kids."

"Middle of no...You know we're just a few hours

from New York City, right? And we have a world-class university just up the road. My alma mater, in fact." Jeanie shot her a saucy look.

"You went to Vassar?" Eleanor looked suitably impressed, though Jeanie was pleased that she didn't seem to find the notion too difficult to believe.

"We're not completely unenlightened upstate." She shrugged. "But just like you, I grew up there. I lived in the city for a while in grad school, but it didn't work out, so I moved back. A small town may not be as tolerant as Manhattan, but then I'm not exactly parading my lifestyle down the streets these days. It's not like there are a lot of options. At least not ones I haven't already dated, and who haven't gone on to date most of my friends."

"Oh." Eleanor gave her a sympathetic smile. "So that's why you booked the singles cruise."

"No, actually." Jeanie bristled at Eleanor's sudden look of pity. "That was more of a lucky bonus. I've dreamed of traveling for years. I was the only art history major who didn't spend a semester abroad. In fact, I've never traveled outside the country, until now."

"Art history? I didn't realize they teach that in high schools."

"They don't. I teach regular old history, I'm afraid. When I first got out of school, I figured I'd be a curator before I hit thirty. I was top of my class and got a few internship offers, but I lacked the right social connections to really move ahead. My parents have never lent their name to an endowment, I'm afraid." Jeanie sighed as the disappointment of her post-college job search flooded back. She shrugged, her smile returning. "Before I went to grad school, I did the requirements for a teaching certificate to make my parents happy. I didn't think I'd ever need it, but then I ended up leaving and it came in handy. I can't complain. I earn an okay living, get summers off, and I'm on this trip, right?"

"Are you always this upbeat?"

Jeanie nodded. "Pretty much."

"Huh." Apparently unable to think of anything else to say, Eleanor leaned her head back against her seat and shut her eyes, remaining that way until they pulled into Tapolca station.

As the bus came to a stop in the middle of the town square, Jeanie studied the landscape with growing alarm. Faded paint and concrete buildings weren't at all what had been described in the tour book. *Eleanor's going to kill me,* she thought as they stepped off the bus. Her only hope was to pretend like nothing was wrong and pray the spa itself wouldn't disappoint. Jeanie took a deep breath. If there were ever a time to try channeling some of Eleanor's quiet confidence, this was it.

TEN

THE BUS DROPPED them off in a muddy square in the middle of town. There was no real station or shelter, just a sign next to a bench amid the crumbling Soviet-era concrete architecture. Eleanor took in the drab green paint of the closest building, anxiety pricking the skin at the base of her neck. It wasn't how she'd pictured it, and glancing at Jeanie, she wondered what she'd gotten herself into. Her companion's look of concern did little to reassure her.

"This way." After a brief survey of the landscape, Jeanie pointed east, and Eleanor was at least relieved to hear more confidence in the woman's voice than she'd seen on her face.

They walked along a main thoroughfare, past buildings with cracked plaster and cars that were mostly a decade or more old. There was little for Eleanor to look at along the way, with the notable exception of

Jeanie's legs. They'd been pressed against her for the entire two-hour ride, putting her so on edge that she'd barely been able to concentrate. Now they were on full display in a short denim skirt as she strode a few paces ahead. Every so often the view left so little to the imagination that Eleanor could feel her temperature spike as she desperately searched for someplace else to look. But try as she might, Eleanor's eyes just kept being drawn back. *What kind of tourist destination is this, without any sights to see?*

"So, exactly where is it that we're going?" She cringed at her own tone. The accusatory edge to her words betrayed her growing unease. Eleanor realized she'd never asked for details, an oversight that was beginning to worry her as she took in the frayed edges of this working-class town.

"The cave baths. They're thermal springs, like a spa."

"A spa?" Eleanor looked around again somewhat dubiously. *This is what passes for a spa town in the old Eastern Bloc?* "Wait," Eleanor felt her shoulders tense as she realized she'd overlooked an important detail. "Thermal springs? I didn't bring a bathing suit. Why didn't you tell me I needed one before we left?"

"Well, Eleanor, there really wasn't enough time. Remember how early the bus left? If you'd run back to the ship, you might've been late." She said it pleasantly enough, nonetheless Eleanor wondered if Jeanie was taunting her for her obsession with punctuality.

"But, I—"

"Besides, you don't have to worry about it."

Eleanor's muscles began to relax. "Of course. Spas provide that sort of thing, don't they?"

Jeanie laughed. "No, silly. But they separate the baths by gender, so suits aren't required. Good thing, too, since mine was stolen."

"Suits aren't…" Eleanor froze. She blinked her eyes shut against the sudden mental image of Jeanie without a swimsuit, but her imagination wasn't so easily extinguished. "I'm not sure—"

"You seem especially tense today, Eleanor. The baths will do you good. Oh, especially if they offer a Watsu treatment."

"A…what?"

"You've never heard of Watsu? I figured you would have, being from the city and all. It's a relaxation treatment where your body is cradled and massaged and stretched while you float, weightless, in the warm bath. It's marvelous!"

"What, while naked?" Eleanor swallowed roughly.

"Well, obviously." Jeanie gave her a look as if to say that she really wasn't as sophisticated a city girl as she'd let on. "You know, I learned a few rudimentary moves last summer from one of the other counselors at the camp where I was working. Strictly after hours, of course." The memory seemed to add a lustiness to Jeanie's smile, and Eleanor found herself curious to know just how pretty this other counselor had been.

"If they don't have any practitioners of it at the spa, I can show you."

"I...I..." Eleanor's words dissolved into a coughing fit.

Jeanie rummaged in her backpack and pulled out a bottle of water. "Here."

Eleanor took the bottle gratefully, taking a few cautious sips as she fought to steady her breathing. She handed it back to Jeanie, who lifted it to her own mouth to drink. Once again, Eleanor's gaze was transfixed, her pulse ticking up as she watched her companion's full lips wrap around the bottle's opening. A single drop of water escaped Jeanie's lips, and Eleanor followed its path with her eyes. It glistened on the edge of her chin, then plummeted to the bronze skin of her chest, snaking its way toward the deep furrow between Jeanie's breasts. Plump and inviting breasts, that would soon be on full display once they arrived at the spa. Sweat beaded on Eleanor's forehead.

Suddenly her chest constricted in the first sign of impending panic. She blinked, hard, and wrenched her head away to stare at the park across the street. Her body was so tense she could feel something in her neck threaten to snap as she did. "Look over there." There were tents and booths set up, and it appeared that some sort of festival was taking place. "You know, Jeanie, I don't see anything in this place that looks at all like a spa. Maybe we should go check out that fair, instead." *And remain fully clothed. Oh God, I can't breathe!*

"Oh, well...I suppose we could. But it has to be around here—oh, there! I see a sign."

"A sign? What sign? All the signs are in Hungarian."

"Yes, I know, but see there, next to the entrance to the festival? I recognize the word for *cave*. It looks like it's right down this street. How lucky that you happened to look over there when you did!"

"Yeah," Eleanor muttered. "Lucky." She battled to maintain control.

They crossed the street and immediately an impressive stone building with flags in front came into view. *That must be the place.* Eleanor's anxiety increased exponentially with each step. By the time they stood in front of the entrance, her body had become an oven and sweat dribbled down the back of her neck. She struggled to control her breathing, counting slowly in her head to keep the panic contained. The rational part of her brain told her that she was getting herself worked up over nothing. *No big deal, just like showering in the locker room at the gym.* But her rational brain wasn't fully in control. Eleanor knew that if she didn't reign it in now, she'd end up in the middle of a full-blown panic attack.

"Eleanor?" By now, Jeanie was several yards ahead of her and holding open the spa's heavy glass door. "You coming, or what?"

With every ounce of concentration focused on keeping her anxiety contained, Eleanor nodded and joined Jeanie in the lobby. It was a bright and airy space with large photographs of the caves displayed on its walls. The caves were just as beautiful as Jeanie had described, and Eleanor studied each detail carefully as her pulse began to slow. Feeling more in control, she went to catch up with Jeanie, who was walking toward an information desk. The woman at the desk looked pleasant. *Maybe she'll lend me a swimsuit.*

"*Jó naput!*" The woman behind the desk called out. "Good morning! You speak English?" she added when the women exchanged confused looks. "Welcome to Tapolca cave! You're in luck. It's quiet here this morning with the festival going on. I think you'll have the place to yourselves."

It was becoming increasingly clear to Eleanor that she did not share the same definition of luck with the people around her. *Having the place to ourselves is a good thing?* She tamped down another tremor of nerves. *Just what I need. A naked woman in my bath, and nothing to distract me.* "So, we pay here?" she asked with as much calm as she could muster.

"Yes," the woman replied. "It's two thousand forint."

Jeanie sucked in her breath. "Two thousand?" she whispered to Eleanor. "I didn't realize it was so much."

Eleanor's lips twitched with amusement. "It's about seven bucks."

"Oh." Jeanie's cheeks flushed and her posture

became defensive. "Everything around the ship has taken euros, so I didn't realize. In that case, it's much more affordable than I expected."

They handed over their payment and the woman gave them back receipts and a brochure. "You can look around up here as much as you like, then you take the stairs down to the boats when you're ready."

"Boats?" Jeanie's face clouded. "Do we have to take a boat to get to the baths?"

"Baths?" The woman's eyebrows shot up. "Oh, no, no. The water in our cave is completely pure. It's forbidden to touch it!"

"But, but…" Jeanie spluttered. "The tour book specifically recommended bathing at the Miskolc-Tapolca cave!"

"Ah, yes." The woman nodded. "But you see, you're at Tapolca, not Miskolc-Tapolca."

Jeanie's jaw dropped. "There're two different caves with the same name? How do we get to the ones with the spa?"

The woman laughed as if Jeanie had told a particularly funny joke. "It's about four hours from here. On the other side of Budapest. But since you're here, our caves are very nice!"

"Oh, God." Jeanie groaned, looking helplessly at Eleanor. "I seem to have made a little mistake."

"You think?" The tension inside Eleanor snapped. After the emotional turmoil of fighting off a panic attack, Eleanor's nerves were raw. *All that worrying for nothing?* She could feel her temper rising, bleeding into her anxiousness. *We're in the wrong place?* The realization made her blood pressure spike. She glared at the woman behind the counter, but it was hardly her fault that this cave shared a name with some other cave. *How did I let myself get taken to the wrong place?*

"I'm sorry. But these things happen."

She stared at Jeanie, dumbfounded by her ability to take this monumental mistake in stride. How could she not be bothered by this? They were two women alone in a strange country, with no idea where they were. *Anything could've happened to us!* "These things happen?" The word came out as a shrill squeak. Every muscle in her body ached from stress and she couldn't rein herself in any longer. "No, Jeanie. When you actually pay attention and put some thought into what you're doing, they don't. First you book the wrong cruise, now you go to the wrong town? These things only happen to you!" As she said this, Jeanie rolled her eyes and started to walk away. "Where are you going?" She couldn't tell if what she felt now was anger, or fear, or remorse, or something else entirely. She was so confused.

"To the boats. Stand around and complain if you like, but I want to see this cave. And I don't like being yelled at."

Guilt flooded her. The hurt feelings were evident in Jeanie's voice. And she had been yelling, just a little. *But she's missing the point!* Eleanor tried to reason away the guilt. This was Jeanie's fault, not hers. *To think how worked up I was getting on the way here, and all for no reason!* The fact that her getting all hot and bothered had nothing to do with Jeanie buying tickets for the wrong bus, Eleanor conveniently ignored.

Her pulse, which had mostly returned to normal, sped up again as she recalled some of the racier fantasies that had suggested themselves to her on the way there. What had she been thinking? With the thoughts she'd been having about her companion the whole way here, there was no telling what she might've allowed to happen once they were alone together in a thermal bath, *au naturel*.

Honestly, I should be grateful, Eleanor thought as she followed Jeanie toward the stairs. *Let this be a reminder to me that Jeanie Brooks is a living, breathing disaster!* Sure, she was attractive, but she'd had more calamity strike in the three days that Eleanor had known her than anyone she'd ever met. Statistically, it shouldn't have even been possible to have so many accidents. The woman was an anomaly, and given her line of work, Eleanor had never cared much for anomalies. But she'd learned her lesson this time. Once they were safely back on the ship, she wouldn't seek out Jeanie again. She was just too unpredictable.

This resolve was firmly in place as she emerged from the stone steps into a cavern of sparkling turquoise water. Eleanor's breath caught, overwhelmed by the beauty. Had she been in a more generous mood, she would have admitted that visiting this natural cave lake was a million times better than any spa could have been. But she was grumpy and determined to stay that way, so instead she managed to keep the awe at her surroundings carefully balanced with her irrational ire toward Jeanie.

There were metal boats lined up at the edge of the lake, and Jeanie was stepping into one as Eleanor entered the cavern. A man was helping her, and he looked up questioningly at Eleanor. "You ride together?"

Eleanor shook her head. "No. We'll go separately, if that's okay."

"Suits me," Jeanie mumbled, clearly just as annoyed as Eleanor over their interaction upstairs.

"Yes, that's okay," the man replied. "There's no one else here."

Jeanie paddled off as Eleanor stepped into her own little row boat. There was an aching in her chest as she watched her go, but it was soon chased away by another shot of adrenaline as Eleanor's foot hit the bottom of her own boat and it began to wobble uncontrollably. She fought to maintain her balance, praying it wasn't a losing battle. The physical effects of her anxiety had taken their toll. Her body was just too wound up at this point from the ups and downs of her emotions to assert much control as the boat dipped and swayed. "Is the water very deep?"

"No," the man told her as he reached out a hand to

steady the boat, "but some of the passages are a little narrow. If you have trouble, there are alarm buttons in the cave walls."

"I'll be fine, but thank you," she assured him, feeling a little shaky inside but needing to put on a brave face.

She tried her best to relax and enjoy the view as she rowed . The cave lake was stunningly beautiful, beyond anything Eleanor could recall seeing before. The galvanized tin boat reminded her of an old laundry tub, but once it had stopped bobbing it seemed sturdy enough, and she maneuvered it without incident through the cave's first wide tunnel. Here and there, lights had been installed in the rock walls both overhead and beneath the surface of the water, and their reflection made the crystalline water appear to glow. At one point, Eleanor caught sight of a red alarm button in the wall and chuckled. A slight buzzing was all that was left of her earlier anxiety, and that was nothing she couldn't control. The danger had passed. She wouldn't need the alarm today.

Jeanie's boat was nowhere in sight, but Eleanor couldn't shake the woman from her mind. Flashes of her face kept popping up in her brain, but not the flirty looks she'd secretly enjoyed on their walk from the station. All Eleanor could remember now was the stricken expression Jeanie had worn when Eleanor had snapped at her. The dull edge of guilt about her angry outburst was getting harder to ignore. Jeanie's impulsiveness wasn't entirely to blame, she belatedly realized. It was that somehow when she was around the woman, she let down her guard. And that was a problem. It opened her up to too many things that were beyond her control. *But it feels so nice, in the moment.*

Conflicted, Eleanor stretched out along the bottom of her boat and closed her eyes, allowing the gentle current to pull her along as she tried to relax. Warding off her panic today had taken its toll. *What was that thing Jeanie had mentioned, Watsu?* Whatever it was, it sounded like something Eleanor's tense, aching muscles would welcome right about now. The thought of Jeanie's hands touching her bare skin, bending and stretching her floating limbs, sent her pulse ticking up once again. *Now* that *would feel good.*

A sudden thump on the bottom of the boat startled Eleanor from her reverie. Her eyes flew open, and her heart sped up from a gentle trot to a full gallop as she found herself completely in the dark. She bolted upright and cried out as her head slammed into something hard. The pain sent stars shooting behind her eyelids. She felt around in the blackness with mounting concern as her fingertips brushed jagged rock just inches around her on all sides. She was desperate to ring for help, but there was not an alarm button to be had. The panic she'd so neatly suppressed burst full force inside her chest, and she felt a squeezing in her lungs as her airways constricted.

There was nothing she could do. She was alone on a deserted lake, about to die.

"Jeanie?" The words barely escaped the stranglehold of her throat. It felt like the only word she knew.

"Eleanor?"

She heard Jeanie's voice calling out, but at this point she was too far gone to feel relief. Instead she remained huddled in the bottom of the boat, gasping for breath, as Jeanie struggled to pull her boat free from the narrow passageway. Sensing more light, Eleanor opened her eyes a crack and saw Jeanie's face above her, brimming with concern.

"It's okay, Elle. You're okay," Jeanie assured her in the cooing tones one would use to soothe an infant. "You'll be fine. Can you sit up and row? We're not too far from the shore."

Eleanor shook her head and shut her eyes tight, fear engulfing her.

"Okay. I'm going to climb into your boat and row us back."

Eleanor felt the boat start to go topsy-turvy as Jeanie climbed over the edge, and a fresh rush of anxiety flooded her. She was barely aware of the trip back to the platform, or of the walk to the bus stop, or of anything much at all except for the constant, soothing drone of Jeanie's voice in her ears. She called her Elle, just like Miriam always did, and it kept Eleanor from falling to pieces.

They were well into their return trip when Eleanor

finally started to feel more like herself. And the more like her usual self she felt, the more she felt like crap. She'd been at her bitchiest, snarky and rude. And why? It wasn't her anxiety that had caused it, not at first. It was because Jeanie had been teasing her—the flirty kind of teasing, which she enjoyed—so why had she responded with all the maturity of some kid pulling a girl's pigtails on the schoolyard? Her mother's words of wisdom echoed in her head from long ago: *He just does that because he likes you!* Eleanor's shoulders slumped as she admitted to herself that she possessed all the emotional sophistication of a seven- year-old boy.

Eleanor glanced to where Jeanie sat beside her, her head resting against the window. She'd drifted off to sleep shortly after boarding the bus, and no wonder. Taking care of Eleanor in her panicked state had been an exhausting job. And she'd done it even though Eleanor had given her such a hard time the entire trip. She'd treated Jeanie unfairly, Eleanor knew she had. And she regretted it, so very much. She took a raspy breath, her physiology still not quite back to normal after the day's ordeal. She studied Jeanie's face, peaceful in slumber, and warm affection flooded her insides. If it hadn't been for Jeanie rescuing her, she'd still be huddled in the bottom of a glorified laundry tub, wedged in a tunnel in the middle of a lake. *After this, is it really possible we could still be friends?*

She owed Jeanie an apology, at the very least for how she'd behaved in the lobby. Jeanie had done nothing wrong, other than make a mistake that anyone could've made in a foreign place. The Tapolca cave had turned out to be amazing, one of those lucky mistakes in which she seemed to specialize. It would've been a great excursion if Eleanor hadn't ruined it—first with her attitude, then with her ridiculous panic attack. Just apologizing didn't seem like enough after all of that. As the bus made its way back to Budapest and Jeanie slept by her side, Eleanor tried to think of what she could do to make it up to her and maybe win a second chance for herself in the process. She'd been so concerned with fighting off any romantic attachment that she'd lost sight of the numerous benefits of making a friend.

ELEVEN

JEANIE SET her breakfast tray on the table, raising an eyebrow as she spotted a white envelope propped against her glass. "What's this?"

Eleanor looked up from her book and shrugged. "Just a little thank you for taking care of me during my...distress...yesterday." She set the book aside, and gestured toward the envelope. "It seemed like something you'd be interested in."

Jeanie opened the envelope and pulled out two passes for one of the most exclusive thermal bath spas in Budapest. She'd heard of the place, but it was so far out of her price range that she'd never dreamed of going. "Eleanor! This is too much. I thought breakfast was your way of saying thanks. Speaking of which, I'm sorry I was late." *Not that it surprises you, I'm sure.* She managed to keep the last part silent. She didn't want to seem ungrateful for the unexpected generosity, but she could still feel the sting of Eleanor's frequent lectures about her time management and organizational skills.

"I hadn't even noticed." The assertion sounded genuine. "And I can hardly count breakfast as anything special when you already know I have the meals included in my ticket, whether they get used or not."

Jeanie eyed the coffee mug and half-eaten slice of toast at Eleanor's place, then looked at her own overflowing plate with some chagrin. "You barely ate one meal, let alone two."

"I'm not a big fan of breakfast. Especially not after…what happened yesterday. I probably shouldn't be having caffeine, either, but I'm really not human without it."

Jeanie laughed. She could relate to that as she required at least three cups of coffee each morning herself. "Wow, two all-access spa passes? Will we have enough time this morning before the ship departs for Slovakia?"

"Yes, just enough. But they're for you, so don't feel like you have to invite me along. To be honest, those passes came with my ticket package, as well, which is why I had two. You can take whomever you'd like, or go alone if you'd rather."

Jeanie waved the comment aside. "Two passes will do me as much good as two breakfasts would do you. Besides, who else would I invite? We're the only two non-old people on the ship, remember?"

"I don't know. Some of them look downright sprightly. That lady over there's kind of cute."

Jeanie snorted. "Yeah, well, no offense to them, but I think I can live a long and happy life without seeing any of these ladies in their swim suits. Let alone out of them." She'd said it flippantly, but as soon as the words were out of her mouth she saw Eleanor's face turn fifty shades of red, and her own cheeks tingled in response. "I mean, not to imply that I want to see you —" *Shit. I'm doing it again.* She'd ignored her mother's warning and indulged in flirty banter yesterday, and look how that had turned out. She'd almost killed Eleanor!

"I'm afraid today's spa is not clothing optional, just so you know." Whether her tone was amused or annoyed was impossible to tell, and Jeanie squirmed uncomfortably.

"Eleanor, I have a confession." One issue in particular had weighed on her conscience overnight, and she decided now was the time to get it off her chest. "That whole naked swimming thing yesterday was just a joke. I'd packed a spare suit for you. I didn't mean to upset you. I...I don't know if that had anything to do with..."

"It was a panic attack," Eleanor said, finally putting a name to it. "I get them sometimes when I'm stressed. It's just something that happens."

Jeanie smiled reassuringly, but her insides burned with shame at the role she'd played.

"You stayed so calm in the cave."

"I'm a teacher. When you're the only adult in a room with thirty teenagers all day, you learn not to show fear."

"You must be a fantastic teacher."

Jeanie cast her eyes toward the table, embarrassed by the sincerity of Eleanor's compliment. She shrugged noncommittally. It's possible it was true, but teaching had never been where her heart was so it was hard to know how to feel. "I'm just used to keeping my head in an emergency."

"Well, you handled mine like a pro. And, come to think of it, you didn't even think my gardening tour thing was weird!"

"I never said it wasn't weird!" Apparently even feeling ashamed of herself couldn't keep all her teasing in check. Jeanie tried to soften her tone. "But your quirks aren't so unusual. You should see some of the students I've had. Have you…um…talked to someone about this?" She wasn't completely certain what "this" might encompass: Anxiety? Depression? OCD? Whatever the label, where Jeanie came from, people didn't talk about things like that out in the open. Not outside of faculty members discussing a student's file. She hoped she wasn't crossing a line by asking.

"Someone like a shrink?" Eleanor's throaty laugh rang out as Jeanie cringed visibly at the blunt word choice. "Jeanie, I'm a Manhattan Jew. Of course I've seen a shrink. That little town you're from has a movie theater, right? You've heard of Woody Allen, at least? Therapy is like a rite of passage for my people."

"Ha. Ha. I was trying to be delicate about it, okay?" Jeanie blushed under Eleanor's teasing grin. "Not everyone takes things like that in stride as well as you and 'your people' do, you know."

"Sorry." Eleanor's expression became serious. "You're right. But yes, I've been working with a therapist for years and it's helped a lot. I have no problem admitting that. It's having the anxiety in the first place that embarrasses me, not getting help for it. Not that *that* makes any sense." She rolled her eyes as she said it, poking fun at herself this time.

"No, I get it." Jeanie's eyes locked with Eleanor's and she felt a tremor run through her at the moment of understanding that seemed to pass between them. She didn't know what to make of it and glanced away, looking at the dining room clock instead while the feeling passed. "Well, I guess I'd better go get my swimsuit if we're going to make it to the spa in time."

Eleanor's eyes narrowed. "I thought your suit was stolen."

"It was. But when I stopped at that shop to replace my backpack and buy you a tour book, they had bathing suits, too. They were buy one get one free, so I grabbed an extra. I told you before that I had one for you. It would've looked really good on you, too." She'd meant to say it teasingly but her stomach clenched as the words tumbled out, realizing how much more suggestive it sounded out loud. Even worse was that she knew that was exactly how she'd meant it. "I mean, it was a very nice one-piece. Tasteful. Almost Amish, really," she backpedaled as quickly as she could.

Jeanie looked away, feeling like an idiot under Eleanor's gaze. All of the desire and confusion that was warring inside her had to be clear as day on her face. Just as she glanced back, Eleanor looked away, but not before Jeanie thought she'd caught the woman checking out the swath of bare skin above the plunging neckline of her blouse. The renewed ruddiness of Eleanor's cheeks gave weight to this suspicion.

"Yes, well, I have my own suit," Eleanor assured her, looking as out of sorts as Jeanie felt. "Maybe you should go with that Amish one for yourself today," she concluded under her breath.

Jeanie bit back a nervous laugh. The teasing between them had started out lighthearted and fun, but now Jeanie felt a tension that could ruin their new friendship before it began. *This flirtation is getting dangerous.*

Back in her room after breakfast, Jeanie fretted as she contemplated the stacks of clothing that surrounded her. Her gaze fell on the two new swimsuits. As much as she loved the sexy two-piece she'd bought for herself the other day, there was no way she would wear it in front of Eleanor, not now. Not with this unspoken *something* that had just passed between them. The one-piece was a safer option. Jeanie's only regret was that it wasn't much more Amish than it was—a Victorian bathing dress, maybe. Or a burkini. *Eleanor should have a burkini, too.* Anything to keep the vibe between them strictly friends-only.

Jeanie was mindful again of her mother's warning. Her naturally bubbly personality often led to being accused of flirting when she really wasn't, but if she were completely honest, sometimes when Eleanor was around, Jeanie knew her actions were way more deliberate than that. She picked up the denim skirt she'd worn to the caves from the top of the pile and studied it reproachfully. If she hadn't been trying to get a reaction from Eleanor, she would have worn something else. She knew Eleanor liked looking at her legs, and the truth of it was, Jeanie enjoyed knowing she was looking. *But that's just the harmless kind of flirting, right?* It didn't have to mean anything, or lead anywhere. It didn't necessarily have to have consequences. But her mother had called it merciless, and maybe she was right.

What about your little joke yesterday, and how that ended up? She'd been pretending to be Eleanor since they left the bus station, and the intoxicating effects of all that charisma had given her a real rush. Still under the influence, Jeanie had thrown out the suggestion of skinny dipping without a thought, but when she saw Eleanor's hilarious response, she'd just kept it up. She was still almost certain that her joke had played a role in the panic attack that followed, even if Eleanor denied it. She hadn't realized the severity of Eleanor's anxiety at the time, but that wasn't really an excuse. There was just something about teasing Eleanor, and even being teased in return, that Jeanie found exhilarating.

The only explanation she could offer was that there was nothing she enjoyed more than cracking the smooth veneer off a polished city girl. It was a skill she'd perfected in college, and it never got old. Plus, Eleanor was particularly adorable when she was out of sorts. Watching a grown woman blush and stutter at the mention of swimming naked had been too much fun to resist. And it wouldn't have been a problem, except thinking back on it, she had to admit that it had been arousing, as well. And *that* was going to be a problem.

Jeanie found it confusing. Despite the obvious spark between them, she'd already written Eleanor off time and again. They were polar opposites. And Eleanor could be sarcastic, and judgmental, and hard to read. But every time Jeanie convinced herself of what a bad idea it would be, she'd be surprised by Eleanor's kindness, or vulnerability, or charming dry wit. And then she'd start the debate all over again.

She liked Eleanor, not just in the grade school euphemism kind of way, but really liked her and valued the possibility of becoming her friend. She enjoyed spending time with her. But the more time they spent together, the greater the temptation to fool herself into thinking there could be something more. And even if she might reconsider a shipboard fling, hard as it would be to end it when the time came, she knew for certain that Eleanor was not on the same page. Despite how well they got on, just the thought of that type of intimacy seemed to trigger her anxiety. And that was the last thing Jeanie wanted to do.

With a sigh, Jeanie shoved her modest one-piece into her backpack with a heavy heart. She was looking forward to the spa trip, but maybe this needed to be their last outing together. Maybe she should spend more time in dance classes, where Eleanor was certain not to go. As much as she wanted to spend the rest of the trip touring Europe with Eleanor, she didn't trust her ability to keep herself in check. She'd done a rotten job of it so far. Spending time with Eleanor was like playing with matches: a terrible idea that was very hard to resist. But resist she would. It was the only thing she could do to avoid hurting them both.

TWELVE

THE WARM WATER swirled between Eleanor's fingers and toes as she moved them slowly back and forth, her body gently suspended at the surface of the bath. She'd never felt more relaxed in her life as she did in this moment, with little more than her nose poking out into the humid air. She held her breath and plunged under the water completely, bobbing to the surface and wiping the water from her eyes.

"See? Doesn't that feel wonderful?"

Eleanor opened her eyes and looked at Jeanie, who was watching her from a nearby side of the octagonal pool. The bath itself, surrounded by marble arches and topped with a towering dome peppered with openings that allowed in dappled sunlight, was easily large enough to hold a hundred people. It was an exclusive spa, and nowhere near capacity this morning, but just enough men and women soaked or swam in the vicinity to make Eleanor feel at ease in a way that she wouldn't have if they'd been alone.

"You know, I really do."

It was an unexpected sensation. When the idea first occurred to her to give Jeanie the passes, knowing she'd likely be invited along, Eleanor had been filled with anxiety. Of course, coming off a panic attack the way she had, such feelings weren't unexpected, but it hadn't been the general anxiety that usually plagued her. Her concern had had a specific and rational source. *Jeanie.* Jeanie, in the intimate setting of a bath, exuding whatever force it was that made Eleanor contemplate ideas and actions that went against all common sense and could lead to heartbreak.

Jeanie tilted her head back, her body floating just beneath the top of the water. Eleanor followed suit. They bobbed along in friendly silence, a safe distance separating them, and Eleanor could almost laugh at her earlier worries.

The trouble was that too often people mistook her outer reserve for a lack of feeling, and that was far from the truth. Eleanor felt emotions as deeply as anyone. She just kept them inside. It was why a shipboard romance, so tempting in theory for a quick physical release, in reality could go so wrong. She would become too attached, especially to someone like Jeanie who seemed to exert a special power over her without even realizing it.

But Eleanor needn't have worried. Jeanie was on

her best behavior today. She probably should have felt more grateful for that fact, instead of vaguely let down. Jeanie behaving herself was rather like being on a diet and having your favorite restaurant run out of chocolate cake. Just because you weren't planning to order a slice didn't mean you weren't looking forward to admiring it from the other side of the glass case.

"So, that's all that Watsu stuff is? Just floating?" Eleanor hoped the other woman didn't detect the disappointment in her voice. It's just that, after the buildup Jeanie had given it, she'd expected something more. *A little chocolate frosting, and some sprinkles.*

"That's not all, but it's all you need to know," Jeanie said, almost primly, in response.

"Hm. After all your talk of learning it from that girl at camp…" Eleanor's voice trailed off. Part of her waited eagerly for a tart response, while the other part wondered why she couldn't leave well enough alone. Jeanie was finally behaving herself, her usually flirtatious personality firmly in check, so why did Eleanor feel compelled to egg her on?

Jeanie bit her lip, looking sheepish. "Yeah, about that…I may have made that story sound more interesting than it was. For one thing, it wasn't one of the female counselors who showed me the technique, it was a guy. And it was an after-hours recreational activity with half a dozen other people. Everything was strictly professional."

Eleanor laughed. "That does put a different spin on

it. So, why were you at this camp? This wasn't so long ago that you were a camper, was it?"

"No, a camp counselor. I've done it almost every summer since college. Between museum internships and teaching, I haven't made the most lucrative career choices. Frankly, I needed the money."

Eleanor felt surprised by the admission. Despite having talked about Jeanie's job before, and knowing that she was traveling on an economy ticket, Eleanor mostly had forgotten the difference in their financial circumstances. Jeanie had replaced her tour book, and paid for her bus ticket to Tapolca cave. It occurred to Eleanor that these gestures had probably caused quite a strain on her budget, but Jeanie had never let on. Her personality stood in stark contrast to Sylvia, who used to bring the money issue up frequently to convince Eleanor to pay for things. Eleanor had usually given her what she wanted, but had grown to resent it, so it surprised her how strongly she wished she could help Jeanie now.

She thought of all the extra meals included with her ticket. *Would Jeanie accept if I offered those to her?* Something told her that she wouldn't. Jeanie didn't seem like the type to accept charity. *Maybe if I just invite her to join me whenever I can?* Eleanor thought that might work, and somehow the thought of spending so much time with the woman didn't make her feel anxious at all. In fact, she was starting to wonder if she hadn't been reading too much into Jeanie's behavior. Could her mental state have led her to perceive a flirtatiousness that wasn't really there? Because it seemed to be thoroughly absent today. Either Jeanie had changed overnight, or Eleanor had been misled by an overactive imagination when it seemed the woman had anything more than friendship on her mind.

"So, Jeanie," she began casually, not quite certain how to guide the conversation around to the subject of dinner in order to invite her, "what are your plans for when we get back to the ship?"

"I thought I'd go to another dance class."

"Oh." Dance classes. The perfect conversation stopper.

"Yes, Marylou wasn't feeling well this morning, so her husband, George, is looking for another partner for this afternoon. I told them I'd be happy to fill in."

"Well, you're making friends, I guess." Eleanor was surprised by the jealousy brewing in her chest. She hadn't expected to encounter any rivals for the woman's time. Suddenly she seemed to be in a competition, and the one thing Eleanor hated was losing.

"We may have been too quick to judge the old people, you know. When you get to know them, they're fascinating! George, for example. Did you know he was a pilot in World War II? It's hard to believe he's in his nineties. He swing dances like he's still a teenager. He and Marylou invited me to join them on a bus tour when we get to Bratislava."

"That's…great." Eleanor wrung her hands together

underneath the water. This was not how the conversation was supposed to go. Jeanie was supposed to want *her* for a traveling companion! *I'll be damned if she's going to go off with some little old couple without a fight!* "So, you're not planning to visit Club Nova, I take it. I can't imagine *that* would be George and Marylou's cup of tea."

Jeanie's eyes narrowed, intrigued. "Club…?"

"Nova," Eleanor supplied, secretly gleeful that Jeanie hadn't heard of it. *This should win me some points.* "It's this really popular underground gay club in Slovakia. They just happen to be hosting their weekly lesbian night. I'm surprised you hadn't heard of it!"

"I'm surprised you had," Jeanie muttered under her breath, seemingly out of sorts over this revelation. Eleanor had gathered from earlier conversations with her that Jeanie liked to stay on top of trends and didn't like feeling left out of the loop.

Eleanor fought back an evil chuckle. "Oh, sure! A friend of mine told me about it." This was true. Her friend Cheryl had visited Bratislava five years before and gave her the brochure as a joke, knowing it was the last place in the world Eleanor was likely to step foot. "It's this really crazy, sort of secret club. Very eastern European. You know, in an avant-garde sort of way." The rapt attention on Jeanie's face told her she was saying all the right words.

"That sounds…" Jeanie's forehead was lined with

deep furrows. "But I did already tell George and Marylou…"

Sensing her best play was not to seem too eager, Eleanor shrugged. "Well, if you already promised. What a shame, though. Here *you* were the one looking forward to meeting single women on this cruise. Ironic."

"Yeah…" Conflict was clearly raging inside her head, and Eleanor figured it was just a matter of time before she caved.

"I wonder what kind of music they're playing in the European clubs these days." Eleanor leaned back and floated in the water, as if she'd already forgotten Jeanie was there. "They always seem to be so far ahead of the States."

"I mean, maybe I could…"

"It will certainly provide me with some interesting stories when picking up women back home," Eleanor added, still talking to herself.

At that, Jeanie seemed to reach the tipping point. "You know, I don't know that George and Marylou are *counting* on me to join them."

Eleanor's body bobbed back upright. "Oh?" *Victory!*

"They felt sorry for me being in the class by myself. I think they just asked me out of pity. I'd hate to feel like I was intruding on their time together."

Eleanor nodded sympathetically. "There's nothing worse than feeling like a third wheel."

"This Club Nova...I suppose I could wander over there at some point in the evening."

"Sure, I could give you the directions. Or, we could meet up for an early dinner and then just wander over together. In case it's hard to find." Eleanor gave herself a mental pat on the back for how deftly she'd managed to turn the conversation toward her original objective of giving Jeanie one of her meal tickets. *Nicely done!*

Jeanie hesitated. "Well...I suppose underground clubs can be hard to find sometimes."

"They're notorious for it," Eleanor agreed.

"And if we meet up for dinner first, at least you'll know I'm not running late," Jeanie added with a laugh. "I suppose your suggestion is the most practical."

Eleanor smiled the smile of a woman who was accustomed to that being the case. As she exited the pool and started to towel off, Eleanor was deep in thought, working through the plan. She needed to find that old Club Nova brochure, arrange transportation, and...*Oh God! What to wear?* She hadn't packed for going to a club. She felt a nervous hum in her stomach. It wasn't the troubling kind, but the garden-variety nervousness that went with putting together a plan, the kind that kept her motivated until she got it right down to the last detail.

Concierge. Of course! Eleanor had almost forgotten that her ticket gave her access to the ship's concierge services. A concierge would know what people were wearing to clubs these days, and where to buy them. Maybe she could even have something ordered for her and delivered to the ship when they reached Bratislava. Eleanor had an easy enough body to dress that a standard size would do, and she'd rather not have to shop if she could avoid it. As she slipped on her shoes, she was too wrapped up in her planning to give the slightest notice to which shoe she'd put on first.

How lucky that I have the concierge to help! Even with all the business travel she'd done, Eleanor wasn't used to traveling in quite such a luxurious way as this. Sylvia would have eaten it up, which struck her as funny. When she'd booked the cruise for the two of them, she'd reserved a nice room, but not like she had now. The dollar had strengthened so much in the past year that her credit had been worth considerably more than before, and Miriam had thrown in every conceivable amenity when booking Eleanor's passage, just to use it up.

As she waited in the lobby of the spa for Jeanie to finish dressing, it occurred to her that it could be a lot of fun to use as many of those amenities as she could to show her new friend a good time. Eleanor was certain Jeanie had never traveled first class before, so it would be a new experience for her. And on her own, Eleanor would just let most of it go to waste—like today's spa trip, which had done miracles to ease Eleanor's anxiety. In retrospect, it would've been a shame to miss it, and she would have if it hadn't been for Jeanie.

Eleanor's mind raced to remember what other envelopes she had tucked away in her folder back in her room. Bicycle rentals, museum tours, so many things to see! As she thought about the possibilities for the weeks ahead, the only thing she didn't give even a passing thought to was the fact that, just a few days before, she'd been equally determined to stay as far away from Jeanie Brooks as she could.

THIRTEEN

JEANIE PACED BACK and forth on the sidewalk, fretting for the thousandth time over the black dress she'd chosen for the club. When she'd seen it in a boutique in Poughkeepsie that promised European fashion for a discount price, the asymmetrical shoulder and daring metal trim had seemed like something straight from a Paris runway. But when she'd put it on in her cabin before dinner, she'd started to have doubts. Was it too short? Too low cut? Would Eleanor take it the wrong way and have another panic attack? And what was the right way for her to take it? Jeanie wasn't sure she knew.

This is why you decided not to see her anymore, remember? Jeanie balled her fists, tugging her hem closer to her knees. *You like her too much to spend time with her!* She was fully aware that none of her thoughts made any sense at all. It hardly mattered. It's not like she ever listened to herself anyway.

Her resolve to not spend time with Eleanor had lasted all of, what, a few hours? One relaxing soak in a pool and the chance to go to a swanky European nightclub and her backbone had dissolved like a jar of bath salts. Either that, or Eleanor had played some sort of Jedi mind trick on her. After all, Eleanor was a woman who was used to getting her way, and thinking back on it, Jeanie had a strong sense that having her go with her to this club was something she really wanted. The thought of that made Jeanie feel warm and tingly inside in all sorts of nice places, even though she knew she shouldn't let it. She grasped her head between the palms of her hands and screamed silently, frustrated with her own wishy-washy confusion.

Tonight's dinner together is what had kicked off this latest round of insecurity. Eleanor had arrived after Jeanie, which was unusual in its self, but she was wearing just another version of her ubiquitous travel wardrobe. That's when it crossed Jeanie's mind that she'd gotten something wrong and was way overdressed. But then a message had been delivered to their table during dinner, after which Eleanor muttered something about going back to her room to change, leaving Jeanie to wait by herself for the car that Eleanor had arranged and second-guess herself into an early grave.

Enough! Eleanor would be back any minute and it

was time for Jeanie to start acting like a grown-up. An interesting, exciting woman wanted to be her friend, so what was the big deal? This shouldn't even be a debate. They'd enjoy the night out as friends, and why not? Just because she'd dated almost all of her friends didn't mean she had to do so this time. *I can do 'friends only', no problem!* Her pinched face relaxed into a smile at her renewed resolve. *Piece of cake!*

Jeanie heard the tapping of heels on the gangway and turned to see Eleanor about half the distance between the ship and shore. Jeanie instantly felt an affinity for cartoon characters whose jaws dropped to the floor and tongues rolled out of their heads like a red carpet, while something literally heart-shaped protruded from their chests. She was almost certain she looked like that now, right down to the steam whistling from her ears. *Damn.* An evening clubbing with Eleanor in this get-up was going to deal a major blow to her goal of keeping her motivations strictly platonic.

This woman sauntering toward her—could it really be the same Eleanor she'd seen at dinner?—would have looked just as at home on a catwalk during fashion week as she did on the ramp leading up from the ship. A black halter top, sheer to the point of being see-through across her midriff, skimmed her waistline. A pair of skin-tight claret-colored pants in—*Heaven help me, is that leather?*—rode low on her hip bones. Her shoes were strappy silver confections with heels so high Jeanie wasn't certain how Eleanor was managing to stay upright on the uneven walkway.

"Mercy!" she whispered. Louder, she added, "You look—"

"Foolish, I know," Eleanor said with a groan. "Maybe I shouldn't go."

"What? No!" Jeanie stared at Eleanor's outfit, then at her own dress. Her earlier fears forgotten, Jeanie's primary concern now was that, next to her companion, her own dress looked exactly like what it was: a discount dress from a shop in Poughkeepsie. "That is definitely not part of the easy-care travel collection."

"No. It's new." Disappointment permeated her words. "I didn't pack for going to a club. This only just arrived during dinner. I asked the concierge to order me something appropriate, but obviously he was completely off the mark. There's nothing appropriate about it."

On the contrary, Jeanie was certain no one had hit the mark so flawlessly since William Tell's arrow sliced through the center of the apple on his son's head. Eleanor looked born for a night on the town. "Seriously, you look—oh my God, is that our car?" A white stretch-Hummer pulled up alongside the curb as both women gaped. "Eleanor, you really didn't need to go to so much trouble!"

"I didn't!" she protested, walking briskly toward the driver, who had walked around to open the passenger door. "Yet another misunderstanding.

Excuse me, sir," this she addressed to the driver, "I only ordered a town car, not...*this*! Are you sure this is the reservation for Fielding?" She waved her arms to encompass the full monstrosity. Jeanie watched, feeling ridiculously turned on by the way she took command of the situation.

"Fielding? Yes," the driver confirmed, and Eleanor nodded. "I'm picking up another party there when I drop you off. They ordered this car, so it was easier just to upgrade you for the trip."

Satisfied with the explanation, Jeanie climbed into the cavernous interior, then popped her head out the door. "Eleanor? You coming?"

Eleanor blinked twice, then shook her head and climbed in beside Jeanie. "This evening is not going at all the way I planned."

"Oh, well," Jeanie said with a shrug, "Do they ever?" She was impressed that Eleanor had even tried to sort the issue out, but when the only response was stony silence, Jeanie bit her lower lip and reflected that maybe for Eleanor, things usually did go according to plan. "Bratislava's got some fancy lesbians, ordering giant cars like this just to go to and from a club," she joked, but got only a partial smile in response. She took to nudging Eleanor's knee with her own until she coaxed a smile. Their eyes met and Jeanie felt it like a shot to the gut.

The car pulled up in front of the nightclub where a bouncer, who was twice the size of a normal human and looked like he might have competed on a Cold War-era wrestling team, stood at the door. Eleanor strode up confidently to speak with him while Jeanie lingered several steps behind. Soon, she could hear Eleanor's voice begin to rise.

"A reservation? For a club? No, I don't have a reservation."

"Sorry, miss. Reservations only. Plus an eight person minimum."

Jeanie's muscles tightened and twitched nervously as Eleanor continued her heated debate with the bouncer. There was a fine line between finding it arousing and being concerned that it could trigger a panic attack. The door to the club opened and a group of very drunk, very *male* individuals stumbled along the sidewalk toward the waiting car. Jeanie stared in confusion as, one by one, they piled into the vehicle that had brought her and Eleanor from the boat.

"Um, excuse me," Jeanie said to one of the stragglers, smiling as a single bloodshot eye struggled to focus enough to sustain contact with hers. "Were you coming out of the lesbian club just now?"

"Yeah. Bloody brilliant!" His slurred speech sounded vaguely British. With a niggling worry building inside, Jeanie asked a few more questions. The answers increased her concern exponentially.

"Eleanor?" Jeanie walked up behind her but she was too engrossed in her argument with the bouncer to notice. Jeanie closed her fingers on her friend's bare shoulder, giving it a shake. "Elle!" she hissed.

"What!" Eleanor turned with a start.

"I think we have the wrong club." Jeanie's voice was calm but insistent.

"What? Why?"

"In case you didn't notice, the car that brought us here just drove off with a dozen men. *Men*, Eleanor. Simon told me they'd just come from inside this club."

Eleanor's brow furrowed. "Who's Simon?"

"The one who's getting married. It's his stag weekend, and they stopped at the club to celebrate."

Eleanor stared at her for a moment. "I swear, Jeanie. Is there anyone whose name you don't learn?" She shook her head, dismissing the question. "That's just stupid. Why would a bunch of guys spend a stag weekend in a club full of women who won't look at them twice?"

"Because," Jeanie explained in a stage whisper, glancing at the bouncer, "it's not that kind of lesbian club." Jeanie waited for a response but got none. "It's a *strip* club." By this point it had become clear that in her confusion, Eleanor had lost the power of speech. "Elle, listen closely. This is a club where men go to eat steak and drink beer while watching women with no clothes on do naughty things to each other. For their entertainment."

Just as Jeanie feared Eleanor's loss of speaking ability might be permanent, Eleanor spoke. "That doesn't even seem...*hygienic*." She had the appearance of a woman whose own appetite had just evaporated. "I mean, don't you think? With the steak and...everything?" She swallowed hard, looking a little green. Staring toward the empty street, her eyes widened. "Jeanie, if you knew what type of place this was, why did you let those men leave in *our* car? Now we're stuck!"

"I'm sorry. I'm not as good at that type of thing as you are. But trust me, Elle, you wouldn't have wanted it anymore. I think I saw Simon throw up as he got in."

Eleanor winced. "This is a disaster. What do we do now?"

"I don't know, we could ask the bouncer. Maybe he could help."

"Yeah, good luck with that." Eleanor rolled her eyes. "He's been super helpful so far."

"Um, excuse me?" Jeanie stared up at the brick wall of a man. "My friend and I are in the wrong place, as I'm sure you already figured out. We're looking for a different club. Club Nova? It's an underground club. For *women*."

The bouncer's head bobbed on his solid neck. "Underground? I think I know it. Straight down that way, about a block."

Jeanie smiled radiantly. "Look at that! Sometimes just asking nicely can work, too."

"Let's go, Miss Congeniality," Eleanor said, rolling her eyes.

After walking the block or so in the direction the bouncer had shown them, they came to what looked like the entrance to an old subway station. Techno music pulsed from within the tunnel, which was lit with stripes of blue neon. As they waited hesitantly at the opening, two women emerged, looking a little tipsy as they clung to each other for support.

"Look, Eleanor. Girls!" Jeanie nodded toward the women. "We're off to a promising start. This must be the place."

"It never occurred to me that the underground club was *actually* underground."

"Clever, huh?"

Inspired by the girls who'd passed by, Jeanie absent-mindedly snaked her arm around Eleanor's waist as they walked down the glowing neon passageway. Her breath caught as Eleanor returned the gesture, and she nearly floated the last few steps into the club. It was filled to capacity, with people standing so close that their shoulders and hips were pressed together. Instead of dancing, they seemed to be turned to face the center of the club, watching something and cheering raucously. It was too dark, with bodies jammed in too tightly, for either of the women to get a clear view.

"Can you see anything?" Jeanie removed her arm from Eleanor's waist and stood on her tiptoes, pressing forward and craning her neck toward whatever everyone else was looking at.

"No, nothing." Eleanor hung back at the edge of the crowd, anxiety etched on her face.

"You okay, Elle? The crowd making you nervous?" Jeanie smiled reassuringly as Eleanor shut her eyes tightly and nodded. "I'll just push through to check it out. You stay here and think calm thoughts."

She elbowed her way through the boisterous onlookers until she found an opening with a clear view. She stopped dead, trying to process what she saw. An inflatable pool sat in the middle of what was usually the dance floor. It was filled with slick, gray mud. Inside were—two? Three? No, make that four—four female-shaped figures, covered head to toe in mud. They were writhing on top of each other in a heap, wrestling one another in their mud-caked underwear, as the crowd whooped and hollered. A long line of ladies, also stripped down to their bras and panties, flanked the edge of the pool, apparently waiting for their turn to jump in.

As Jeanie took in the scene with growing horror, one of the women belly-flopped into the muddy pit, sending beads of gray goo flying through the air. With a wet *plop!* A droplet landed on the tip of her nose, and a wave of nausea overtook her. Jeanie shoved her way back to the edge of the crowd and grabbed Eleanor's wrist, yanking her back toward the blue neon tunnel as Eleanor tripped after her in her high heels.

"Jeanie, what was it? Where are we going?" A trace of panic infused Eleanor's words.

"We're leaving."

"Why?" Eleanor raced after Jeanie to the opening of the tunnel, taking the stairs two at a time until she joined her at the surface. "Jeanie, what happened? And what's that on your nose?"

Jeanie made a sickened face as she wiped the tip of her nose with the palm of her hand. Then she attempted, in as few words as possible, to explain what she'd seen in the underground club. When she'd finished talking, Eleanor stared at her in dumbfounded silence.

"Mud?" she managed to ask, and Jeanie nodded. Eleanor shook her head slowly. "Steak, strippers, and mud. I fucking hate Bratislava."

Jeanie felt her body shake and soon found herself doubled over in laughter. "Oh my God, Elle," she gasped. "You know what this means?"

Eleanor raised an eyebrow slowly. "No?"

"It means," Jeanie replied between ragged breaths, "that as long as you live, you can never tease me again about messing up that trip to Tapolca. Or throwing your book in the river. Or reversing the dates for the cruise. Not after this!"

"Fine, you're right." Eleanor's shoulders shook as she joined Jeanie's laughter with her own. "No matter how much you plan, things can go still go horribly wrong. I guess tonight proves *that*."

Eleanor nudged Jeanie's bare shoulder with her own. It felt soft and warm, and unconsciously Jeanie leaned toward her until the whole of their arms were pressed together. *So comfortable.* They stayed that way for some time, and it was only as Jeanie went to slide her arm across Eleanor's back to draw her even closer that she realized with a start how intimate she'd allowed the moment to become. With every fiber of moral strength, she pulled away. "Come on. Let's go back to the first club and see if we can call for our car."

As they walked, the sound of a classic Depeche Mode melody wafted down a cobblestone alleyway. They both paused, listening. "I love this song!" they exclaimed in unison.

"Should we go check it out?" Jeanie asked, pointing down the alley toward what appeared to be a small club.

Eleanor studied it cautiously, then shrugged. "Why not? What's the worst that could happen?"

FOURTEEN

"I MAY BE willing to revise my opinion of Bratislava." Eleanor plunked two glasses of beer on the table and slid into the seat across from Jeanie. "I think these cost a dollar each. Maybe less."

Jeanie took a sip, and nodded her approval. "And it even tastes good. Between this and the music, the city just may be redeemed. Any place with a Depeche Mode tribute band can't be all bad."

Eleanor watched, unblinking, as Jeanie licked a thick line of foam from her upper lip with the tip of her tongue. She swallowed down half her glass in a single swallow as she pried her eyes away from the enticing spectacle, trying to focus on the band instead. Their music was good, but the view was hardly a fair substitute for her companion's lovely face. Looking from one to the next, Eleanor reflected that these were the four least hip-looking musicians she'd ever seen on a stage. The lead singer sounded exactly like the real deal, but he looked like a Slovakian actuarial accountant. This is what it would look like if she rounded up some guys from at work and forced them to be in a talent show.

Eleanor gulped down the rest of her beer and motioned to the bartender for another round. "I still think it's funny that you're a fan of this music. You were just a kid when they were popular."

Jeanie shot her a look of mock insult. "Me, a kid? You're, what, maybe five or six years older than me? You were just a kid yourself."

"Maybe." She looked at Jeanie slyly, knowing she wouldn't expect what was coming next. "But I was old enough to sneak out of the house and use my fake ID at a Chelsea night club after a bartender friend tipped me off that the band had gone there to hang out after their concert at Madison Square Garden." She sucked in her cheeks to stop from laughing as she watched Jeanie struggle to make sense of this new information.

"The band. You mean the *actual* band?" Jeanie's eyes grew wide as Eleanor nodded. "I...you know, I don't even know where to begin. Sneaking out? Fake ID? A friend who was a bartender? This is not the same Eleanor Fielding I've met. How old were you?"

"Fifteen, I think? Yeah, they were having some drinks at a place a few blocks from me. It was before cell phones, of course, and my friend didn't want to wake up my parents by calling the house, so he ran over on his break and threw rocks at my window until I came down." Eleanor chuckled at the memory. "Sometime around four in the morning, some guy brought in a guitar and the band did an unplugged version of *Personal Jesus* that was nothing short of inspirational."

"Wow." A new look of admiration sparkled in Jeanie's eyes. "Of course, being Jewish, I'm betting no one ever told you that you'd burn in hell for listening to that song."

Eleanor propped her elbow on the table and rested her chin in her hand. "Really? Someone actually said that?"

Jeanie nodded. "A few. Small town, remember?"

"Jesus! Oops, sorry." Eleanor giggled into her hand. She studied Jeanie curiously, wondering why she'd stayed. Jeanie blinked and Eleanor realized she'd been looking at Jeanie far longer than she'd intended. She slid her head further down her arm, resting it close to the table, to hide her pink cheeks.

"So, Eleanor Fielding had rebellious teenage years."

"You could say that." Eleanor raised her head back up and made a funny face in acknowledgment. "Figuring out you'd rather hang out with the guys and sleep with the girls can do that to the best of us."

"Oh, was that the reason?"

"Sure, what else? Don't tell me you never rebelled." Eleanor cocked an eyebrow, staring intently until Jeanie giggled.

"What?" She batted her lashes innocently. "I really didn't!"

"Right, because it was so easy coming out in a town where people think you go to hell for singing song lyrics?"

Jeanie closed her eyes in thought. "No, not *easy*. But the main church in town got a new minister with more enlightened views, so that helped a lot. My family was supportive. It could've been worse. Besides, I caused enough trouble just being my impulsive self that I didn't need to rebel, too."

"That I can believe," Eleanor said with a laugh. She looked down at her second empty glass, then noticed Jeanie's were in a similar state. "Another beer?"

"Yes, but it's my turn to buy. I'll be right back." She swiped the two empty glasses from the table and headed to the bar.

Eleanor watched her go. Studiously avoiding looking at those gorgeously tempting legs, her eyes focused on the asymmetry of Jeanie's neck line, the long sleeve on one side, the bare arm and shoulder on the other. It was the type of look that would usually start her anxiety ticking. So off-balance. So disorganized. But right now all she could remember was the silky smoothness of Jeanie's arm against hers, and the sudden chill when it was gone. Eleanor squeezed her eyes shut, shifting her focus to the music coming from the band.

The plunk of a glass on the table brought her mind

back to the present. She opened her eyes and frowned at the drink in front of her, which was definitely not another beer. "What is this?"

Jeanie was back in her chair and already sipping from her own glass. "I'm not sure, but it's really good. The woman in front of me ordered one, and the bartender couldn't believe I'd never had one, so he poured two of them—on the house! Wasn't that nice?"

Nice? What was it about this woman that she seemed to bring out the *nice* in everyone she met? Eleanor could only dream of having people respond to her in that way. On the verge of telling Jeanie how extraordinary she was, Eleanor thought better of it and decided instead to stick with the comfort of sarcasm. "So you're just going to drink it down without knowing what it is?"

Jeanie tilted her head and gave Eleanor a searching look. "What, you figure the bartender is trying to poison us? It's just a drink, Eleanor. And it's really good." Her brows knitted as she drained the rest of the glass and waved at a passing waitress to bring two more. "So, tell me something. What happened to you, that you went from this rebellious teenager sneaking into clubs to someone who can't even take a chance on a new drink?"

Eleanor stiffened defensively. *Stick-in-the-mud Eleanor.* She'd heard this accusation enough from Sylvia —and several others before her. The last thing she needed was Jeanie, friendly, sweet Jeanie, whom everyone seemed to fall in love with at first sight, to pile it on, too. She felt Jeanie's hand cover her fingers, and flinched.

"Elle, I'm really sorry. I didn't mean it to sound judgmental. I just really want to know."

The look in Jeanie's eyes told her it was true, that her interest was genuine. At that, the tension drained out of her. She relaxed her hands and felt Jeanie give her fingers a friendly squeeze before pulling her hand away.

"It's not like I don't know how I come across," Eleanor replied, her quiet tone nearly drowned out by the music.

"But to go from then to now, something big must have changed?" Jeanie's voice was quiet, too. Encouraging.

"Not any one thing, to be honest." Eleanor sighed. "To start with, I did enough dumb stuff that I finally got in trouble, which I hated. Being a rebel is one thing. Getting caught and grounded is a different story." She rolled her eyes at the stupidity of her younger self. "And some of the people I was hanging out with got in a lot more trouble than me. Drugs, stealing. I wasn't involved, but who's to say I wouldn't have been, eventually. My grades started to slip, and my parents saw what was going on and gave me an ultimatum. If I didn't get my act together, I'd be on my own to pay for college."

"Ouch! That was harsh."

Eleanor waved away the pity. "Not really. It worked. I got my act together, got into college. Then the second semester of my freshman year, I had my first panic attack."

"You haven't always had them?"

"No. The first time it happened, I thought I was having a heart attack. It just started out of the blue. Well, I mean, I've always been competitive and a perfectionist, with a family history of anxiety, so that's a recipe for disaster. But truthfully, it's just something that can happen around that age to some people. Bad luck, I guess."

"But you've been working on it?" Jeanie's eyes shone with empathy.

"For a long time. And despite what you've witnessed this week, it's gotten way better than it was. Just not good enough for everyone, especially girlfriends. Like Sylvia, for instance." Eleanor cringed as she said the name. Why ruin the evening by bringing that up?

"Sylvia? Oh, you mean the ex who cheated with the French tart? Sounds like she came with more of her own issues than a magazine subscription."

Eleanor erupted into a hearty laugh. *Oh my God, I love this woman!* She sucked in her breath as she became aware of the thought. *Not like that!* Just, how could anyone not love the way Jeanie could sum up a situation so perfectly, so completely dead-on? She was right, her ex had plenty of shortcomings of her own, a fact that Eleanor was prone to forget. Sometimes blaming herself felt more true, even when it didn't match the facts. Still, it wasn't exactly an isolated occurrence.

"You're probably right about Sylvia, but that doesn't explain them all."

"All, huh? Have there been a lot?"

Eleanor gave a half shrug. "*are* your issues?" Eleanor looked at her frankly and waited.

Jeanie made a face. "It's getting late. We should probably head back to the ship, don't you think?"

Interesting answer. Eleanor's gaze remained steady.

"I don't want to talk about this, okay? It's embarrassing." Jeanie muttered, squirming under Eleanor's stare. "Can we go?"

Eleanor didn't push for more. Instead, she rose from the table and held her hand out to help Jeanie, who swayed as she took a step. "Whoa! Your suspicion of that drink might not have been so crazy. My head's spinning!"

She leaned against Eleanor for support. It was the side of her dress that had a sleeve, so only fabric brushed Eleanor's skin, which she considered a blessing. Eleanor's own head wasn't quite right, not only from the alcohol, but from the effects of allowing so many emotions to escape. She helped Jeanie toward the door, and they were just about to step outside when the band started a new tune.

"Oh, I love this one!" Jeanie stopped in place and swayed tipsily in time to the slow rhythm.

Eleanor watched with apprehension, wondering just how far gone her friend might be. She sucked in her breath as she felt Jeanie's arms envelop her.

"Dance with me, Elle?" The yearning in Jeanie's eyes was undeniable.

She didn't say no. Instead, Eleanor put her arms around Jeanie's waist to steady her and as she did she took a step, and for the briefest moment it felt as if they were dancing. Tousled blond curls tickled against her neck as Jeanie rested her head on Eleanor's shoulder and pulled her closer. Warm, moist breath caressed her and she shivered, Jeanie's lips so close that she could imagine the silky feel of them against her bare skin.

As if responding to her thoughts, Jeanie shifted her head upward and for the briefest of moments their lips brushed. The sensation was like breath over a dandelion as you closed your eyes to make a wish, so soft it was barely there at all. Eleanor took another step and they swayed together, in time to the music.

Maybe I don't have to say no. Her fervent desire echoed within as hope flooded her that this time things could be different, *she* could be different. *Maybe just this one time I could dance.* She didn't have to be stick-in-the-mud Eleanor, anxious in her own skin. Maybe there was something of the fearless, rebellious Eleanor still hiding somewhere inside.

Who am I kidding? Eleanor knew it was no use. It had been half a lifetime, and that version of herself was gone for good. With every ounce of restraint she possessed, she peeled Jeanie's body gently from hers and positioned her to face the door as she took another step. Jeanie groaned tiredly, but didn't argue.

A cab waited back on the main street and they climbed inside. As Jeanie drifted into a light sleep, Eleanor gave her bare shoulder a tiny nudge, so that her head would rest against the taxi's window instead of on her. Even that faintest brush of her fingers against Jeanie's skin made Eleanor wish for things she knew she couldn't have.

What am I doing? Am I falling for her? I can't fall for her! She'd said it herself in the club. Everyone fell in love with Jeanie, and she was too sweet to turn them away. *Incompatible.* Sure, they might go on a few dates, even have sex once or twice, before Jeanie realized that she was no different that the rest: completely wrong for her. It was a heartbreak she could do without. Eleanor closed her eyes and rested her head against her own window, but she could still see Jeanie's face. Beautiful, carefree Jeanie deserved someone she could dance with, and Eleanor would never manage that type of risk.

FIFTEEN

THE ROOM WAS SHROUDED in semi-darkness when the alarm on her tablet began its relentless screeching, and for once Jeanie was grateful that her cabin lacked a view. In her hungover state, she didn't think she would survive more than the barest hint of sun. Grabbing her robe, she braved the journey from her room to the shared bath down the hall, and was relieved to find it unoccupied. She hadn't looked at the clock and couldn't recall exactly how many times she'd snoozed her alarm, but the lack of a line for the shower hinted at it being well past breakfast. *Just as well.* Jeanie's stomach lurched in opposition at the slightest thought of food.

My God, what was in that drink? Eleanor had been right to be cautious. She usually was. *Smart, sensible, sexy Eleanor.* Under the hot stream of the shower, Jeanie froze. She hadn't intended to think the word *sexy*. Her brain had just been searching for a third word that started with the letter 's'. That she heartily agreed with the word it had chosen wasn't the point. Eleanor was strictly off limits in that regard. They were becoming friends, and the last thing Jeanie wanted was to screw that up.

She thought back to the night before and groaned. Toward the end of it, her memory became a little fuzzy. She had the vague impression that she'd tackled Eleanor and forced her to dance. She was pretty certain the resulting choreographed tango to a Depeche Mode love ballad, ending in a passionate kiss to the raucous applause of a roomful of Slovakians, was purely embellishment. The tackling part, however, felt real enough to be true.

I can't be trusted. Jeanie scowled at herself in the bathroom mirror as she toweled herself dry. After promising herself, after even promising her *own mother*, that she wouldn't lead Eleanor on, what did she turn around and do? Tackle her and force her to tango. *I'm a merciless flirt!*

Usually possessed of a healthy self-esteem, this morning Jeanie hated the person who stared back at her from the mirror. Why couldn't she have more control? She knew Eleanor wasn't interested in anything more than friendship. Why ruin a good thing by complicating it with a meaningless holiday fling that they'd both probably regret?

What if it's more than just a fling? Jeanie stared quizzically at her reflection, as if it had been the one to suggest the idea. Her face brightened. Reflection-Jeanie might have a point. Most of her previous relationships were better classified as flings anyway, with as quickly as they usually were over. Yet she couldn't remember feeling about any of them the way she did about Eleanor. Captivated by their conversations, amused at Eleanor's many foibles, and when their bodies so much as brushed past one another, it felt wonderfully intoxicating. Maybe she wasn't just mindlessly flirting with Eleanor. Maybe she wanted something more?

So what if you do? Jeanie looked at her reflection in shock. What a time for it to pick to start arguing with her, right as she was almost convinced! Her reflection's voice sounded different this time, too. Less like her, and more like Eleanor. *That figures*. It was a reasonable question, and Eleanor was the queen of practicality. Jeanie gave the question some thought. As hard as it was to believe, the cruise was nearly halfway through. In another week, she and Eleanor would be heading their separate ways. Not that their separate ways were all that far apart. It was only a couple of hours from her house to Manhattan. Hell, if she drove into Poughkeepsie proper, she could take the train straight to Penn Station.

Be practical! This time the voice was Eleanor's, through and through. It was a short distance to travel, but they lived worlds apart. Eleanor was a sophisticated career woman, a Manhattan native, who clearly made a good income. Jeanie had saved for years for a single vacation. Assuming it did work out between them, where would they live? Eleanor would never leave the city, and Jeanie could never afford New York on a teacher's salary. *Two different planets.* Besides, she'd been down that road before.

Of all the women she'd dated, she'd only been in love once, her junior year of college. *Rochelle.* They'd planned their whole future together after graduation, only Rochelle's parents didn't approve. They thought Jeanie was just a gold-digger, even though at that point she was a student at Vassar in her own right and not just some townie. But their little princess could do better, so they'd packed Rochelle off to study in Italy, and Jeanie was too short on funds to follow. They'd tried long distance for a while, but then Rochelle met an art patron with her own gallery in Rome, and that was the end of that.

It won't work, Jeanie! Her reflection agreed, but failed to provide any useful tips for how best to maintain their *just friends* status for the rest of the trip. It wouldn't be easy. Every minute they spent together, her attraction was harder to fight. The tension between them right now was perfectly balanced, keeping them apart. But if something shifted the slightest bit, heaven help them. There was no telling how things could go.

The fact that she'd been arguing with herself in the

mirror for fifteen minutes reminded her that she was half-crazed from lack of coffee, so she dressed quickly and went up to the snack shop in search of a cup. The ship was already speeding away from Bratislava on its way to Vienna. Jeanie's spirits lifted at that thought. Vienna was the city she most wanted to see. So much art! So much history! Her schedule would be so full once they arrived that the whole Eleanor issue might resolve itself. Eleanor didn't seem like a big fan of museums. Their paths would barely cross. It was much easier not to fall in love with someone if you didn't see them.

As she approached the snack shop, her stomach tightened on the off chance that she would run into Eleanor while there. A love for morning coffee was one thing they definitely had in common, though like all the other things she'd already thought of, it was hardly the basis for a relationship. It could, however, become the opportunity for an awkward conversation. Jeanie still couldn't recall exactly how affectionate she'd gotten the night before, or whether any apologies might be due.

The snack shop was empty. After a surge of relief, Jeanie detected a lingering disappointment, too. That wouldn't do. A few minutes of feeling lonely and she was likely to start searching Eleanor out. The ship was small. She'd find her in no time. She picked up her coffee and resolutely carried it to the one place on the ship she knew Eleanor would not be: dance class.

Entering the room, she waved at George and Marylou, then promptly joined the circle they'd all formed around the room. The instructor explained that, in honor of their arrival in Vienna, he would be taking a break from the usual swing dancing class to teach a few traditional Viennese folk dances, instead. They took partners around the room, changing frequently as each new step was taught, and Jeanie's spirits were lifted measurably as she learned the quaint steps and made new friends in the process.

As the class drew close to the end, the instructor introduced one final dance, the polka. With a room of mostly experienced dancers, they caught on quickly to the basic steps, so to make it more fun, he suggested a twist. Each couple would dance just two times through, then the gentleman would fling the lady down the set to the next gentleman, so that she, and he, could dance with someone new.

The music was fast, so fast that Jeanie soon felt like she was flying, leaping from partner to partner without a care in the world. She threw her head back breathlessly and laughed as she spun and bounced her way around the room. The tempo shifted, and with the song nearing its end, Jeanie's current partner let her go. Dizzy and disheveled, she landed in the arms of her last partner as the room went silent, and gasped as she looked up. It was Eleanor.

EARLIER THAT MORNING...

Eleanor stretched her legs in front of her on the lounge chair, tilting her head back to soak up the early morning sun on the observation deck. The cup of coffee clutched between her pale fingers was likely to be just the first of many today. She'd slept little, and fitfully. Her night of tossing and turning could be boiled down to one mistake: When slow dancing in the dark with a woman you're determined not to fall in love with, never listen to the lyrics.

Song lyrics lie.

She was hardly what anyone would call a romantic, but even Eleanor had her weaknesses. One of them, embarrassed as she would be to admit it, was going weak in the knees when a few well-turned phrases were paired with a catchy melody. When done at just the right time, in just the right way, even her skeptical self could be a complete sucker for a love song. Last night had been one of those times. It was the only explanation she could accept for how she felt.

Wanting someone to talk with, who understands you, and loves you—what sane person *didn't* want those things? Declaring your desire for someone to hold you through the night hardly qualified a person for a medal in profound thinking. And yet the combination of a pop song almost as old as she was with the solid warmth of Jeanie falling into her arms in that club had broken her completely, thrusting her across the boundary from daydreaming about the impossible to believing it could happen. At some point last night, she'd dared to think that she and Jeanie could have a chance. And then she'd kissed her. Or maybe the other way around, Eleanor wasn't sure. But either way, it had gotten out of hand.

It was as foolish as wishing on a star to think it could ever come true. The whole reason so many love songs resonated with people was because everyone was searching for love. It didn't mean they ever found it. If everyone were finding what the lyrics promised, why would they bother taking time out from their bliss to write a song? It was a dream that didn't exist. A lie. There was no version of events where an uptight Manhattan actuary and a free-spirited teacher from Poughkeepsie fall in love and live happily ever after. Not this side of a Hollywood movie. They were too different, and this was the real world. In the real world, women like Jeanie needed more than Eleanor could give.

Eleanor glared at her coffee and set it, virtually untouched, on the table at her side. Caffeine wasn't going to clear her foul mood. She needed exercise. It had been a week since her last trip to the gym, and she could feel it in every tense muscle. Spying the tennis court on the far side of the deck, Eleanor went to check it out. Her shoulders slumped at the empty court, a cruel reminder that even playing tennis required having a partner. She was the only person on the deck, except for a couple of old-timers chatting by the shuffleboard court. Probably playing hooky from dance class and hoping their wives didn't catch them and drag them back in. *See? That's what love looks like in real life.*

She understood their plight. Dance class was the last place she wanted to be, as well. The men didn't look up to engaging in a tennis match, and Eleanor had no interest in shuffleboard, so she left the deck in search of some other way to pass the time. The ship's library was her next stop, but it mostly held travel guides and romance novels, and both held equally dangerous associations of a certain leggy blond who was best not dwelt upon too long. For the first time that she could remember, she couldn't find a single thing she wanted to read.

Stifling a yawn, her thoughts turned back to the cup of coffee she'd left to grow cold on the upper deck. Another cup would help, but what she really needed was to move around. The thought of Vienna brought a smile to her lips. The ship was set to arrive in the afternoon, and if she timed it right, she could Rollerblade the paths at Donauinsel, Vienna's island recreation area, before dinner. Surely that would help to straighten her head. She'd found a comprehensive list of parks and recreation facilities in the tour book Jeanie had given her. It occurred to her that their itineraries for the city were unlikely to overlap. Despite the woman's glowing tan, she seemed like more of an inside girl. Eleanor should have found relief in the realization, but didn't.

As she wandered down one of the ship's deserted passageways, a cold tingle worked its way down her back. With the rest of the passengers in class, the ship was quiet. *Too quiet.* It was the kind of quiet that made her feel uneasy, like something was hiding in wait. Objectively she knew it wasn't true, but she'd be more likely to maintain composure in the presence of a bit of ambient noise.

Drawing closer to the ballroom door, she was reassured by the sounds coming from within, but frowned as a raucous polka reached her ears instead of the expected big band jazz. Intrigued, she cracked open the door and slipped inside for a closer look. She instantly regretted her choice.

Finding the room in chaos, Eleanor squealed as one of the dancers careened into her side, knocking her off balance. Before she could straighten up and scoot back into the hall, she felt the grip of a hand on her arm, her body sliding against her will into the out of control crowd. Her heart pounded, trapped in the bobbing and swirling, and unable to fight her way out of the circle. She sighed in relief as the music slowed and she came to a safe rest in the arms of one final partner. Her skin burned at the contact, her body vibrating to its core, and Eleanor knew who it was before she even saw her radiant face shining up from her arms. *Jeanie.* She held her breath, unsure what to do.

"Hi." The word escaped despite the breath remaining trapped in Eleanor's lungs.

"Hi." The awkward silence stretched into eternity. "I thought you didn't dance."

Eleanor recoiled as if slapped, imagining the reprimand buried in those words. *You didn't last night.* Silent accusations were usually the first step in the downward spiral of her relationships. She stiffened, projecting a confidence she didn't feel. "I was just passing through."

"Oh." It was an implausible excuse, but Jeanie appeared not to notice.

"So I assume you have a full schedule for Vienna? Museums and...such?"

Jeanie nodded. "You?"

"Some outdoor sports." Relief washed over her. *Saved by our plans.* "I guess that means we won't be seeing each other much."

The faint smile on Jeanie's lips suggested that she felt much the same. "No, I guess not. Well, I hope you have a good—" Jeanie's words were cut short by a crackling noise from a speaker on the wall.

"Attention passengers! Due to a disabled ship in Vienna, our assigned berth will be unavailable today. The captain has been advised to take a detour to Melk in the Wachau Valley overnight. We will continue on to Vienna in the morning. Thank you for your understanding."

"Wachau Valley?" Jeanie shook her head. "I've never even heard of it."

Eleanor's brow crinkled. "I may have...but I don't have anything planned for there at all." Her stomach tightened at the prospect of a full twenty-four hours without a schedule. Just when she thought she was in the clear, with activities to keep her busy—and far, far away from Jeanie—another wrench was thrown in the works.

SIXTEEN

THE SUN WAS high in the sky as the ship docked along the south side of the river, coming to rest on the outskirts of a small village that was nestled at the base of the verdant hills of the Wachau Valley. This stop was not a part of any of the usual tour routes, and as Jeanie walked along the cobblestone path toward the cluster of half a dozen stuccoed buildings with red roofs that made up the town, she doubted whether the place was even large enough to merit a dot on the map. Not that she was carrying a map.

She'd nearly opted to wait for the sightseeing coach that the ship's captain had ordered to keep passengers entertained during the unexpected detour, but her friendly steward, Thomas, had tipped her off to a bicycle rental shop in town. The paved cycling path that ran along the river and through the vineyards was, he claimed, the very best way to explore the region.

She'd been on the verge of looking for Eleanor and inviting her along, but thought better of it. She couldn't bear a repeat of that clumsy encounter between them at the end of class. Neither one of them had known what to say to the other, and they'd both fled in relief as soon as they could. She hadn't experienced such a painful social interaction since she was thirteen!

Jeanie balled her fists, pumping them harder as she increased her speed into town. Her inability to figure out what made that woman tick was a bottomless well of frustration. *Do I like her? Do I not? Does she like me?* She wouldn't have to grapple with all this if they could just stop running into each other so much. River boats weren't the floating cities that ocean liners were, but they weren't tiny. There had to be someplace to hide!

The shop she was searching for was the last building on the street, conveniently marked by a flag fluttering outside with a picture of a bicycle on it. The woman at the counter spoke enough English for her to figure out quickly what Jeanie was looking for, and after filling out the paperwork, she showed Jeanie out the backdoor to choose from an assortment of bikes.

Jeanie was just testing out the height of one of the seats when she heard a jingling sound from the back door. Her head swiveled, expecting that the shopkeeper was returning to see how she was getting on. Her stomach clenched as she saw Eleanor instead, and she watched warily as the usually confident woman took a single step outside, froze in place, swirled back around, and promptly closed the door.

She's hiding from me! Jeanie nearly laughed out loud at the ridiculousness of it, conveniently forgetting that her plan to deal with Eleanor for the rest of the trip was essentially identical.

"Eleanor?" Jeanie approached the door and tried again, louder. "Elle, I know you're there!"

The door creaked open and Eleanor stepped outside. "Oh, Jeanie. I didn't realize you were here." Her expression dared anyone to prove otherwise.

The hell you didn't! But Eleanor was a rational woman. If she'd decided to hide, there must be a good reason. With a sinking feeling, Jeanie once more attempted to recall how their night in Bratislava had ended, but failed. "I'm afraid of the answer, but I've just gotta know. Elle, please, be honest with me." Jeanie swallowed roughly. "Did I do something really awful at the club? Or on the drive home?"

"No," Eleanor assured her, and Jeanie let out a relieved breath. "Of course not. You mean, you don't remember?"

Jeanie shook her head. "Not a thing, at least not after trying to stand up from the table and my head starting to spin. We didn't..."

"Didn't what?" Eleanor appeared to have stopped breathing.

"Dance?" Jeanie squeaked, her heart racing at the sudden discomfort on Eleanor's face. "I just... I sort of remember... I didn't force you to dance a tango in front of everyone, did I? And then everyone started to clap when we were done?"

"What?" Eleanor dissolved into laughter. "No, of course not!"

Jeanie let out a sigh of relief. "Oh, thank God! For a minute, I thought..." An image of Eleanor's lips brushing hers flitted through her mind. It felt so real, and yet..."Never mind. It was obviously all just a vivid dream."

Eleanor chose a bike from the row and wheeled it toward the gate. Jeanie followed, throwing her leg over the bar and hoisting herself onto the leather seat of the one she'd chosen. Tension hung in the air as each seemed to weigh whether to ride together or apart.

Eleanor smiled apprehensively. "Well, have a nice ride."

"Yes, you too." The tension that drained from Jeanie's body formed an almost visible puddle on the ground at this unspoken pledge to ride their separate ways.

They mounted their bikes and began to pedal. But instead of heading in opposite directions, they each headed the same way down the road, side by side though on opposite sides of the pavement. After several yards, Eleanor stopped her bike. "So," she said with a sigh, "I take it you're heading to the winery, too?"

"No, not particularly. I was just riding this direction because it's downhill. I don't have to go this way, if you'd rather I didn't," Jeanie offered, sensing Eleanor's displeasure.

"Well, I had been planning to follow a winery tour from my guide book, but maybe I should go the other way," Eleanor offered politely.

They'd been walking on eggshells all morning. Back and forth. Jeanie couldn't take it any more. "Listen, I like you. Okay, Elle? I've said it. If that's what we're tiptoeing around, then now you know. I do." Jeanie looked away, embarrassment burning her cheeks even while she felt relief for putting the unspoken thing between them into words.

"Thank you for being honest," Eleanor said, looking prim.

Jeanie fixed her with a long, pointed stare. "That's all you have to say?"

Eleanor began to squirm. "What? Okay, fine," she grumbled. "Me too."

Jeanie acknowledged her confession with a nod. "See isn't that better to have it out in the open?"

"Not really."

"Come on, Elle, we're adults. There's nothing wrong with admitting to being attracted," she added when Eleanor continued to look unsure. "We've acknowledged it, and now we can ignore it and move on."

"Just…like that?"

"Of course! We'd be fools to act on it, and I'm not

an idiot, and neither are you. We both know that we've been thrown together in this artificial environment and that there's absolutely no way that any of this translates to the real world." Jeanie felt a stab of regret. "I mean, maybe if we had met somewhere back home…"

Eleanor raised an eyebrow. "Where could we *possibly* have met in our real lives?"

"Nowhere!" Jeanie laughed, and Eleanor joined in, relieving the tension. "See? That's the point. I mean, at least if we'd met in a bar in Poughkeepsie, for example—"

"Why would I be in a bar in Poughkeepsie?"

"You wouldn't! And I never go into Manhattan, if I can help it. See, we wouldn't have had the chance to become friends in real life, let alone anything else. But that doesn't mean we can't continue to be friendly while we're on this trip, does it?"

Eleanor smiled. "Of course not."

"So now that we've got that out in the open," Jeanie added pleadingly, "do you think we can manage to ride on this bike path together, or should I turn around and go the other direction?"

"I think we can manage." Eleanor pushed off with her foot and began to pedal. "In fact, I'm really glad we talked this through. I feel surprisingly better."

"Good." Jeanie pedaled alongside. "Because I wasn't looking forward to riding uphill."

Eleanor gave her a funny look. "You know it'll be uphill on the way back, right?"

"Sure, but I've got *hours* before I have to think about that!"

"We really are complete opposites, you know. We'd be disastrous together."

"Completely disastrous!" Jeanie agreed with a shake of her head, as the two women pedaled along, side by side, in perfect harmony.

The road followed the twists and curves of the Danube, staying mostly flat even while the hills beside them grew increasingly steep. Here, a short rock wall separated the bike path from the lowest of several terraces, the vines growing so close to the edge that the grapes swung above them just a few inches from their heads. Jeanie reached out as they rode past, snapping off a cluster with her fingers as she passed. She slowed to a stop and rested the bike against the wall as Eleanor joined her.

Jeanie popped a juicy green grape into her mouth. "Wanna try one?"

"Jeanie, you're not supposed to pick those!" Eleanor's tongue clicked reproachfully.

Jeanie eyed the acres of grapes that seemed to stretch all the way to the sky. "I doubt they'll run out." She plucked a grape from her cluster and flicked it Eleanor's head. "Live a little, Elle." She giggled as the grape bounced off the corner of Eleanor's lip. A shiver ran down her spine as their eyes connected, Eleanor holding her gaze as if daring her to try again. With a slow, deliberate twist, Jeanie armed herself with another grape. She took aim, still not breaking eye contact, and flicked the orb at her target. Eleanor caught the grape between her teeth and Jeanie clapped in delighted surprise.

"That's not bad," Eleanor commented, liking her lips. "Can I have another?"

"Eleanor Fielding, eating stolen grapes." Jeanie clucked her tongue as she tore the cluster in two and handed over one half. "So rebellious!"

They walked silently along the edge of the path, pushing their bikes and eating grapes. Eleanor gave Jeanie a sidelong look. "I feel guilty."

"For what?"

"Stealing the grapes."

Jeanie stopped and turned, studying Eleanor's face and finding a glimmer of something—perhaps it was fear—deep within her amber eyes. "Oh, sweetie. You're not kidding, are you."

Eleanor shook her head. "My stomach's all in knots. Maybe we should see if there's a farmhouse and offer to pay?"

"Fine, I'll come along, but I think I'll leave this particular conversation to you. Do you speak German?" Jeanie winced as Eleanor shook her head no. "This'll be interesting. Come on, let's go."

Just ahead was a break in the wall, with a small path that led from the road and disappeared between the vines. They pushed their bikes out of view, leaning them against the wall on the opposite side of the vineyard, and started up the path by foot.

The gravel crunched and skittered beneath their steps as they climbed, until they reached the top of the first terrace. Here, another path led off in both directions. Jeanie looked one way and then the other, then shrugged. "Which way now? And please don't say up."

"No, going up won't do us any good. Who would build a farmhouse that high? And we didn't see any buildings on the ride, so heading back that way doesn't make sense. We should go to the left."

"You're very logical. What?" she added as Eleanor shot her a dirty look. "That's a compliment! You're good at thinking things through."

Eleanor shrugged. "It's pretty much my job, I guess."

"Making sure no one takes any risks?"

"Not *any* risks. You have to take some, all businesses do. I just figure out what's likely to happen in the future, given different sets of circumstances, and guide my clients toward the risks that are worth the pay off."

"Sounds important."

"I don't know. It's not like what you do isn't just as important."

Jeanie stared ahead, painfully aware of her disappointment in her own accomplishments compared to Eleanor. What did she do all day except keep kids in line and lecture them on things that had happened in the past that they didn't care anything about? Maybe she could've been more, if she hadn't thrown in the towel. She shuffled along the path in a funk, but perked up as she spotted a curl of smoke in the distance. "Oh, look! I think it's a chimney. That must be the house."

As the building came into view, they soon realized that it was much more than a house. The cottage with the chimney was just one of several buildings, and the footpath they'd taken was far from the only access to the complex. In fact, a wide drive led up from the main road, and there were dozens of cars parked on a grassy clearing. A tent had been set up beside one of the buildings. It was filled with rustic wooden tables, and the sounds of an accordion and assorted brass instruments filled the air, along with the chattering buzz of the crowd.

"I think I know what this is." Eleanor reached into her satchel and pulled out her tour book. She rifled through the pages while Jeanie looked on, finally opening to the section on the Wachau Valley. "Huh. I don't see it on the map. But this is obviously a winery of some kind, and I'm almost positive they're having a new wine festival."

"A festival? That's perfect!" The prospect of approaching a crusty old farmer and confessing to stealing grapes had set Jeanie's usually steely nerves jangling. This gave them an out. "If we buy tickets to the festival, it'll more than make up for the grapes. Besides, if they're serving wine, I'm sure they'll have food, too. And I'm starving."

Jeanie took Eleanor by the hand as they went in search of a place to buy tickets. She smiled contentedly. After laying their issues out earlier and realizing they were on the same page about where their friendship stood, Jeanie felt free to indulge in friendly gestures without worrying that Eleanor would interpret them as flirting. *What a relief!* As they stood in line for tickets, Eleanor's thumb caressed Jeanie's palm, while Jeanie gave Eleanor's fingers a squeeze. Neither seemed to pay the least bit of notice to how thoroughly their hands remained clasped.

SEVENTEEN

"LOOK AT ALL THIS FOOD!" Eleanor's mouth watered as she surveyed the rough-hewn tables that groaned under the weight of more platters than she could count. Cold meats, cheeses, crusty breads, dozens of side dishes, and bowls overflowing with grapes and other fruits, stretched the entire length of the tent. Though she suspected that her stomach would suffer for it later, the knowledge didn't deter her from piling more items onto her plate.

"You didn't get any grapes," Jeanie pointed out as she grabbed a cluster of purple ones from a bowl.

"It was a conscious decision. I'm making up for the ones we stole." Eleanor chuckled as Jeanie rolled her eyes before adding a second cluster to her own plate. The teasing didn't bother her today. It was just such a relief to be on good terms again.

They found seats at a table for two toward the

center of the tent. Though it was only late afternoon, with several hours of sunlight left in the day, it was darker beneath the heavy canvas covering. A trio of tea lights flickered in clear glass holders that sat on the bare wood of the tabletop. Tiny white bulbs twinkled on strings overhead. That, combined with the persistent oom-pah from the band, gave the festival's atmosphere a lively party vibe.

"Can you believe how lucky we were to find this place?" Jeanie's smile beamed from ear to ear, and for once Eleanor found that she couldn't argue with her companion's astonishing good fortune.

"I'll admit that spontaneity can have the occasional benefit," Eleanor replied. "If I'd been relying only on my tour book, I never would have known this was here. It wasn't on the map, and according to the book, there aren't any festivals in this region until late August."

Jeanie's smile grew even wider, her teeth sparkling in the candlelight. "See? I'm a good influence on you. If you hadn't let me ride along with you, you wouldn't be here right now."

Eleanor's jaw dropped in mock offense. "Oh, you think you should get all the credit?" She thought for a moment. "What about me? If I hadn't been about to have a panic attack over those stupid grapes, we'd never have left the trail. We would have passed right by and never known it was here."

Jeanie pursed her lips. "But I'm the one who took

you seriously when you said you were feeling anxious. I should get credit for that."

"Except that I was only feeling anxious because you stole the grapes in the first place! You don't get extra credit for being the cause of my anxiety, as well as its cure." Eleanor gave a snort. "Good influence, my ass!"

"Fine," Jeanie said with a pout, "at least you can admit that we make a good team."

"Actually, I can't argue with that." Eleanor laughed as Jeanie's eyebrows shot up. "Seriously. Traveling with you has been an unexpected pleasure. For the most part." Even Eleanor felt surprised by the realization, and how easy it was to admit now that they had cleared the air.

A server came by pouring wine, her full-skirted *dirndl* brushing the chair backs as she walked through the crowded tent. Jeanie and Eleanor held out their glasses as she went by, then held them up to inspect the light golden liquid. Jeanie sniffed the glass and wrinkled her nose. "Interesting."

Eleanor inhaled as well, an almost vinegary odor tickling her nostrils. "Well, I guess we should try it." She lifted the glass to her lips and grimaced as the first drop hit her tongue. Across the table, Jeanie's face mirrored her own. "Wow. That's really…"

"Sweet? Goodness. We won't have to worry about me drinking too much today, that's for certain." Jeanie waved her arm in the direction the server had gone.

"What are you doing?"

"Just going to see if we can get something else. There she is!" Jeanie hopped up from the table. "Be right back."

Eleanor watched with amusement as Jeanie tracked down the server, her hands gesticulating excitedly as she explained the situation. Moments later, she returned with two new glasses. "Maria, that's the server—oh, and she was an exchange student in New Jersey, isn't that nice? Anyway, she thinks we'll like these much better."

The fact that she'd gotten exactly what she wanted in record time and learned the server's name and life story in the process no longer struck Eleanor as in the least bit odd. As Eleanor sipped the dry white wine, she reflected that this was one of the many ways in which they made a good team. Eleanor would've fussed and fumed at everyone in sight for hours over the issue, and with half as good a resolution in the end.

As the guests finished their meals, the musicians moved from beneath the tent to set up again in a clear, flat courtyard. The band's leader made an announcement in German, which neither Eleanor nor Jeanie understood, but obviously many in the crowd did because soon after several couples had left the tables and reconvened on the open space. The opening notes of an Austrian folk melody reverberated above the din of after-dinner conversation, and the couples took hands and began to dance.

Jeanie broke into a delighted grin. "Elle, look! It's the dance that we learned this morning in class!"

"The dance *you* learned, you mean. I told you, I was just passing through."

Though she had no interest in dancing herself, Eleanor was intrigued enough to wander with Jeanie to the edge of the courtyard to watch. Glimpsing Jeanie's shining face, Eleanor's heart sank. It was obvious the woman was itching to dance. Now that she'd shaken off her anxiety over their attraction to one another and was truly settled on just being friends, Eleanor found herself examining her actions through the lens of what a typical friend might do. In this case, it seemed reasonable that a friend would ask Jeanie to dance, and Eleanor felt a pang of guilt at her failure to oblige.

As the dancing continued, Eleanor studied the dancers' movements with a frown. Dancing was chaotic and unpredictable. That was the reason Eleanor avoided it like the plague. So many variations, so many choices to make with each new beat of the music. It overwhelmed her. But what she saw in the courtyard wasn't like that at all. "It's a pattern. They just keep repeating the same thing."

Jeanie nodded. "It's called a *Ländler*. There are a few variations, but it's basically just a set of steps that repeats." She cocked her head to one side. "Careful, or someone might get the wrong impression and think you were willing to give it a try."

"Well, maybe I am." Though Jeanie's mouth gaped at the admission, no one was more shocked to hear these words than Eleanor herself. Fighting the nervous flutter in her belly, she stuck out her hand. "Come on. Show me how it's done."

They stepped into the sea of dancers and after facing her and bobbing a quick curtsy, Jeanie took both Eleanor's hands in hers. "You're sure?"

Eleanor nodded, focusing on the warm, sure grip of Jeanie's fingers to fight back her worry. Soon they were stepping in time to the music, several counts of simple walking steps, followed by a series of turns that left Eleanor dizzy and on the verge of giggling. When the whole crowd around them stomped and clapped with the rhythm of the music, Eleanor jumped in surprise, then burst out laughing as the music came to an end.

"See?" Jeanie gasped for breath, laughing heartily herself. "Wasn't that fun?"

"I doubt I'll be tempted by any of the other swing dancing stuff, but this wasn't half bad."

The crush of dancers leaving the courtyard prompted Jeanie to place a guiding hand at Eleanor's waist, and though it was an innocent gesture, Eleanor felt a tremor of desire pulse through her at the touch. *Friends,* she reminded herself, and felt relieved once again that they'd talked this through already and reached the same conclusion. If they hadn't, her thoughts and feelings might have tied her up in knots all night. As it was, the decision was already made.

She couldn't help feeling attracted to Jeanie, but that's as far as it would go. Still, Eleanor felt a fleeting regret for what could've been if they'd had more common ground. There was no intersection between her real life and Jeanie's, but if there had been, Eleanor wasn't blind to the fact that it might've been nice to see where things between them would go.

They reached an open space apart from the crowd and Jeanie's hand lingered at her waist just a fraction of a second before dropping. The look on her face made Eleanor wonder if a similar thought had occurred to Jeanie, too.

The sun was low in the sky as they sought out the footpath back down to the road. The walk seemed to take less time, partially because it was downhill, but also because they walked with purpose this time. The ride back to the village was very much uphill, and they would be lucky to get the bikes returned and be back on the ship before dark. At the opening in the stone wall, Jeanie grabbed her bike by the handles and pushed it onto the road. She was just mounting the seat as Eleanor pushed her own bike to the road, stopping with a groan.

"Jeanie, hold on a sec. My tire's flat."

"What?" Jeanie frowned as she dismounted and knelt alongside Eleanor to inspect the damage. "Shit. That's a big gash."

Eleanor stared helplessly at the hole, cursing herself for her carelessness. *So stupid, Eleanor!* She felt her chest tighten for the second time that day as the anxiety tried to take hold of her. She fought the urge to scream at herself, or at Jeanie—though she'd done nothing wrong. The cold nerves coiled in the pit of her stomach as she realized there was nothing she could do to get herself out of this mess.

"There's a patch kit in the bag beneath my seat. Would that help?"

"What?" The vice squeezing Eleanor's lungs loosened and air rushed in.

Jeanie rummaged through the small pouch and pulled out a repair kit. "The woman at the shop suggested it, and since *someone* I know keeps reminding me of the importance of planning ahead, I bought one. There's a can of foam or something in here, too, to fill the tire once it's fixed."

Her friend's surprise preparedness prompted her to chuckle, but her smile faded as she held the patch up to the hole. "It's way too small. We'll never get it to work. Maybe you can ride ahead for help?"

"Me? Uphill all that way alone?" Jeanie squeaked. "Honestly, Elle, I was counting on your encouragement to get me back. That, or just being too embarrassed to fail in front of you. You're a much stronger rider than I am. Maybe you should go, and I'll wait here."

A new stab of anxiety shot through her. "Leave you

here alone? In the dark?" Eleanor shook her head vehemently. "Too risky."

"I could go back up to the winery and wait there."

"Of course." Eleanor smacked her forehead with the palm of her hand. "I don't know why I didn't think of it before. We should *both* go back to the winery, and see if someone can give us a ride. It'll take over an hour by bike even if we hurry, but it's just a few minutes by car to get back to the village."

The hike back up the hill took longer than the first time as they both rolled their bicycles with them since the bike path was inaccessible by car. When they arrived back at the winery, the dinner crowd had disappeared. Their server from the afternoon had changed out of her *dirndl* into jeans and t-shirt and was scrubbing down the tables under the tent with a bucket and rags.

"Excuse me, Maria?" Jeanie called out, and Eleanor had never been so grateful for her companion's innate friendliness.

As soon as she heard her name, the server looked up with a welcoming smile. "Ladies, you're back! Did you forget something?"

"No, I'm afraid we had a little trouble with our bikes," Jeanie replied, gesturing to Eleanor's flat tire.

Maria's smile faded and her brow creased in concern. "Oh dear! Are you staying nearby? Is there someone I can call for you?"

"Actually, we were hoping for a ride," Jeanie

explained. "If it isn't too much trouble. You see, we're on a river boat that leaves in the morning, and we have no way to get back."

"Oh," Maria said, her concerned expression deepening. "Normally, I'd be happy to. We have a farm truck large enough to hold the bikes. But the headlights aren't working and with the festival, I haven't had a chance to get them fixed."

Eleanor's shoulders slumped. "Well, thanks anyway."

"But I could take you in the morning," Maria added. "When does the ship leave?"

Jeanie looked searchingly at Eleanor, obviously unsure.

"Nine o'clock," Eleanor supplied.

"The sun's up well before then. We have a small inn here, above the main building of the winery. It's mostly booked because of the festival, but someone canceled this evening, so there's one room left."

"We'll take it." Eleanor replied. "I'll pay for the room," she added firmly to Jeanie. "I insist. It was my stupid tire that blew."

Jeanie flashed a grateful smile, but there was concern in her eyes, and it didn't seem to be the financial kind. As they followed Maria toward the inn, Eleanor felt it, too. Swiveling her head, she saw that it was completely dark at this point. The black sky was filled with twinkling stars, the moon a half circle hidden behind gray clouds. There wasn't a single sound coming from the main road. This was their only option for the night, and there was just one room left. Eleanor knew she should be thankful for their good luck, but all she could hear echoing in her head was a question of vital concern: *How many beds will there be?*

EIGHTEEN

THANK GOODNESS, two beds! Jeanie let out her breath and felt her racing pulse begin to slow as she surveyed the room she and Eleanor had been assigned. She felt Eleanor's presence close behind her, and heard her companion suck in a gulp of air. "What's wrong?" she asked, turning to look at her. *Surely she wasn't hoping for a different sleeping arrangement?*

"Are those supposed to be beds?" Eleanor's forehead scrunched tightly, her eyebrows nearly touching, as her eyes scanned the room.

Jeanie laughed. "They're single beds, Elle. Don't tell me that you, the world traveler, has never seen a single bed before. They're all over Europe!" She deemed the fact that she hadn't known they existed until seven days ago, irrelevant under the current circumstances. Not when it gave her the upper hand.

"I'd heard rumors," Eleanor muttered. "It's fine. It's just for the night."

"Oh, come on, Elle. You have to admit that this room's adorable." It was decorated in a traditional, rustic style, with woven red and white coverlets on the narrow beds and exposed wooden beams in the white stuccoed walls. Jeanie thought it was cozy, and a million times nicer than her dreary room on the ship.

"Adorable?" Eleanor scoffed. "At least it's better than a twenty-mile walk in the dark."

They had no luggage, but Maria had gone in search of extra nightclothes and toiletries. There was a knock on the door and, upon opening it, Jeanie was presented with a towering pile of white cotton and two toothbrushes in plastic wrappers. She handed a toothbrush to Eleanor, and shook the pile of clothing onto the bed.

"Look at this!" She held up one of the voluminous cotton nightgowns to her chest and spun around to show Eleanor.

"The last time that thing saw the light of day, the Habsburg Empire was probably still going strong."

"Here, there's one for you, too." She tossed the other nightgown onto Eleanor's bed. "They're a little old fashioned, but they'll do for tonight."

Eleanor nodded. "It's better than nothing." Her cheeks flushed pink and she quickly looked away while Jeanie failed to bite back a teasing snicker. Eleanor rolled her eyes. "You know what I meant. And just so you know, if Maria shows up with *dirndls* for us to wear in the morning, I'm drawing a line."

They quickly changed for bed, taking turns in the tiny bathroom. After they'd both climbed into their beds, Jeanie turned off the light. She could hear springs squeak as Eleanor tossed and turned in the darkness. "Everything okay over there? Do you need me to turn on the light?"

"No." Eleanor gave a deep sigh. "It's just, each time I move I feel like I'm going to fall off the edge."

Jeanie giggled into her pillow, conveniently failing to mention that she'd done the same thing her first night on board the ship.

"It's not funny. Seriously Jeanie, I feel anxious that I'm going to fall off."

Jeanie stopped laughing. She'd fallen off her bed more than once during the week. There were just so many clothes on her floor that she'd continued to sleep soundly until morning. "When you say *anxious*, Elle, do you mean that figuratively, or—"

"I mean chest tightening, hard to breathe, starting to feel panicked just talking about—"

"Okay, okay, I get the picture." Jeanie snapped on the light and hopped to her feet. "Come on, out of bed."

"What?" Eleanor blinked in confusion. "It's not going to get better if I sleep on the floor."

"You're not sleeping on the floor." Jeanie fixed her with her most exasperated look. "We're pushing the beds together, over in that corner. That way you'll have the wall to make you feel safe on one side, and me on the other." She felt her cheeks tingle as images of this scenario populated her mind. Some of the possible outcomes were *quite* appealing. And strayed well beyond *just friends* territory.

Eleanor swallowed hard. "Jeanie, I'm not sure if that's—"

"Elle, don't worry." Jeanie forced herself to banish her more lascivious thoughts from her mind. "When you hit the edge of the mattress, your body will know to stop. But just in case, this way you can't fall all the way off." She gave the beds a final shove and looked at Eleanor in satisfaction.

Eleanor stared at the resulting space thoughtfully. "It's not quite as big as the bed in my stateroom, but I think it will work."

Jeanie frowned at the word *stateroom*. She'd known from the start that Eleanor didn't share her economy accommodations on D Deck, but for the first time it occurred to her to wonder exactly how fancy her friend's room was. After all, just the mention of it had certainly gotten Thomas' attention in a hurry. Her curiosity piqued, Jeanie wondered if there was some way to get to see it, but every plan that occurred to her she quickly dismissed as wildly inappropriate if she intended to keep up her end of their no-relationship bargain.

As she turned off the bedroom light and climbed

back into her half of the bed, it struck her that she may have been too hasty in stipulating that there was *no* chance for her and Eleanor. *Just because we didn't meet before in real life, does that really mean we wouldn't have met in the future?* In retrospect it was a stupid rule, but Eleanor had really gotten on board with that idea. Eleanor, who was currently tucked under her coverlet like a stiff board, seemingly afraid to breathe too hard lest their skin accidentally brush past one another in the night. *It's no use.* They'd reached an agreement, and that's how it was going to be. Jeanie rolled onto her side and tucked her own blanket under her chin. *I'll just have to learn to live with my second guessing,* she thought as she closed her eyes.

The next thing Jeanie was aware of was the incessant crowing of a rooster somewhere in the distance. As she pried one sleepy eyelid open halfway, early morning light cast gray shadows around the unfamiliar room. There was a slight chill in the air, but Jeanie felt remarkably warm, and so luxuriously relaxed that she thought she might never want to move from this spot. She closed her eye and snuggled deeper into the bed, breathing in the clean scent of jasmine. The pillow she clasped to her body was so comforting, sweetened with the fresh scent of jasmine. So soft and silky. So...*alive.*

Jeanie held her breath, but found that the pillow in her arms continued to inhale and exhale rhythmically. Her eyes flew open to find a mass of short, messy curls resting on her chest against the starched white of her borrowed nightgown—a gown which had started out looking so Victorian the night before, but looked decidedly less so in its current condition, with buttons popped open and the front splayed so far apart that she could see the outline of her nipple peaking through, and feel the gentle tickle of Eleanor's breath across her skin.

Cautiously, Jeanie shifted her focus and discovered that the hem of the gown had shifted up as well, and that her limbs were so entwined with Eleanor's that she wasn't sure how to get them undone. They were completely and inextricably wrapped around one another at every possible point, like vines that had grown together in the night. And infuriatingly, they were so evenly sprawled across both beds that it was impossible to tell who'd started it. *Someone's to blame!* Jeanie held her breath again, her heart racing, as she slowly eased each of her body parts back to her own mattress and prayed that Eleanor would continue to sleep. If she woke up, it wouldn't matter how little evidence there was. Eleanor was sure to assume it was Jeanie's fault.

Safely back where she belonged, Jeanie closed her eyes and pretended to sleep. While waiting for Eleanor to stir, she thought about how they would get back to the ship, about the places she would tour in Vienna later that day, about anything and everything that she could, other than the memory of waking up in the sweet perfection of Eleanor's embrace.

THE BRIGHT GREEN tennis ball bounced hypnotically on the end of Eleanor's racket as she waited for Jeanie to join her on the court. Around her, passengers sat on the observation deck and grumbled. The bell from the village church had just tolled two o'clock, but the ship still sat motionless in place. The disabled ship in Vienna that had led to their initial detour also yielded an impromptu safety inspection of their own vessel, and maintenance had yet to clear them for departure.

The best estimate from the crew was that they'd be lucky to reach Vienna before nightfall. In the meantime, without tours or classes to pass the time, the atmosphere aboard the ship grew increasingly restless. Were she the dancing type, Eleanor might have done a jig at discovering that Jeanie played tennis. As it was, she'd had quite enough dancing the day before to last her. Maintaining the *just friends* status quo was much easier without the intimacy of the dance floor.

The flutter of a white skirt caught Eleanor's eye and she looked up to see Jeanie, dressed in a pleated white dress, white shoes, and even a white scarf around her head to tie back her curly locks. *Who dresses like that for tennis?* It was like something from a fashion magazine. The only place she'd seen a getup like that was on trophy wives at her sister's posh suburban tennis club. And none of them knew how to play.

Eleanor groaned inwardly, regretting her decision to challenge Jeanie to a game. She'd assumed the fact that Jeanie mentioned bringing tennis clothes meant she knew her way around a racket. Now she realized it was just Jeanie's excuse for a costume change. Eleanor sighed. She'd been looking forward to a little friendly competition to work out some stress, but she suspected she wouldn't find it here. *I'll have to go easy on her.*

Jeanie took up her position on the court and grasped her racket. Eleanor lobbed the ball squarely across the net. It had been as gentle a serve as she could muster, but Jeanie still missed. And dropped her racket. "Oops!" she called out with a shake of her head. "I guess I'm a little out of practice."

As Jeanie bent to retrieve the fallen racket, the top of her tennis dress gaped to expose her chest. Eleanor's throat went dry. It was a familiar view, one Eleanor had woken up to just that morning. Her stomach clenched as she recalled the chilly morning air and the rooster's cries, and the shock of finding every inch of herself wrapped tightly around Jeanie's slumbering frame. Her sleepy eyes had been met by a plateau of sun-kissed flesh, sloping upward in a gentle curve, with just a shadowy outline of a nipple as the skin disappeared beneath white cotton. Eleanor had stared for some time at the lovely view, until it occurred to her disoriented brain exactly how she'd come to be enjoying it. Then she froze in place, afraid that any movement would wake Jeanie, between whose breasts her face was currently nestled, her lips resting in a puddle of drool. It was a safe bet that many of the frustrations she sought to work out on the tennis court had their start at that moment.

Eleanor blinked hard and looked away from her friend, who by this point had gotten the racket and was now exposing the better part of her thighs and buttocks as she scurried to retrieve the ball. She'd never been so thankful for a pair of sunglasses to hide behind. "Why don't you serve?" Eleanor blushed as her voice crackled in her parched throat.

"But it's still your turn."

"It's just a friendly game, Jeanie. We don't even have to keep score."

Jeanie stood up and smoothed her dress, seemingly unaware of the effect it had had on her friend. She tossed the ball in the air and swung, the racket connecting with a solid thwack. Eleanor jumped as the bright green orb sped over the net, swinging and narrowly missing as the ball came at her at twice the velocity she'd expected. *Lucky shot?* Eleanor's pulse ticked up. *Maybe not.* That had been one hell of a serve.

The next time she was more prepared, and managed to return the serve. Jeanie made an impressive dive toward the ball and sent it sailing back. Eleanor swung and missed. "Wow." She rested her hands on her knees, panting in disbelief. She had *not* expected to give up two points in a row. "Where did you learn to play?"

"Summer camp, when I was a kid."

"Oh?" Her breath caught. *Me, too.* "Not Pine Meadows, was it?" What a coincidence that would be! *And if our paths crossed at camp, then maybe—*

"The sleepaway camp? As if!" Jeanie chortled. "For your information, Miss Fancy Pants, it was a day camp in the church basement run by one of the high school gym teachers." She smacked the ball with the racket.

Eleanor missed the ball again and scowled. *Damn, she's good!* "Did you play other sports? Like lacrosse?" Miriam had played lacrosse and was about Jeanie's same age. Could she have been on the opposing team at one of the games? Eleanor had gone to every game. If they could have bumped into each other there, surely that would count?

Jeanie served. "No, nothing like that."

"Scouts?" Eleanor swung at the ball and it soared across the net.

"Nope." This time Jeanie swung and missed, and Eleanor grinned.

They took a break, grabbing bottles of cool water. Jeanie leaned beside the net while Eleanor paced. They grew up just a few hours apart, could their paths really never have crossed? The more she thought about it, the less probable it seemed. Eleanor hated improbabilities. She needed to dig deeper.

"You said you lived in Manhattan, after college?"

Jeanie nodded. "Yeah, for a bit while I was in grad school."

"Washington Square?" It was the neighborhood closest to New York University. If she'd been a student there, she would have been just a few blocks from Eleanor's office in lower Manhattan. There were a hundred ways they could've met!

"Washington Heights," she replied with a snort, naming a neighborhood clear on the opposite end of the island that was close to the City University of New York.

Eleanor's fingers twitched in agitation. "Have you been to Central Park?"

"Of course I have. Who hasn't been to Central Park?" Jeanie cocked her head, fixing Eleanor with a searching look. "Did you have a particular day or location in mind?"

Eleanor's heart skipped a beat. Jeanie was a bright woman and had clearly caught on to what Eleanor was doing. "Of course not. I was just curious." She leaned her back against the net.

Jeanie slid closer, still eying her studiously. "And you're sure you've never been to Poughkeepsie?"

"Couldn't find it on a map." Eleanor's heart ached with regret. "I guess there really is no way we could've met."

"Seems like it," Jeanie agreed, pushing herself up from the net. Eleanor thought she caught the whispered words 'what a pity' as they both took their places on the court.

They were partway into the next set when Rolfe wandered up and tapped on the glass barrier separating the tennis court from the rest of the deck. "Ladies?" he called.

"Rolfe!" Jeanie cried. "Any news on when we'll be leaving for Vienna?"

The steward shook his head. "Soon, hopefully. But the captain's decided to host a dinner tonight, to apologize. Everyone is invited, even economy passengers," he added with a smile to Jeanie. He shifted his eyes to Eleanor. "And since you're in one of our VIP rooms, if you arrive early, I can seat you at the captain's table. And a guest. If you're interested."

"The captain's table!" Jeanie clapped her hands in glee.

Eleanor took in Jeanie's beaming face and laughed. "I'm not sure I have much of a choice! That sounds very nice. Thank you, Rolfe." She felt a flush of pride as she got the name right without a moment's hesitation.

"Oh my goodness. That's such an honor! See what happens when you make friends, Elle?" Jeanie commented when the steward had left. "It can be very worthwhile to be nice to people."

"I'm sure my paying twenty thousand euros for a VIP stateroom had nothing to do with the *honor*." Eleanor blushed as Jeanie's face blanched at the revelation of the price. "But I see your point," she added awkwardly.

They returned to their game and had just finished another set when the lurch of the ship made Eleanor pause mid-serve. "I guess we're finally underway!"

"I'm not sure I'll be able to play if the deck's going to keep swaying like this."

Eleanor nodded in agreement. "We should probably head in to get ready, anyway."

"Already? Dinner's not for another few hours."

"But we're supposed to get there early," Eleanor warned, her body telegraphing its usual tension at the prospect of running late.

"Fine, you win," Jeanie agreed. "The argument, that is. Not the match. I was the clear winner there."

"The hell you were! It was a tie!" Eleanor's eyes narrowed as Jeanie began to laugh.

"I thought you said we weren't keeping score." Her laughter echoed across the deck as she retreated to the door.

Eleanor watched her go, much more hot and bothered than she would have liked. Jeanie's competitive streak was as strong as hers, and a real turn on. But they'd gone through every place she could think of, and the answer was still the same. There was absolutely no way they would have met in their everyday lives. Like it or not, it was the rule they'd established. Unless there was someway they could've met in the real world, there was no way their relationship could move from where it was now. *Two friendly acquaintances on a cruise.* Eleanor picked up her racket and left the court with a heavy heart, but there was no getting around it when they had both agreed it was for the best.

Back in her room, Eleanor turned on the shower and stripped off her tennis clothes in front of the bathroom mirror. As the steam fogged the glass, she closed her eyes and caressed her shoulders, allowing herself for the briefest of moments to imagine that it was Jeanie's fingers instead of her own. A half smile teased her lips as she imagined them both naked, stepping into the shower and—*Stop it!* She forced her eyes open and stuck her fingers into the spray, contemplating whether, in her current mood, she should adjust it a little colder. Just as she was stepping in, there was a loud knock at the front door. Donning one of the fluffy white robes that hung next to the shower and grasping the top demurely to keep it closed, she sprinted through the sitting room and spied a familiar figure through the peephole of her door. *Jeanie?*

She opened the door. "What's wrong?" she asked as she took in the sight of her friend standing in the hall, wrapped in a brightly patterned floral robe and clutching a heap of clothing to her chest.

"May I come in?" Jeanie scooted past, entering the room. "There's a line a mile long for the showers on D deck. I've been waiting twenty minutes already and I'm starting to freak out."

"What do you mean there's a line?"

"Every little old single lady on the ship is trying to get first dibs on the captain's table."

"You mean, you don't have your own shower in your room?"

Jeanie shot her a sidelong look. "In case you hadn't guessed, the economy rooms aren't exactly like this." She gestured with one hand as she turned to take in the room. "My God, is this like a living room, or something?"

Eleanor nodded, her awkwardness returning as her eyes fixed on the short hem of Jeanie's robe, and the long bare legs beneath.

"Wow." Jeanie whistled. "Wait, do I hear running water?"

"The shower! I had just turned it on when you knocked."

Jeanie's cheeks colored. "I'm sorry. Go, take your shower! Just, do you mind if I do, too?" Her eyes widened as Eleanor began to choke in response. "Oh, Jesus, Elle! I meant when you're done!" Jeanie burst into laughter as Eleanor's face turned beet red.

"I knew that. Obviously," Eleanor muttered, coughing once more. "I've just got something caught in my throat." *Like my dignity.* "Yes, fine. Wait here and you can use it when I'm done." She could still hear chuckling coming from the living room as she scurried back to the steam-filled bathroom and shut the door.

NINETEEN

JEANIE DABBED at her eyes with her fingertips, her laughter having moistened the corners with tears. She still couldn't stop. *The look on Elle's face!* She'd never intended to imply that they should shower together. In her rush to get ready for dinner, flirting with her punctuality-obsessed friend had been the furthest thing from her mind. She was just trying not to be late! Of course, now that she had a moment of quiet to think about it…with the sound of running water coming from the next room…and knowing that Elle was in there at this very second, all naked and…sudsy…

A ribbon of steam escaped the crack in door, wafting into the bedroom and tickling Jeanie's nostrils with its jasmine scent. A wave of heat hit her as if her internal thermostat had just been adjusted to a thousand degrees. She tossed her change of clothing and toiletry bag on the edge of the bed and fanned her flushed face. All she could think about was soap. Jeanie flopped backward onto the bed and snuggled a throw pillow to her chest. It, too, smelled of Eleanor's shampoo. When she closed her eyes, she imagined herself back in the inn and tried to recapture the peaceful perfection of waking in Eleanor's arms. Tears pricked her eyes, but this time they weren't the happy kind. She tossed the pillow aside. Because of her stupid rule, Eleanor was off limits.

The relentless pulse of the shower burrowed through her eardrum, planting one tantalizingly inappropriate vision after another into her brain. Needing a distraction from whatever was taking place behind the closed bathroom door, she set about exploring the stateroom. It was bigger and more elegant than she had imagined, though somehow that didn't surprise her. Of course Eleanor—who lived in midtown and had spent her summers at sleepaway camps, with her important job and fancy travel—had a room like this. Jeanie wasn't jealous. She didn't begrudge Eleanor her money. If anything, it filled her with sadness, because it was just one more thing they didn't have in common, one more reason that under ordinary circumstances, their paths would never cross.

The memory of Eleanor's tennis court antics teased a smile from Jeanie's lips. She'd guessed what Eleanor was up to the minute she'd started listing every conceivable space they might have occupied at the same time in their lives. *Central Park, for heaven's sake!*

That was a real needle in a haystack. Her heart fluttered to think that Eleanor was as torn up about the situation as her. What she wouldn't have given to have found that connection! All they needed was one place on the map they could point to, just a shred of proof that they had the potential to be more than just a meaningless fling after their ship reached its final port.

Meaningless? Impossible! Everything about Eleanor held meaning to Jeanie. They were nothing alike, but maybe that wasn't a bad thing. She'd found some of Eleanor's habits annoying at first, sure, but what was wrong with being on time or planning ahead? Those were lessons Jeanie could do well to learn. Jeanie squeezed her eyes shut to stop them from watering. There was so little time left! And day by day, the more time they spent together, the less she wanted it to end.

What if they *had* found that needle in a haystack, out on the tennis court that afternoon? Jeanie snickered as the scenario played out in her imagination. She would've hopped over the net and given Eleanor a kiss like nothing either of them had ever experienced before. Desire shot through her just to picture it in her head. Half the old grannies on the observation deck might've fainted dead away at the sight, and she wouldn't have cared.

Her tongue touched her lips. The taste and feel of Eleanor's mouth against hers was all she'd been able to dream about since waking up in her embrace. *We ended up on the cruise together, isn't that good enough?* Why were they wasting the time they had left struggling to stay at arm's length instead of taking a chance and seeing where it led? Jeanie cursed under her breath. *What possessed me to come up with this idiotic rule?* Now they were stuck with it. Eleanor didn't seem the type to renegotiate rules once they were set.

She walked to the French doors in a huff, wrenching them open and stepping out onto the private balcony. The fresh air calmed her, and she took a deep breath as she tried to readjust her attitude. The evening was off to a magical start as they cruised the Danube. Its beauty lifted her spirits. The sun was just disappearing behind the terraced hills of the Wachau Valley. Fluffy clouds, turned brilliant pink in the golden light of sunset, filled the sky. In a few hours, they would arrive in Vienna, the city she'd dreamed of visiting for over a decade. She rested her forehead in her hands, working her fingers through her hair as if they could push the regrets right out of her head. Why dwell on what she couldn't have when so many of her dreams were coming true?

There was a rustling behind her and she turned to see Eleanor, fresh from her shower, snug in her robe with a towel wrapped around her head. Her serious expression gave Jeanie a start and set her nerves jangling as she tried to think of what she could have done to bring it on.

"Where did you get this?" In her hands, Eleanor held Jeanie's toiletry bag.

"That?" Jeanie winced as she recalled the pile of stuff she'd thrown on Eleanor's pristine bed. "Oh, Elle. I'm so sorry I left all my stuff—"

Eleanor waved her off. "No, that's fine. But where did this bag come from?"

Jeanie frowned, still uncertain where this was headed. "The Katonah Country Club. It's just some little freebie I picked up last summer."

"Katonah?"

Jeanie nodded. "It's a tiny place, maybe thirty minutes from where I live. I'm sure you've never heard of it."

"My sister and her husband live in Katonah."

Jeanie's eyes widened at this unexpected revelation.

"They bought a house there last year. She plays tennis at the Katonah Country Club every Saturday. I've joined her a few times. I even got the same free bag." Eleanor's eyes met hers and Jeanie saw her own dawning sense of the meaning of this discovery reflected therein.

"The summer camp where I work is in Katonah. We take the kids to the country club for tennis lessons." Jeanie laughed giddily. "Do you know what this means?"

Eleanor took a step onto the balcony. "We could've met at the club."

Excitement welled up in Jeanie's chest. "Or at the coffee shop across the street."

"The one with the red awning?" A smile teased

Eleanor's lips. "I've been there at least half a dozen times."

A worrying thought struck Jeanie and she frowned. "But I'm never there on Saturdays."

Eleanor's shoulders slumped. "You're not?"

"Camp only runs on weekdays." *Why am I making this harder than it needs to be?* She thought for a moment and her spirits lifted. "But I'm friendly with the barista at the coffee place. She might've chatted with you one day and decided to introduce us."

"Me, chat?" Eleanor cocked an eyebrow. "With a barista?"

"Okay maybe not." Determined not to give up, Jeanie took a step toward her. "Does your sister play tennis during the week?" She smiled when Eleanor nodded. "Well I chat with everyone, so maybe I would've met your sister at the club. I'd definitely mention being single, because you know I'm always telling people personal things that I shouldn't. And then she would've mentioned her sister being single, too. And then she would've invited me for dinner the next time you came to visit." It was a ridiculous scenario, but it was her last shot. Jeanie held her breath.

"That's exactly what Mimi would do."

Jeanie's breath rush out in a laugh. "It is?" She'd been convinced Eleanor would shoot her down.

"Are you kidding? Ever since Sylvia left, my sister can't stop herself from interfering with my love life. A blind date, a dinner ambush. Hell, she's the reason I ended up here." They were just inches apart now. "One way or another, the point is—"

"We could've met," Jeanie breathed.

Their bodies were so close that Jeanie could feel the shower steam that had been trapped against Eleanor's skin by her terry cloth robe. She closed her eyes and let the jasmine-scented warmth envelop her. It was impossible to tell who made the first move to close the distance. It was less of a conscious choice and more like they were two magnets that, after pushing against each other since the moment they'd met, somehow suddenly flipped and became impossible to pull apart.

Jeanie's arms clasped behind Eleanor's neck as their lips met, Eleanor's hands at her hips, pulling her close. She lost herself in the indescribable sweetness of those lips. From somewhere in the depths of passion, it occurred to her that they tasted unexpectedly of honey. She grasped Eleanor's bottom lip between her teeth and confirmed it was so.

Their chests rose and fell rapidly, bursts of hot breath scorching bare skin as they devoured one another. The tips of Jeanie's fingers snaked beneath the towel that covered Eleanor's head. It dislodged and fell to the ground as she twisted the damp locks with her hands. The thin fabric of her robe slipped from her shoulder and down her arm, momentarily exposing her bra-clad torso to the breeze before it was mostly covered by Eleanor's searching lips. A shiver coursed through her at the searing touch, and at the same moment she felt the press of icy metal behind her as her back made contact with the balcony's railing. The contrast of heat and cold nearly made her come apart. "Oh, Elle!" she gasped.

ELEANOR'S SENSES returned at the sound of her name being wrung from Jeanie's trembling lips. Her heart throbbed like a kettledrum. With some surprise she realized that she was standing in nothing but a robe, with a half-naked woman pressed against her face, in full view of the entire world. It was not a situation she could ever recall having found herself in before, and her brain froze, momentarily uncertain what to do.

"What's wrong?" Jeanie's voice rumbled in her chest and made Eleanor's mouth, which was still attached the base of her throat, vibrate.

Eleanor straightened up, self-consciously shifting Jeanie's robe back into place on her shoulders while avoiding eye contact. "I got a little carried away."

"Funny. I thought we were just getting started." The huskiness in Jeanie's voice made Eleanor venture a shy glance at her face, and the desire she saw there sent a tremor through her core. Jeanie reached for the edges of her robe to pull her close again, but Eleanor lightly swatted her hands.

"Jeanie, we're in public." Eleanor's face burned hot and red.

"This?" Jeanie's laugh was as crisp and clear as the evening air. "This isn't public. It's a completely private balcony, Elle. No one can see."

Eleanor felt her resolve waver as Jeanie wrapped her arms around her and nuzzled the sensitive spot just behind her ear. "What about people along the riverbank?"

Jeanie's soft laughter tickled against her neck and made her knees go weak. "What people? There's no one but us, Elle. And even if someone happened to be looking from shore, they'd need binoculars." Jeanie let the robe slide down from her shoulders, exposing the pink whisper of lace that contained the swell of her breasts. "And if they thought to bring binoculars, well, don't you think their preparation deserves to be rewarded?"

Eleanor shivered as she ran her finger down one thin strap of Jeanie's bra, her defenses melting. "I guess I am a fan of people being prepared." She moaned as she felt Jeanie's tongue touch her lips, luxuriating in the tender caresses for a moment longer before gently pulling herself away. "Jeanie, what are we doing?" Her nerves twitched alarmingly.

"That seemed obvious." Jeanie gave a sultry pout

that shifted to a sly smile. "I know it's been a while Elle, but exactly how long *has* it been?"

"That's not what I meant. I meant, are we just getting caught up in all of this…*spontaneity*?" She pronounced the last word with a hiss of distaste.

"Spontaneity?" Jeanie laughed. "We've dragged this out a week! This is me at the height of patience, following every rule. And don't pretend you don't know what I mean. You knew the conditions, same as me. Find one way we could've met in real life—and you did!"

"Fine. The off chance that we could've run into each other during a tennis match might have fulfilled the bargain, but is it enough? It doesn't change the fact that we're opposites in every way. I read a study recently, and statistically speaking, most relationships—"

"A study? Have you ever considered that it's okay to do things without reading a study first and gathering up the stats? Elle, I know you love your numbers, but let's not over analyze this, okay? We only have one week left, and there are better things we could be studying."

Eleanor's breath hitched as one of Jeanie's long legs, bare beneath her robe, caressed her own. "And after the week?"

"Can we just leave it undefined?"

Eleanor shook her head no, though the truth was,

she was seconds away from agreeing to anything that would lead to more of Jeanie's skin touching her own.

"Okay. How about no strings attached, and the possibility of renegotiating terms at the end?"

"For an insane plan, you make it sound surprisingly reasonable."

"I was doing my best to impersonate you. So, you agree?" Jeanie grinned as Eleanor nodded. She gently tugged at Eleanor's reluctant hand and led her to the middle of the balcony, then took her in her arms and slowly started to spin.

"What are you doing?"

"Teaching you to waltz."

"Jeanie." There was a warning edge to Eleanor's voice. "We only have an hour to get down to the captain's dinner. It's going to take longer than that to teach me to dance."

"Fine, dancing can wait. I wouldn't want to pressure you into something you're not comfortable with." Jeanie's lips puckered as she thought. "I have a much better idea." She walked Eleanor backward until her legs bumped against one of the bistro chairs.

Eleanor's heart raced as she felt a tug at her robe, and she held her breath as it fell open, leaving her fully exposed. "You figure stripping in full view of the entire Wachau Valley will put me at ease?"

"Where's that rebel I've heard so much about? Anyway, like I told you before, no one can see." Jeanie eased the robe off her completely and draped it over the metal chair, then pressed lightly on Eleanor's shoulders until her bare bottom came in contact with the covered seat. "Sit down here."

Eleanor's chest rose and fell rapidly as her breathing changed to nervous gasps.

"Elle, are you okay?" Jeanie's seductively playful smile vanished, instantly replaced with concern. She looked searchingly at Eleanor. "You're not starting to panic are you? I'll stop!"

"No!" Eleanor forced her breath to steady and shook her head vehemently against the idea of stopping. "No, I'm all right. The nerves are just the regular kind." Every inch of her naked body burned with arousal in the cool breeze. Stopping was no longer an option.

"If you're sure." Jeanie hesitated, then tossed a cushion from the other chair to the ground and sank slowly to a kneeling position between Eleanor's bare thighs. Her floral robe gaped open, affording Eleanor a clear view of her bra and panties as she moved. Then Jeanie leaned forward, pressing her silky skin against the length of Eleanor's body, the top of her head reaching just below Eleanor's chin.

Eleanor's pulse raced as Jeanie tickled the hollow of her throat with butterfly kisses. She grasped the sides of the chair with both hands as Jeanie's lips made a path further down, moaning as she felt the weight of her breasts lifted with soft hands, velvet lips suckling one hardened bud as the pad of a thumb traced circles around the other. Her stomach muscles contracted as she felt the gentle nip of teeth on her nipple before those teasing lips continued their downward glide.

She felt a nudge beneath each knee urging her legs upward, and she shifted so that her feet rested on the balcony rail. It reminded her of the first time she'd sat in this space, alone and defiantly determined to stay that way for the duration of the cruise. She stifled a laugh. If she'd been told a week ago that she'd be sitting in this spot, naked and exposed to the world while the sexiest woman she'd ever met traced a line from her navel to the crease of her thigh with her tongue…Eleanor's muscles contracted again, the balls of her feet pressing into the rail. She never would've believed it, until Jeanie Brooks came along.

This was the effect Jeanie had on her. What they were doing on this balcony could tick off the checklist of Eleanor's greatest fears: intimacy, exposure, a real and immediate possibility for public humiliation. There was every reason in the world to have a panic attack on the spot, but she wasn't afraid. Not even a trace of nervousness remained. She was aware of nothing else but the unquenchable desire for this to never end.

Eleanor arched her back and moaned with pleasure as Jeanie's mouth covered the sensitive mound of flesh between her thighs, her tongue parting the folds with practiced perfection. If anyone stood on the river banks with binoculars trained on them right now, Eleanor fervently hoped they enjoyed their view. There was no worry so great that it could make her move a single inch. An entire village could fill the banks of the Danube to watch, and Eleanor wouldn't care. She was too far gone, lost in the exquisiteness of Jeanie's touch, to notice anything else.

As the overwhelming sensations reached a climax like she'd never experienced before, Eleanor cried out and didn't care if the whole ship could hear. She shook from head to toe, feeling more relaxed and satisfied than she could ever remember. It was nearly dark, the golden intensity of the sunset replaced by the faintest pink glow at the edge of the blackened sky. Jeanie rose from the cushion and straddled Eleanor's knees, leaning forward to nestle her head in the crook of Eleanor's neck. Eleanor held her tightly, stroking her fingers up and down the robe that still clung to Jeanie's back.

"We'd better get ready for dinner," Jeanie whispered against her ear.

Eleanor frowned, confused. She'd entirely forgotten about dinner, or the need to arrive early if they wanted to be seated at the captain's table. Lounging naked with Jeanie on her lap, it was possible she'd forgotten how to move. "Now? But, that's really not fair to you." She slid her hands beneath the loose robe and massaged her fingers along Jeanie's hips.

Jeanie sucked in her breath at the touch. "It's okay. I know you don't like being late."

"True." Eleanor explored Jeanie's rounded buttocks, her fingers searching and teasing. "But we don't really have to get there so early."

Jeanie arched her back. Her breasts pressed into Eleanor's chest. A mewling sound escaped her throat as Eleanor shifted her hands. "Elle, I have a confession. This could take longer than you think."

Eleanor looked at her quizzically while her hands continued their explorations beneath the lacy wisp of Jeanie's panties undeterred. "What do you mean?"

"Remember that embarrassing thing I wouldn't tell you the other night? Well, this is it. I almost never manage to…you know."

"Never?" Eleanor's fingers slid with purpose through the wetness between Jeanie's legs, seeking just the right spot.

"Not never, but it takes me forever. If it even happens at—oh, mercy!" Jeanie screamed as her fingers clenched against Eleanor's shoulders.

Eleanor jumped, her hands flying away from Jeanie's body in alarm. "Oh, God. Jeanie, I'm sorry." Her heart raced as she caught sight of Jeanie's widened eyes and pinched face.

"Why are you sorry?" Jeanie panted. Her irises had gone dark as the night sky. "Never mind that! Why did you stop?"

"You screamed." Eleanor frowned. "I was afraid it hurt."

"Just now? Uh, no." Jeanie dissolved into laughter. "Surprised is all. I was just trying to explain my humiliating affliction to you and...I mean, I don't think I've ever had that happen so fast in my life!"

"Oh!" Eleanor's anxiety faded as she realized what Jeanie was trying to say. "You mean, that worked?"

"Uh, yeah. You could say that. What did you do?"

"Well, I just...I read a study that you're forty percent more likely to have an orgasm if you combine pressure on the—" The rest of Eleanor's explanation was muffled as Jeanie covered her mouth with a kiss.

"You know what?" Jeanie kissed her again. "As long as you can do it again, I don't need an explanation." She smiled slyly. "Was there anything else in that study?"

"Possibly." Eleanor failed to hold back a smirk as her arms encircled Jeanie's waist. She desired nothing else but to pick up right where they'd left off. "But what about dinner?"

"Does this fancy place of yours come with room service?"

"There's a personal concierge on call twenty-four hours a day. But I thought sitting at the captain's table was a once-in-a-lifetime opportunity."

The muscles in Jeanie's face twitched as she considered. "So is this." She shifted her body and stood, then led Eleanor by the hand back through the

French doors and into the privacy of the suite. "I'm pretty sure if I have to regret something from this trip, I'd rather it be missing out on the captain's table." Their lips met and lingered, then Jeanie pulled away. "You call room service. I'll be right back."

Eleanor frowned. "Where are you going?"

"Just need to get a...bag. From my room."

"A bag? What, are you planning to move in? Geez, I mean I know we have certain stereotypes to live up to, but—"

"No, I'm not moving in!" Jeanie's cheeks flushed pink. "I'm not getting my suitcase. It's a different bag." She raised her eyebrows meaningfully. "I'm almost positive I mentioned it to you when we first met."

Eleanor swallowed roughly, recalling their very first conversation. "Oh. That bag." The mysterious contents of that bag had spiced up her dreams all week. She felt a thrill of anticipation as Jeanie cinched her floral robe around her and disappeared down the hall. "Hurry back!" she called, and the jingle of Jeanie's laugh echoed back, making her heart skip a beat.

TWENTY

"MORNING, SLEEPY HEAD!" Eleanor's sing-song voice was unexpectedly chipper in the pre-coffee dawn.

Jeanie groaned and stretched her arms and legs, luxuriating in the spaciousness of Eleanor's bed. She felt the mattress dip as Eleanor sat beside her. Cracking one eye to half-staff, she saw that she was already fully dressed, and was waving a stack of white envelopes like a fan in one hand. "What are those?" she mumbled as she yawned.

"Tickets, VIP passes. Whatever Miriam needed to add to use up my credit. Basically, anything you want to see in Vienna, it's in here somewhere."

Jeanie grabbed Eleanor's tunic in her fist and gave it a pull until they were close enough for their lips to meet. "What if all I want to see is you? Preferably without so many clothes." They kissed deeply, tingles running along Jeanie's spine as she felt the covers around her shift as Eleanor's hands ventured underneath the sheets to caress her naked skin. "I didn't expect you to be up and dressed already," she said with a pout.

"It's a good thing for you that I am. We've got a full schedule ahead of us today! You said you were dying to see Vienna."

"You're right. The fact that we're in Vienna and not some less interesting town is the only thing that could coax me out of bed today." Jeanie began to move the covers back.

"Wait! Take this first." Eleanor held out her robe and Jeanie took it from her hand and slid it on under the covers. "Just a precaution. No matter how much we say we want to go touring, if you start parading around the room the way you are now, it'll never happen. So, where do you think we should go first?"

"Can we start with the Kunsthistorisches? That's the biggest of the art museums, and their Italian Renaissance collection is superb. There's a painting by Caravaggio on display there that I wrote a paper on in college. I can't believe I'm finally going to see it in person!"

"Oh, is that where the famous Klimt painting is, too? I love that painting!"

"You mean *The Kiss*? No, that's at the Belvedere." Jeanie hesitated. "It wasn't on my list, but we could go there, too, I guess. If we have the time."

"How can that not be on your list? It's famous! In fact, it's probably the only painting I know."

Jeanie shrugged. "Twentieth century art is a little outside my main interests. Plus, well, honestly...it's hard for me to respect a painting that every college freshman has a poster of in their dorm room."

"That hardly seems…okay, wait. Actually, I did have that one hanging in my dorm."

"Exactly. Everybody does. What can I say? I'm an art snob. Klimt's okay, but I'm much more interested in seeing *David with the Head of Goliath*."

"And would that be a severed head?" Eleanor's mouth puckered in distaste.

Jeanie laughed. "There's a reason people don't hang copies of my favorite art above their sofas. But I'll make you a deal. We can either walk the half hour out of our way to see that one Klimt, or we can come back here tonight and do our own version." Jeanie responded to Eleanor's puzzled expression with a sly grin. "That's where you picture the painting in your head while we make out on the balcony. Clothing optional."

"I think I like that version of *The Kiss* much better than the one I had in my dorm room."

"I thought you might say that. Hey, what time is it? I should take a shower if we have a few minutes. Someone distracted me from it last night."

Eleanor grinned wickedly as she fished her phone

out of her pocket to check, her smile dissolving into a frown as she looked at the screen. "Damn it."

"What's wrong?"

"There's an urgent email from my boss." Eleanor stifled a frustrated scream. "Seems that our Vienna client is having some sort of crisis and needs to set up a meeting right away. And since I'm here..."

Jeanie's shoulders slumped. "He wants you to do it?"

"I'm so sorry." Eleanor looked crestfallen.

Jeanie wrapped her arms around Eleanor's shoulders and gave her a squeeze. "It's okay. You go to your meeting, I'll spend the day at the museum. It'll take forever for me to see everything on my list, anyway. You'd probably get bored."

"Oh, that reminds me! I found an app where you can enter all the exhibits you want to see and it'll plot the most efficient route for you through the museum."

Jeanie chuckled and squeezed her tighter. "Of course you did."

"Oh, better yet, I think one of these envelopes has a voucher for a private tour. Just take the stack. You really don't mind me going?" Eleanor smiled as Jeanie shook her head. "Thanks, Jeanie. Hopefully it won't take too long. I'll text you when I'm done and we can meet up at Café Sperl for coffee and *sachertorte*."

JEANIE SAT on a gray plush sofa in the middle of the Italian Renaissance gallery, staring with awe at the painting she'd waited over a decade to see, which hung on the wall just a few yards away. She massaged her right calf as she sat. The muscle twitched and pulled beneath her fingers, the side effect of three hours spent walking through the halls of the Kunsthistorisches on a VIP tour with the museum's Assistant Director. The whole experience felt like a dream.

When she'd arrived at the museum, Jeanie had been hesitant to make use of the pass Eleanor had given her. It hadn't seemed right, taking advantage of a privilege that didn't belong to her. But the spectacularly ornate galleries of the museum had soon become overwhelming, and Jeanie realized the best way to see everything she wanted would be with a guide to help. She'd expected some young docent, an art history student on a summer internship like she herself had done, so when a woman in her fifties had shown up instead and introduced herself as Dr. Birnbaum, second-in-command of the entire museum collection, Jeanie had been both thrilled and humbled.

At first, Dr. Birnbaum came across as business-like and a little bored, and Jeanie felt a stab of guilt for taking her away from what had to be more important work than showing a tourist around. The woman had started by taking her to see some of the more famous pieces in their collection, including a stop at a special telescope so that Jeanie could view the museum's celebrated Gustav Klimt wall paintings in all their painstaking detail. And they were stunning, no matter her opinion of other pieces of his work. But as they approached the entrance to an entire Klimt gallery in the twentieth century wing, Jeanie had grown increasingly antsy.

"I don't suppose we'll be making it to the Renaissance wing anytime soon?" Jeanie had asked, and her tour guide had looked at her in surprise.

"You're interested in those? Most Americans seem to prefer the...*prettier* paintings, and some of the pieces in our Renaissance collection can be a little gruesome."

At that, Jeanie had pulled up the museum app on her phone and showed her the wish-list of paintings she'd put together. Dr. Birnbaum had broken into a broad grin as she perused the list.

"These are some of my favorites, as well! I never get to see them as much as I'd like. Showing them to you will be a treat."

Soon, they were deep in discussion about their favorite artists and paintings. Jeanie had felt overwhelmed by Dr. Birnbaum's knowledge, but her guide had been impressed by her, as well, so much so that after they'd seen all of the paintings on Jeanie's list, the assistant director suggested a surprise stop. The museum had just acquired a new Caravaggio painting that was not yet on display. Dr. Birnbaum took Jeanie into a private room where the painting awaited restoration, and explained the process to her in detail while allowing Jeanie to examine the work to her heart's content. As she examined the brush strokes with a magnifying glass, the experience had overwhelmed her to the point of tears.

Sitting on the sofa and viewing her favorite work of art from so close she could nearly smell the paint, Jeanie once again felt tears welling up, but this time they were from sadness instead of joy. In the years since she'd given up on graduate school and returned home to teach, she'd rarely had much of a chance to reflect on what she'd left behind. But now, surrounded by the masterpieces she loved, a sense of loss weighed heavily on her. She'd be back home soon, back to teaching American history in front of a class of bored high school students, where conversations with colleagues rarely strayed into deeper territory than complaints about the freshness of the lettuce at the cafeteria's salad bar.

Spending the day with an art expert and getting a glimpse into her world had been a dream come true. In fact, Jeanie could never thank Eleanor enough for giving her the opportunity. But it had also been a reminder of all the dreams she'd given up on. The longer she sat, the more her regret weighed on her, until finally Jeanie stood to go. She needed some fresh air.

Outside, the afternoon was sunny and warm. She made her way across Maria-Theresien-Platz, the large public square that separated the art museum from its twin building that housed the natural history museum. As she went, Jeanie passed people from every walk of Viennese life. There were mothers pushing babies in strollers, tourists with cameras, and workers on their lunch breaks eating picnic-style in the grass. Next to the towering statue of the Empress Maria Theresa in the center of the square, Jeanie spotted a familiar figure resting on the stone steps.

"Dr. Birnbaum?" Jeanie waved as the woman looked up from the thick three-ring binder that was balanced on her thighs.

"Oh, Miss Brooks! How nice to see you again. Are you finished in the museum?"

"Yes. I thought I'd take a walk. I have another hour before I need to be at Café Sperl to meet my friend." *Friend?* Jeanie paused, realizing she wasn't certain how best to describe her relationship with Eleanor at this point. Would *girlfriend* be presumptuous? It felt so right, but hadn't they agreed that this was no strings attached? Jeanie fought back a sigh. "Thank you again for the tour."

"But of course! It really was my pleasure. I hardly ever get over to that part of the museum these days, and it was a nice break from all this." She gestured at the paperwork in her lap.

"Rough day at work?" Jeanie smiled with her usual friendliness as she propped herself against the step.

Dr. Birnbaum nodded, giving an exasperated sigh.

"To think when I started this job, I thought all I would do is look at paintings all day. Instead it's nothing but requisition forms and reports to the board, and a lot of headaches."

"I envy you, though. What an amazing place to work!"

"You're right. Most of the time it is. Today, though..." The woman shook her head. "There's a new education program starting in September and the person I had lined up to run it just fell through. It's so late in the process that most of the other top candidates have already accepted other positions, and none of the recent applications I have here will do."

"Oh, no. I'm sorry to hear that." Jeanie gave her a sympathetic look.

"There are so many restrictions. I honestly don't know where I'm expected to find someone with a background in art history and knowledge of curriculum planning, who's fluent in English. And if that's not enough, because of the way the grant was funded, they have to be a citizen of a country outside the EU. It's like searching for a needle in a haystack."

"I'm sorry, did I hear you correctly?" Jeanie's heart rate increased as she ran over the list in your head. "It sounds like you're looking for an American teacher with an art history degree who wouldn't mind relocating to Vienna."

Dr. Birnbaum nodded. "Yes, that would work nicely. Do you know someone?" she added jokingly.

"Actually, I do. Me!" Jeanie laughed at the woman's surprised expression. "There's really a job opening for this September?"

"Yes, there really is!" She rummaged in her bag and pulled out a card. "Here's my contact information. If you truly think you'd be interested, send me an email tonight and I'll make sure you get the information on how to apply. I can tell just from our conversation on the tour that you know everything you'd need to about art. If the rest of your resumé is as strong, you'd be the best candidate I've come across, by far. What a stroke of good luck!"

As Jeanie raced from the plaza toward the café, she could hardly wait to tell Eleanor the amazing news, though it didn't occur to her to question how Eleanor might react.

JEANIE PAUSED in front of the stone facade of Café Sperl and her heart skipped a beat as she spotted Eleanor through the window. She'd been desperate to tell her all about her conversation with Dr. Birnbaum, but only now did she feel a little nervousness about what her response would be. *Will she think I'm too impulsive?* Given Eleanor's aversion to risk, that was a safe bet, though Jeanie thought she could convince her. More worrying was what a job offer half way around the world would mean for this new relationship between them that they had yet to define. Jeanie tamped down her concern as best she could. Like riding her bicycle back up the hill, it was an inevitable complication that she could deal with when the time came.

She walked past tables filled with locals and tourists alike, seated in solid wooden chairs covered in the same deep red upholstery they'd worn for over a century. The room buzzed with activity, a popular destination for a classic Viennese lunch. She slid into the seat across from Eleanor and leaned over to kiss her cheek, careful to avoid spilling the steaming coffee that already awaited her at the table. "I hope you haven't been waiting long."

"No, I just got here a few minutes ago." The nervous edge to Eleanor's manner that had softened during her time away from work was more visible this afternoon. "I ordered coffee for both of us already. Have you eaten?"

Jeanie shook her head. "No, and I'm starved."

"I hear the schnitzel's good, but I can't decide between apple strudel or *sachertorte* for dessert."

"Why decide? We'll order one of each and share!" Jeanie was pleased to see Eleanor's face and shoulders began to relax as they chatted about the menu choices. "How was your meeting?" she asked once it seemed like Eleanor was relaxed enough to discuss it. She was dying to share her news, but wanted to be sure Eleanor was completely at ease first.

"Oh, you know. It was a typical meeting. The clients ranted and complained for a few hours, and at the end they offered me a job." She said it nonchalantly, as if job offers in exotic locales happened every day.

The wheels in Jeanie's head began spinning at this unexpected turn of events. *A job offer in Vienna?* Jeanie could barely contain her grin. *This could solve everything!* No matter what they'd agreed the night before, Jeanie knew that when they returned to New York, there was no way she wouldn't want to continue seeing Eleanor. Choosing between a possible life with Eleanor back home or a dream job in Vienna seemed like an impossible task. But what if she didn't have to choose after all?

Eleanor's face held an expectant expression and Jeanie emerged from her musings with a frown, realizing that she'd missed what was said. "Sorry, what was that again?" She pushed all thoughts of jobs and relationships aside and trained her focus on Eleanor's words.

"I said that I had the plan all figured out for the next two days here. Of course there's a walking tour of the city that's not to be missed."

Jeanie groaned. "Another walking tour?"

"I promise this one's good, and I'll even let you hold onto the book. If something looks terrible, just skip over it. As long as I don't know about it, it shouldn't bother me too much."

"That wouldn't be cheating? And you'd really trust me to be in control?" Jeanie's heart fluttered at the thought.

"I really would." Eleanor smiled bashfully, all trace of her uptight work persona disappeared. "And no, it's not cheating to look for ways to keep your sanity intact."

"In that case, taking a stab at another walking tour sounds acceptable."

"Just so long as you don't try to take a stab at me! Once we finish that, we can relax a little and take a carriage ride—"

"Oh, I've always wanted to do that!" Jeanie squealed.

"There's a concert with the Vienna Boys' Choir tomorrow night that I have passes for—"

"Careful, I could get used to traveling like this." It was only when the words were out of her mouth that Jeanie remembered Sylvia, who *had* gotten much too used to traveling like this. She tensed, but relaxed again when her faux pas went unnoticed.

"Oh, and the butterfly house!" Eleanor's eyes lit up in excitement.

"The what?"

"It's a fancy glass house in the middle of town, like a greenhouse where they used to grow palms in the winter. Now it's filled with butterflies, and you can go inside and they fly all around you. They even land on you!" A self-consciousness skirted across Eleanor's radiant face. "I mean, it's not an art museum or anything...I thought it sounded interesting, but maybe it's not something—"

"Elle, it's perfect! I can't imagine a more beautiful way to spend part of the day." *Or anyone I'd rather spend it with.* The honesty of the thought caught her off guard. Her heart soared as she listened to Eleanor outlining all the plans she'd made for them to spend their time together. Jeanie thought again of her possible job offer, and all the implications. So much change and risk. So much potential for loss. She looked at Eleanor, whom she'd never seen look so excited before, and knew she couldn't share the news with her yet. There were still too many unknowns to worry Eleanor with any of it now. She set the news aside for another day. For now she would eat schnitzel and *sachertorte,* and hold Eleanor's hand as they explored all that Vienna had to offer. Difficult decisions could wait.

TWENTY-ONE

"WE'LL ARRIVE in Nuremberg in an hour." Jeanie placed a cup of coffee in front of Eleanor on the bistro table, where she sat in her usual spot to enjoy the early morning sun. "What are you thinking about?"

"Vienna." She said the word in a dreamy sigh as she picked up her coffee. It had become a habit over during the last few days to sit on the balcony each morning to sip their first cup of coffee. The new ritual produced a peaceful feeling inside her that was unlike anything else she could remember. "All the times I'd been there before, and I had no idea what a beautiful city it was." *Because of you*, she thought, but kept the words unsaid, uncertain how Jeanie would take them. They'd agreed to keeping their relationship strictly no strings attached while on the trip, and she wasn't about to break the rules. But in just four days the cruise would end, and then they could renegotiate. *If we want to.*

She felt ice in her belly at the uncertainty of it, but surely they were both agreed on what they ultimately would choose. *Right?* Eleanor knew that things would be different when they returned home, away from the artificial paradise of vacation. It would be harder. But it seemed impossible not to give it a try. As much as she'd fought with Miriam about the pros of remaining single, Eleanor couldn't imagine not continuing to see Jeanie when they returned home.

Their lifestyles were different, but that was something they could overcome. Eleanor just needed to remember that Jeanie was on a different budget than her. Unlike previous girlfriends who had used her for her money, Jeanie was very uncomfortable letting her pay. It was good, in a way. Eleanor preferred simpler things. And Jeanie understood her. Most of her past girlfriends had been driven crazy by Eleanor's odd behaviors, but even the worst of her panic attacks didn't seem to phase Jeanie. She took it all in stride. Plus, since Jeanie had entered her life, she'd felt more like her old, healthy self than she had in years. It was a feeling worth holding onto as long as she could, if only she knew whether Jeanie felt the same way, too.

But she must! Eleanor pondered what continuing to see each other at home might look like. The distance between them, while not a deal breaker, added a layer of complication. Would she meet Jeanie at Penn

Station on Friday after work for date nights? Or make weekend trips to Poughkeepsie? She shuddered at that prospect, city girl that she was, but she'd be willing to do it if it meant more time together. After all, if Jeanie lived there, how bad could it be? But maybe she would consider giving city living another try? *I'm getting way ahead of myself here…*

She glanced at Jeanie, who was watching the changing scenery along the river bank with a blissful look on her face. Though Jeanie was naturally chatty, the fact that they could so easily sit in companionable silence for long stretches meant the world to the more reserved Eleanor, who sometimes needed to be alone with her thoughts. She reached out and tucked a long golden lock behind Jeanie's ear. "What are you thinking about?"

"The Ferris wheel last night. I'm trying to figure out how you did it."

"Did what?"

"Timed it so perfectly!"

"I swear, I didn't." Eleanor chuckled, knowing exactly the moment to which Jeanie referred.

"I don't believe you."

It'd been their last night, with more sights left to see than time remaining in Vienna. Though its voucher sat among the other envelopes, they'd nearly skipped over the Riesenrad Ferris Wheel, picturing a child's carnival ride. But they'd wandered past it in the late afternoon and discovered that it was something altogether different from what they'd imagined. The giant Ferris wheel was of the elegant nineteenth century variety, equipped with enclosed cabins large enough to hold several people at a time.

And rather than a single trip around in a crowded public cabin, they'd discovered that Eleanor's voucher entitled them to a half-hour ride in their own private space, complete with a bottle of champagne. That alone was more romance than Eleanor was generally capable of planning with plenty of advance notice, let alone anything she could come up with on the fly. So the fact that their cabin reached the top of the wheel at the precise moment the sun slipped below the horizon, just as their bodies seemed drawn together by an unstoppable force...That exact moment when they kissed at the top of the Ferris wheel at sunset was the first time in her life that Eleanor had seriously considered the possibility that magic might exist after all.

"Really," she repeated her denial under Jeanie's suspicious gaze. "I swear. I'm a planner, but even I'm not that good."

Jeanie shrugged, still looking dubious over the denial but willing to let it go for the moment. "I can hardly wait to see what you have planned for us in Nuremberg to top that."

Eleanor groaned at the mention of their next destination. "How about we skip Nuremberg and find something to do on the boat." She traced a finger suggestively along Jeanie's shoulder, toying with the strap of her bra. "I can think of a few ideas."

"Elle," she scolded, and moved as if to swat Eleanor's hand away. Instead their hands clasped and became entwined.

"What?"

"Tempting as that sounds, this is our final stop before we leave the ship and take the coach to Prague for our last two nights. I was just kidding about topping Vienna. I didn't mean to put any pressure on you! Besides, Nuremberg might not be a major city, but it would be a shame to skip the sights. Oh, like Albrecht Dürer's house—"

Eleanor's eyes crinkled. "Who?"

"The famous German Renaissance artist." Jeanie shook her head as if it were obvious.

"I'll just have to take your word for that," Eleanor teased.

"Fine. Maybe he's a little obscure. But there's St. Lawrence's Church, and St. Sebaldus' Church, and the Church of our Lady—"

"And the Nazi rally grounds, and don't forget the Palace of Justice where the war crimes trials took place."

"Oh." Jeanie's face fell.

"I'm sorry Jeanie. I know for most people this is just a little city in Bavaria with Gothic churches and Christmas markets, but as a Jew, the history here is less charming."

Jeanie squeezed Eleanor's fingers where they rested against her shoulder. "And as a history teacher, I probably should have thought of that without you having to point it out. I'm sorry."

"No need to be. Not everyone feels that way about it. My sister Miriam would find it completely fascinating. In fact, she'll probably kill me for not taking pictures of it all for her. But I just wanted to explain my lack of enthusiasm for this particular destination. If there are things you want to see without me, it's fine. In fact, I'll give you my camera and *you* can get the shots for Miriam."

Jeanie sat silently for a moment, then straightened up with a grin. "Buy your sister some postcards, because I have a better idea. Hold on a minute." She went inside and emerged a minute later with her tablet in hand. "Have you ever heard of urban exploration?"

Eleanor frowned at the unfamiliar term. "I don't think so."

"Basically, people go and look for abandoned places, like hotels and hospitals, or amusement parks, or mansions—and then go inside to explore and take photographs."

"So...trespassing?"

"No! Er...not always. Maybe. Technically." Jeanie handed Eleanor the tablet. "But it's really about finding and documenting places that have been forgotten."

"Why would anyone want to wander around ramshackle old buildings?"

"Because they're amazing! It's like claiming your own piece of the past. How could that *not* be appealing? Here, look for yourself."

Eleanor squinted at the image on the screen, and saw what appeared to be a manor house or castle, with two stone pillars leading to an overgrown garden. "Okay?"

"Isn't it awesome? That's an abandoned castle right here in Germany. It used to be a private residence, then a hotel for a while, but it's been empty for years. If you flip through the pictures, you'll see it still has furniture inside and everything!"

"Fine, I'll give. You're right. This is pretty amazing." Despite her usual risk aversion, Eleanor's interest was piqued as she looked through the hauntingly beautiful pictures. She could almost feel herself walking down the cobweb-encrusted halls, and it was deliciously thrilling. "This is nearby?"

"Probably…"

Eleanor frowned at Jeanie's vague reply. "What do you mean by that? Do you or don't you know how to get there?"

"Well, it's definitely in Germany…"

"Germany's a fairly large country, Jeanie."

Jeanie shot her a look. "I *know* that. It's just that the serious urban explorers are notoriously secretive, and the one who runs this website is no exception.

They never tell you exactly where the places are because they don't want a bunch of people going in and destroying them."

Eleanor nodded. "I guess that makes sense."

"But this particular guy likes puzzles even more than he likes secrets. He hides clues in different places around his website, and if you figure it all out correctly, you end up with GPS coordinates that will get you within a mile or two of where you need to be."

"And you've figured out all the clues?" Eleanor asked, impressed.

"No, I'm terrible at these things, but I have really good luck—"

"Yeah, I've noticed that." Eleanor chuckled.

"Well in this case, even though you're not supposed to tell anyone if you figure out the clues, someone let it slip in the online comment section that castle is near Nuremberg. And I just happened to get lucky and see it before they deleted the post. Unfortunately, I'm still missing the actual coordinates, but…"

Eleanor's pulse ticked up as her enthusiasm grew. "I'm very good at puzzles…"

Jeanie grinned mischievously. "I was hoping you'd say that!"

They went inside and Eleanor grabbed a notepad from next to the phone and tucked a pencil behind her ear, then returned her attention to the page on Jeanie's tablet, her thoughts already deep into the first set of clues. Jeanie settled in beside her on the sofa and watched silently as she worked, smiling encouragement. Though it was far from anything she'd expected to do that morning, as Eleanor solved the puzzles one by one, she couldn't help but think how she and Jeanie made the perfect team.

TWENTY-TWO

ELEANOR STUDIED the final photograph on the web page, then let out a victory whoop. "That's it!" Pride bubbled up inside as she pointed to the spot on the screen where the final clue had been hidden. "There's a repeating pattern here. Do you see it?" She enlarged the picture as Jeanie squinted in confusion. "I'm sure it's there. I can check it again, though."

"No, I trust you. We really have all the coordinates now?"

"Yes, and I just entered them into a mapping program and it looks like it's about an hour's drive from here. So that sounds right, don't you think?"

"It's gotta be!" Jeanie bounced excitedly on the edge of the sofa. "The concierge called a few minutes ago to say that our rental car is ready, and he was able to find most of the supplies that the website recommended. Flashlights, water bottles, a blanket, some rope—"

Eleanor felt her cheeks tingle. "You know, I was fine with asking for all of it, right up to the rope. Then it just started to sound kinky. You should have seen the look he gave me. Then he muttered something about the interesting sounds coming from this room at night. I think the walls are thinner than they look."

"Oops." Jeanie snickered into her hand. "That was probably my fault."

"Hmm, you think?" Eleanor winked, enjoying the sudden rush of color her teasing brought to Jeanie's cheeks. "I just hope we don't need anything else before the end of the trip because I'm not sure I can look him in the eye again." Eleanor handed the tablet back to Jeanie and picked up her satchel, glancing around one last time. "Okay, I think we're ready!"

Jeanie squealed, clapping her hands. "We're really doing this!"

"We really are!" Eleanor's voice betrayed the same surprise that she felt inside. "I can't believe I'm going along with this crazy idea of yours."

"You're okay with it, though? No anxiety or anything? Because we don't have to go."

As she reflected on the question, the genuine concern on Jeanie's face enveloped Eleanor like a warm embrace. The truth was, she felt great, every bit as thrilled with their upcoming adventure as Jeanie was, and without even a hint of the anxiousness that usually was buzzing just below the surface even on her best days. On impulse, she drew Jeanie close and kissed her lips. "Honestly? I feel like I'm fifteen again, getting ready to sneak out of the house to go clubbing after curfew."

"That's good?" Jeanie remained hesitant.

"Jeanie, you have no idea. I didn't think I'd ever feel like that again. I doubt that I would've, if I hadn't met you." As she spoke, Eleanor grabbed up her shoes and shoved them onto her feet without so much as a thought given to what she was doing or how.

The rental car was waiting at the top of the gangway as they disembarked, a late model Mercedes that struck Eleanor as a bit more extravagant than was necessary, though she reminded herself that in Germany it might be seen as less of a luxury car than in the States. She didn't want to make Jeanie uncomfortable with the money she'd spent, though the other woman seemed too consumed by her excitement to pay much attention to what they were driving. The supplies they'd requested were already packed for them in the trunk. As soon as Eleanor plugged the coordinates into the GPS on the dashboard and settled herself into the driver's seat, they were on their way.

The city streets of Nuremberg gave way to narrow roads that wound through thick forest. Every so often they came upon a village seemingly ripped from the pages of the Brothers Grimm, where narrow cobblestone streets were lined with timber-framed buildings and street lamps of wrought iron. Then back they'd go into the forest, driving across babbling streams via stone bridges that almost certainly housed trolls underneath. Everything they passed felt like it belonged in a fairytale.

After about an hour, a voice from the GPS alerted them that they would soon be approaching their destination on the right. Eleanor slowed the car, then pulled over into a narrow space off the side of the road. She opened the door cautiously and looked around. There was no house in sight, and no clue that they were even close. "Jeanie, does this look right?"

Jeanie joined her outside the car and shrugged. "I guess so."

"What do you mean, you guess so?" Eleanor frowned. "Is this usually how it is?"

Jeanie pursed her lips as she considered. "I'm not sure. I've never actually made it this far."

Eleanor's eyebrows shot up in alarm. "You mean, you've never done this before?" She felt her muscles tense, preparing for the familiar weight of anxiety to descend, but to her amazement, it never came. Despite being in the middle of nowhere in a foreign country with no idea where she was going, Eleanor remained remarkably calm and clearheaded. "Okay. So let's figure out what to do next."

Slowly, Eleanor turned in a circle where she stood, scanning the surrounding area. Through the brush, she spotted what appeared to be a stone pillar. "Jeanie, look at that."

"It's like the one in the picture!" Jeanie walked closer and pushed aside the overgrown vegetation. "And here's a second one. I think this is it," she said, motioning for Eleanor to come closer.

Eleanor's heart raced with excitement as she surveyed the gravel path beyond the two pillars, which appeared to have marked the entrance to a carriageway at some time in the distant past. It was heavily covered in weeds and low hanging branches, but still appeared passable, and Eleanor had little doubt that the abandoned castle lay at the other end. "Let's grab the supplies before we go."

When they'd made it several yards up the path, Jeanie took her by the hand. "I dreamed of doing this, you know. But I never would've made it this far on my own. Too many details!"

"Whereas I can manage details just fine." Eleanor squeezed Jeanie's hand as they continued to walk. "It's coming up with the idea in the first place that I can't do. Even if I had been aware of this type of thing, it would never have occurred to me to do it. We're the perfect team." At the sound of her earlier thoughts spoken out loud, her usual nervousness, strikingly absent on their adventure so far, returned with a flutter. Had she risked too much by revealing feelings that might not be returned? But as Jeanie snuggled close to her, Eleanor's body relaxed.

"We really are. I like that you can take charge and turn my crazy ideas into reality."

They continued contentedly along the path, and it wasn't until their destination came into sight that Eleanor's nerves began to fail her. The old mansion was a sprawling stone castle with a massive peaked roof line dotted with towers and turrets. Far from being derelict, it appeared to be in pristine condition. Seemingly hundreds of windows gleamed in the mid-afternoon sun, and the way the light reflected from the heavy lead glass made it appear like lights were on inside. "You're sure this place is abandoned?" As she said it, Eleanor's flesh began to crawl and she could have sworn someone was watching them.

"Positive. You saw the pictures yourself. Those were only posted a month ago." Jeanie's words soothed her nerves somewhat, as the building from the photos was clearly uninhabitable.

Ahead of them were the two pillars they'd seen in the photographs, marking the entrance to a lush green lawn and formal garden. A chill ran along Eleanor's spine. "If that's the case, who mowed the grass?" The garden beds were overgrown, but the lawn, which had been little more than a jungle of weeds in the photos, was cropped to within an inch or two of the ground.

"Just because it's abandoned doesn't mean it's completely forgotten," Jeanie reasoned. "Maybe there's a caretaker who mows once or twice a year."

Eleanor was stunned at Jeanie's nonchalance. "Or

maybe the owner's come back and is calling the police as we speak. I feel like someone else is here."

Jeanie laughed. "What on earth would they call the police on us for, walking on the grass?"

"Jeanie, I'm serious. What if someone's here?" Just then, a rustling noise from nearby bushes made her jump several inches off the ground and set her heart racing. "What was that?" She flinched at the panic in her voice. *Calm down.* She repeated the order to herself silently half a dozen times. Jeanie was right, they'd done nothing illegal. She'd come this far, and there was no way she was going to give into her panic now without a fight.

The bushes shook again, and this time the sound was accompanied by the emergence of a white whiskered chin, followed shortly thereafter by the rest of a very plump goat. As a second goat followed, Eleanor broke out in a fit of laughter. "They just about scared me to death. Naughty goats!"

"Actually, Elle, I think they were being naughty. Just look at the satisfied expressions on their faces. Clearly they were getting up to something in there."

"Jeanie, they're goats."

"So? Where do you think baby goats come from?" Jeanie's eyes twinkled with mischief. She set down the bag of supplies she'd been carrying and popped open the top button of her top. "Tell you what, come over here and I'll explain all about it."

Jeanie's low, sultry voice sent a shock of desire

through Eleanor's body. "What, out here?" She swallowed hard and furtively looked around, still not convinced they were alone. "Maybe we should check inside, just to make sure no one else is here first."

The promise of exploring the castle proved a powerful enough distraction that Jeanie was instantly persuaded. She picked up the bag and slung it over her shoulder again, walking toward the grand front entrance without further argument. She left her button undone, and Eleanor wasn't about to complain about that.

"Do you think we can just go in the front door?" Eleanor eyed the solid slab of wood that hung on massive iron hinges.

"We can try." Jeanie turned the knob and gave the door a shove with her shoulder, but it didn't budge. "There's gotta be another way."

Eleanor's pulse quickened. "We won't have to break in, will we?"

"Absolutely not!" Jeanie shook her head vehemently. "The first rule for urban explorers is you don't break in. You look for an unlocked door or an open window. We know someone got in recently, so we'll just keep looking. Speaking of pictures, though…" Jeanie reached into one of the roomy pockets of her pants and pulled out her phone.

Eleanor watched in amusement, pausing for the first time since they'd left the ship to fully appreciate Jeanie's outfit. She wore khaki cargo pants and some sort of fishing vest over her partially buttoned white shirt, with a dark brown hat on her head that made her look for all the world like a female Indiana Jones. *Only Jeanie would have just the right costume for exploring an abandoned castle.* Affection surged through her, and she grinned. The broad smile was still plastered on her face as Jeanie looped an arm around her waist and snapped a picture of the two of them.

"Oh, that's a good one!" Jeanie grinned as she looked at the screen.

"It's not half bad. Miriam would love a copy to post on her wall."

"I'll text it to you and you can send it to her."

Eleanor checked her own phone. "No good. I don't have any bars. You can send it later."

Jeanie tapped on her screen. "Never mind that. I'll just share it with her directly. Is this her?" She turned the phone and Eleanor nodded when she saw that Jeanie had located the correct profile for Miriam on her favorite social media hangout. "Okay, done!"

"She'll love that." Eleanor squinted as the sun glinted off a single window on the first floor that appeared out of alignment with the rest. "Jeanie, look there! I think we found the way in."

Climbing through the open window wasn't nearly as difficult as Eleanor had feared, and in no time both women stood in a hall of weathered gray stone, with matching staircases spiraling upward in graceful arcs on either side. The landing above was brightly painted in red and gold, the walls covered in a bold plaid wallpaper to match which, though peeling in places, managed to retain most of its former elegance. Eleanor's breath caught in her chest as she took it all in, and it felt to her like time was standing still.

"Race you to the top!" Jeanie took off with a laugh toward the staircase closest to her, and after a moment of hesitation, Eleanor raced up the one on the other side, taking them two steps at a time. They arrived breathless at the top at almost exactly the same moment. "I won!" Jeanie declared.

"Oh no, you didn't!" Eleanor's competitive spirit flickered and grew to a full flame. "It was a tie, at the very least."

"You want to go again?"

"No, I don't think so," Eleanor replied between panting breaths. One time up those stairs at full speed was really more than sufficient.

"Fine. Then how about hide and seek?"

"What, are we twelve?" Eleanor teased, but the playful spark behind Jeanie's eyes was already sending heat throughout her body and making her heart pound harder than any race.

"Here's a flashlight. Close your eyes and count to a hundred." Jeanie's footsteps echoed through the empty halls as Eleanor shut her eyes and began to count.

When she reached one hundred, she was alone in the silence. She felt exhilaration, but no fear. Exhilaration, and an intense desire to win. She knew Jeanie wouldn't make it easy for her, either, and she was glad. When it came to competition, they were exactly alike. Eleanor wouldn't have wanted it any other way.

There were hallways leading off in both directions, and Eleanor chose one at random. She didn't find Jeanie, but she did manage to get a comprehensive tour of the old house, turning up room after delightful room of richly carved woodwork and solid oak paneling that hinted at the manor's former glory. As she explored the rooms, she couldn't help but chuckle over what she was doing, playing a spontaneous game of hide and seek in an empty mansion. She'd started the day moping about a place she didn't want to see, and somehow Jeanie had transformed it into something she'd never forget. She couldn't remember the last time she'd played, and relaxed, and enjoyed the moment. That's just what it was like when Jeanie was around.

Eleanor returned to the top of the staircase where they'd begun and struck out down the opposite hall. This time she didn't have to look for long. The second room she entered was the winner, a large space that may have once been a music room judging by the grand piano that still stood in its center. It had been a fine instrument in its day, with keys of real ivory, but Eleanor didn't pay it much attention. She was too focused on the gorgeous woman who leaned against it, looking entirely too self-satisfied for someone who'd just lost at hide and seek. Though Eleanor had to admit that she had every reason to look pleased with herself, considering how industrious she'd been in Eleanor's absence.

The blanket from their supply bag was spread out invitingly on the floor, flanked by three flickering candles that Eleanor couldn't remember requesting from the concierge, but must have been left behind by a previous expedition. The food they'd brought for lunch was arranged on paper plates, but one look at Jeanie and it was clear to Eleanor that food was the furthest thing from her mind.

Her eyes connected with Eleanor's as soon as she entered the room. They were dark with passion and sparkling with mischief, and the combination sent a shock wave of desire rippling through Eleanor from the top of her head to the tips of her toes. She'd found time for a costume change, and now wore nothing but the white shirt that brushed the tops of her thighs. More of the buttons had come open, enough to reveal that if she'd been wearing a bra earlier in the day, it was gone now. The view beyond that was obscured, but discovering whether her panties had met a similar fate was a mystery Eleanor was eager to solve.

"You found me." Jeanie nibbled her lower lips coyly as Eleanor approached. "I guess that means I lost."

"Is that so? Because it looks to me like you were looking forward to getting caught." Eleanor wrapped her arms low around Jeanie's hips, her hands resting at the hem of the white shirt. She worked her hands beneath the fabric and grinned as her fingers touched bare skin. *Mystery solved!*

"Maybe." Laughing, Jeanie threaded her fingers through Eleanor's hair and pulled her closer until their lips met, their tongues tasting and exploring one another greedily. Breaking from the kiss, Jeanie traced a line from Eleanor's mouth and along her jawline until her lips rested against her ear. "You're way over-dressed," she whispered, the warmth of her breath sending tingles down Eleanor's spine. With one swift motion, Jeanie grasped the hem of Eleanor's shirt and whisked it over her head. Her pants quickly followed, joining the rest of their clothing in a discarded heap somewhere in the recesses of the shadowy room.

"Lunch?" Eleanor gestured toward the blanket, guiding Jeanie toward it and encouraging her to sit.

"Now? If you hadn't noticed, we're both nearly naked in the middle of a house that isn't ours. What if someone finds us?" Jeanie's sudden bashfulness made Eleanor burst out laughing.

"There's nobody else here! Unless goats can climb through windows, we've got the place to ourselves. We can take as long as we want." Her body trembled in anticipation. "So we should probably eat first, to keep up our strength."

Jeanie gaped at her. "I can't believe you're the one trying to convince *me*. I thought I'd talk you into a quickie, at best, and you'd be terrified of getting caught the whole time!"

"That does sound more like me, doesn't it?" Eleanor took half a sandwich from the paper plate and handed it to Jeanie. "I don't know what to tell you except that in the past few days you've persuaded me to think approach risk-taking from a different angle. I'm beginning to see the appeal."

"I'm astounded! And starving." Jeanie took a bite of her sandwich. "Aren't you going to eat?"

"Maybe later. I have other plans right now." She knelt on the blanket and settled in, grasping one of Jeanie's feet in her hands. With one hand she gently massaged Jeanie's arches, while the other hand stroked lazily along her ankle. "You have the most gorgeous legs I've ever seen."

Jeanie giggled, covering her mouth with one hand as her cheeks flushing pink. Their eyes connected and her expression grew serious. "Between your take-charge attitude and this new, adventurous side of you, I'm honestly not sure which one turns me on more." Her hand dropped from her face to the collar of her shirt, her fingers trailing down along its front edge until they reached the last few buttons, popping each one deliberately until the shirt fell open completely.

Eleanor drank in the delicious sight as her fingers trembled along their slow, circular path across Jeanie's leg. Everything about this moment was almost too much to believe, from her own new sense of daring to the shared connection that vibrated between them. Eleanor bent her head and pressed her lips to Jeanie's ankle bone, using every ounce of patience she possessed to maintain a measured pace. As she flicked her tongue along the smooth, salty flesh of Jeanie's calf, she averted her eyes from the temptation of her goal, so recently revealed, so close. But they had the rest of the day ahead of them, and two more days in Prague after that. Regardless of how uncertain their future, Eleanor refused to be afraid to savor every moment.

TWENTY-THREE

"ELLE? I have a problem. Can you come down here when you get this message? Room twelve." Jeanie set her phone down beside her on the narrow cot, her eyes darting from the mountain of clothing on the floor to the mangled bag that had been delivered to her door. It was completely destroyed, and she had no idea how she was going to get her things off the ship, let alone home. *Why did I pack so much stuff?*

"Jeanie?" Eleanor's head poked through the doorway. Her eyes widened at the chaotic state of the room, but whatever her opinion, Jeanie admired that Ellie managed to hold it back. "What happened to that?" she asked instead, pointing to the suitcase's shredded remains.

"There was an accident. They were holding it for me, only it was too big for the usual luggage storage area. They put it in a machine room instead, and one of the machines tried to eat it."

"They *will* find you a replacement, right?" Indignation crept into her tone.

"They're trying, Elle. But they have a lot of other, more important things to—"

"Excuse me!" Eleanor's authoritative voice echoed in the small room as someone passed by Jeanie's door. "Thomas, wasn't it?"

The porter, who had frozen in place, looked in from the hall. "Ms. Fielding." His face blanched. "What a pleasure to see you again." He looked terrified.

"Ms. Brooks needs a new bag immediately. Maybe two bags," she added, looking again at the pile. "Could you call up to the concierge and have it arranged? We'll need someone to take care of packing everything as well. You can have them put with the luggage from my room. The Empire suite, in case you'd forgotten."

Jeanie choked back a chuckle as the man nodded and scurried off, nearly tripping over his feet as he went. "Wow." Eleanor's commanding presence sent heat searing through Jeanie's loins. "I love it when you do that. Seriously, if I didn't think you'd scared that poor man so badly that he'll be back in ten seconds with twice what you asked for, I would strip naked right here and now and let you have your way with me."

"Mm, tempting. But where?" Eleanor surveyed the room dubiously. "There's a bed that isn't big enough for one person, let alone two, and you've built a textile homage to Mount Everest that's taking up most of the floor. Looks like we'll have to save fooling around for the hotel room in Prague. Or maybe for the ride there?" She waggled her eyebrows suggestively. "Did I mention we're going by limousine? They always have those tinted windows between the passengers and the driver, plus the backseat is at least as big as that thing." Eleanor pointed to the bed.

Jeanie turned her head to look, giggling as Eleanor took advantage of the opportunity to nuzzle her lips against the newly exposed flesh of Jeanie's neck. "Why, Eleanor Fielding, I do believe you're serious!" Jeanie squirmed with delight, digging her fingers playfully into Eleanor's hair, encouraging her not to stop. "Have I really succeeded in corrupting you so completely in so little time?"

"What, are you shocked?" Eleanor kissed her way downward, following the plunging neckline of Jeanie's shirt.

"Not as much as I probably should be. More like impressed." Jeanie lowered her voice to a whisper. "I'm also really glad I decided not to put on any panties under this skirt." She burst out laughing as Eleanor's head shot up, her eyes wide with surprise. "What, you thought you were the only one to come up with that idea? What else do people *do* in a limousine for three hours?"

Eleanor studied Jeanie's skirt as if hoping to

develop x-ray vision that would confirm the presence of undergarments, or lack thereof. Eventually she gave up with a roll of her eyes. "Come along, my naughty vixen. Time to go."

"The car doesn't leave for another hour. I'm not even packed yet."

"You know how I hate to be late. I'm sure the driver would be fine with us waiting in the back until it's time to go." There was little doubt what Eleanor had in mind for passing the time.

"And if he doesn't like it, I'm sure you can convince him otherwise." A thrill ran through Jeanie at the prospect.

As Jeanie followed Eleanor into the hall, her cell phone vibrated to alert her to a new email. When she saw the subject, her pulse began to race. Though it had only been a few days, the time that had passed since her visit to the Kunsthistorisches felt like an eternity. Jeanie had been so caught up with Eleanor that she'd nearly forgotten the application she'd submitted for the museum education position. It had been a far-fetched dream and easy to write off. Her hands shook so wildly as she read the email from Dr. Birnbaum that it took her a second time through to fully understand that she'd been invited to interview with the museum's General Director in Vienna the following week.

"Jeanie, you coming?" Eleanor stood inside the elevator, holding the door open for her.

Jeanie picked up her pace. "Be right there!"

Jeanie's head spun as she tried to absorb what had just occurred. The life she'd always wanted might actually be within her grasp! A job in a museum and the chance to live abroad: it was everything she'd always wanted. But as she stepped into the elevator and caught Eleanor's eye, she felt the jolting realization that that wasn't the only thing she wanted anymore. She wanted Eleanor, not just for a few more days, but for something more. Her heart felt ready to burst from the emotions that overwhelmed her simply by looking at this woman, whose cheeks were still flushed from their stolen kisses in her room. *I think I'm falling in love with her!* She wanted the job, but she wanted Eleanor, too.

A cold lump settled in her gut as she realized that she had no idea how Eleanor felt in return. Beyond champing at the bit to devour each other in the backseat of their limo, Eleanor's desires were difficult to ascertain. True to their agreement, they hadn't talked about their future beyond this trip. Officially, everything between them remained no strings attached, and Eleanor had made no secret from the beginning that a relationship held little interest for her. How likely was it that rational, analytical Eleanor had changed her mind in a week?

There was no getting around it, this was a topic she and Eleanor would need to discuss, and soon. Would Eleanor even want to see her when they returned to New York? And if she did want to, would she change her mind if Jeanie moved far away? She didn't want to risk losing Eleanor, but she couldn't pass up a shot at fulfilling her dreams, either. Jeanie's usual confidence was replaced by doubt. *What if this opportunity ruins everything we've managed to build?*

IT WAS late in the day when the bellman arrived at the door with Eleanor's single compact suitcase and Jeanie's new set of matching bags in tow. Jeanie's economy ticket had entitled her to a budget room on the outskirts of town, but she'd been more than happy to pass it up in favor of staying with Eleanor in a five-star hotel. She would have slept anywhere as long is it meant a few more nights together. It was what would happen after that time was up that left Jeanie feeling so distressed.

Jeanie rummaged in her pocket at the sound of the bellman's knocking, and pulled out a crumpled five euro note, pressing it into Eleanor's hand. "Here, take this."

"What for?"

"The tip! Part of it, at least. I don't know what the going rate is at a place like this, but almost everything he's bringing up here is mine. The least I can do is cover the tip." The gesture was symbolic, considering the room cost per night what Jeanie made in a week, but it was a gesture that was important to her to make it, all the same.

"You're too much, you know that?" Eleanor gave her a quick peck on the lips. "Absolutely adorable."

While Eleanor went to deal with their bags, Jeanie stood at a window in their suite and took in the view. Their living room overlooked the Vltava river, offering an unobstructed view of the iconic Charles Bridge, as well as the fortified Prague Castle that sat high atop the opposite bank. The sun had sunk low behind the hills, turning both sky and water to shades of lavender and gray. Flood lights illuminated the castle walls, and the glow of lamplight from the many arches of the bridge reflected in the water below. It was a magical view, one of many she'd enjoyed on her trip, and the last she would share with Eleanor. That knowledge weighed heavily on her.

What am I going to do? Jeanie sighed. The drive from Germany to the Czech Republic had provided precious little time for reflection. Not that she was complaining, since the relative privacy of the limousine had given her and Eleanor plenty of time to make some excitingly sensual vacation memories. It just hadn't been conducive to a lot of deep thought or conversations about the future.

Jeanie hadn't booked her return flight to New York until two weeks after the end of the cruise. Her plan had been to use the time, with the help of a train pass and a list of backpacker hostels that catered to budget-conscious travelers, to check off several additional art museums from her wish list. It would be relatively easy to fit in a return trip to Vienna long enough for her interview. But if they offered her the job, what then? Could she take it and leave Eleanor behind?

If only she had more assurance that Eleanor returned her feelings. Jeanie thought she did, but she'd been wrong about things like that in the past. Jeanie couldn't ignore the fact that no matter how promisingly they began, almost every relationship she'd been in had devolved rapidly from passionate romance to just good friends. Her connection to Eleanor felt different, more vibrant and real than any she'd had before, but the possibility existed that if she passed up Vienna to pursue a relationship with Eleanor, the heat between them could fizzle before the first fall frost.

She smoothed the worried lines from her face as Eleanor reentered the room, flashing a smile more cheery than she felt. "Everything set?"

Eleanor nodded. "I had him put the bags in our bedroom. It's getting dark, so we can't do much more tonight than find a place for dinner, but tomorrow's wide open. What would you like to do?"

"You mean you haven't already picked out half a dozen walking tours for us?" Jeanie teased.

"Strangely enough, no. After yesterday's urban exploration, I think I'm starting to appreciate your more spontaneous approach to sightseeing."

"Yeah, I know *exactly* what part you appreciated

most about that. Well, as it happens, I do have something in mind that we could do. But don't get too excited. It's most definitely *not* a clothing optional kind of a place."

Eleanor pretended to pout. "In that case, I'm not sure if I want to go."

"You'll want to go, I think. We're just a few blocks from Prague's old Jewish quarter. There's a synagogue there that's the oldest in Europe, and it's open for tours."

"And how do you know about a synagogue in Prague?"

"Well, I *am* a history teacher." Jeanie donned her most serious, superior look.

"I'm impressed!"

Jeanie giggled, unable to keep up the pretense. "Your sister told me."

"My sister? How have you been talking to my sister?" It was hard to tell if Eleanor was upset, or just caught off guard.

"I sent her that picture yesterday from my phone of the two of us, remember? So she responded with a friend request. I mean, I couldn't exactly turn her down."

"I suppose not." Eleanor rolled her eyes skyward and shook her head. "That's Miriam. Heaven forbid I have a girlfriend she isn't friends with."

Jeanie felt a thrill at the word girlfriend. Now *that* was a serious word. Her heartbeat quickened. If

Eleanor thought of her as her girlfriend, then she definitely intended for them to keep seeing each other. Suddenly, Jeanie's imagination was flooded with images of them strolling arm in arm through the streets of New York, which rapidly morphed into Vienna. Jeanie would work at the museum, and Eleanor would take the job her client had offered. They could find an apartment together, and spend the evenings dancing to the folk music that seemed to play in every plaza.

The more she thought about these daydreams, the more real they started to feel. They occupied her thoughts the rest of the night, and into the next day. As they walked the few blocks from the hotel to the Old New Synagogue, Jeanie's brain continued to whir, searching for an opportune time to bring the subject up. She'd convinced herself so thoroughly that her plan could work that her doubts had all been chased away. All she needed was a chance to present Eleanor with the plan in a way that she would understand.

"You're awfully quiet." Eleanor nudged Jeanie's shoulder with her own. Their skin didn't touch—they'd both worn shirts with sleeves in consideration of the sacredness of their destination—but Jeanie felt the same jolt of physical awareness as if they had.

"Sorry. Just thinking." *Just thinking how to ask you to drop your whole life and move to Vienna with me in a way that sounds rational and not at all impulsive.*

"No need to apologize. I like the quiet sometimes.

Although with you, I should probably worry that you're plotting something."

Jeanie laughed nervously. "Me? No, I wouldn't—oh, look! There's the synagogue." She breathed a sigh of relief at the excuse to change the subject.

They purchased tickets and were met inside by a female tour guide, who led them around the inside. Jeanie looked around curiously as they went, it being her first visit to a synagogue. "The shape reminds me of a medieval church."

The tour guide nodded. "Very perceptive. When it was built in the thirteenth century, Jews were forbidden from being architects, so it was designed by Christians. They patterned after a monastery church, which was the only thing they knew."

"It's amazing it survived for so long," Eleanor said.

"It is," the tour guide answered. "Especially since so many were destroyed during the holocaust. But not ours, thanks to Rabbi Loew and his Golem!"

Jeanie frowned and looked to Eleanor for an explanation, but she looked just as confused.

"You've never heard of the Golem?" The guide asked in surprise. "It's a very old story. He was a creature that Rabbi Loew made from clay and brought to life to protect our community from anti-Semitic attacks."

"He didn't do such a great job, all things considered," Eleanor muttered.

"No, maybe not," the guide said in a quiet voice.

"But he may have saved the building, anyway. When Nazi soldiers came through destroying many of the city's other synagogues, they were afraid to touch this one. See, according to the story, the Golem rests up in our attic, ever since the good rabbi deactivated him and placed him there. The soldiers had heard the story, and they were terrified."

Jeanie's eyes grew wide at this piece of history she'd never heard. "Is he really in the attic?"

The guide smiled mysteriously. "No one knows. We don't go up there. In fact, the lower portion of the stairs were removed long ago so there's no way up. Come outside now, and I'll show you the gift shop, and then you can tour the cemetery on your own."

Jeanie looked at Eleanor with concern, thinking of her reaction at the memorial in Budapest just after they'd met. "Will that be okay? If you don't want to see it, we don't have to."

"It's alright. Those graves are much older, and the people in them died naturally."

"That's true," their guide confirmed. "The last burials were over two hundred years ago. We simply ran out of room. The graves are layered and the stones stacked so close they're almost on top of each other." They exited the synagogue and their guide pointed out the entrance to the cemetery. "Be sure to stop at Rabbi Loew's grave and leave a note."

"A note?" With her limited knowledge of the faith,

Jeanie wondered if this was a typical Jewish custom she was unaware of.

The guide smiled. "With your secret wish on it. If you leave him a note to say what you wish, sometimes the rabbi will answer it." After pointing them to a stand near the cemetery that sold postcards and souvenirs, the guide departed.

"Look, Elle!" Jeanie picked up a clay figure the size of an egg. "It's a Golem!"

"It's probably made in China."

Jeanie stuck out her tongue. "I like it. And the card attached to it guarantees it provides protection from evil."

"And since they wrote it down, it must be true."

"I don't care. I'm buying it." Jeanie handed over her money and took the figurine. "Do you have room in your pocket? My outfit doesn't have any, and I'm afraid he'll break if I put him in my bag."

"Did it occur to you to wonder how he'll protect you from harm if he can't protect himself from being crushed by a water bottle?" Eleanor ducked as Jeanie swatted playfully at her head. Laughing, she slid the tiny Golem into her pocket.

"Do you think it's true?"

"That your made-in-China Golem will protect you from evil? Probably not."

"Not that! I meant do you think the stories the guide told us are real?"

"Which parts? The clay creature? A dead rabbi who

grants wishes? Or just the whole religion thing in general?" Cynicism coated her words.

"Whatever you'd like to share, I guess." Jeanie looked curiously at Eleanor and waited.

"I don't know," she answered finally. "I've never been very religious. I did what was expected of me when I was a kid, but since then, I haven't thought about it much. I doubt there are Golems, and I don't believe much in wishes. The rest?" Eleanor shrugged, a look of uncertainty in her eyes. "I'm not sure. I hadn't been inside a synagogue in years, but it was unexpectedly nice. It felt peaceful."

"Well, I believe in wishes. And I think we should make one." She took Eleanor's hand and led her through the crowded maze of headstones in the direction their guide had pointed out. If she didn't want this day with Eleanor to be her last, she knew what wish she needed to make.

They found the large marker made of a pinkish stone, covered on every surface with tiny pebbles and slips of torn paper. "I assume the notes are wishes," Jeanie said, "but why the pebbles? In fact, all the stones have pebbles, but there aren't any flowers."

"Flowers die. Stones last forever. When you leave a pebble it stays there, and people who come by later know that someone visited, and that the person who died is still remembered."

Jeanie thought about the explanation for a

moment. "That's nice. I'd seen it in movies and always wondered. So, how do we do it?"

Eleanor regarded her quizzically. "Leave a stone? You just pick one up and put it down." She knelt as she spoke and scooped a pebble off the ground, then placed it on top of the rabbi's grave. She chuckled as Jeanie carefully mimicked her actions. "And that's it. It's not magic or anything."

"What about the wishes?"

"I doubt those are magic, either."

Jeanie rolled her eyes. "That's not what I meant. Do I just write it down and leave it here?"

Eleanor shrugged. "We're way outside my expertise here. I'm afraid you'll have to wing it."

Jeanie dug in the bag and produced the receipt from her purchase of the Golem, along with two pens. She tore the paper in half and offered one piece to Eleanor, who shook her head. "Oh, come on." She beamed as Eleanor took the paper and one of the pens. Turning her attention to her own wish, she began to write.

"What are you putting?"

Jeanie gave Eleanor a sidelong look. "I can't tell you!"

Eleanor's brow wrinkled. "Why not?"

"It's just the way it works. Everyone knows that." Jeanie continued to write. *Please let us be together.* It was a small piece of paper, and those were the only words she could fit. Jeanie wondered if it was enough. She wanted to go into every detail about meeting Eleanor, and the job in Vienna, and how she felt, but there was no room. The rest would have to remain implied. Hopefully the magical, wish-granting rabbi would understand.

Jeanie folded the paper. She wanted so badly for her wish to come true. All of it, the new job, the new life, but especially the part that she'd written. She wanted to be with Eleanor. The gravity of the moment weighed on her, causing her hands to tremble. Her fingers could barely hold the paper steady as she tucked it into a crack in the headstone.

She watched as Eleanor did the same, folding her note and slipping it into a crack on the other end of the stone. Jeanie held her breath, wondering if they'd wished for the same thing. Eleanor's hands remained steady and calm throughout, and Jeanie couldn't decide if that was a good sign, or bad. A scrap of white poked out from the rose-colored stone, and Jeanie stared. She'd give anything to know what it said.

TWENTY-FOUR

AS THEY WALKED in the direction of Charles Bridge, on their way across the river toward Prague Castle, curiosity gnawed a hole in Jeanie's belly. Finally, she couldn't stand it anymore. "Just tell me. I can't take it anymore!"

"What?" Eleanor looked confused by the non sequitur.

"Your wish! What did you write?"

"But you said we couldn't tell." Eleanor's calm voice drove Jeanie mad. "I thought that was supposed to be a rule, or something."

"I don't care about the rules," Jeanie whined.

"Oddly, that's what I like most about you."

"I want to know!" Jeanie was too wound up to notice the compliment.

Charles Bridge was just ahead, a wide footbridge made of stone and lined with statues. It was crowded in the late afternoon with tourists and people returning home from work, and Jeanie clasped Eleanor's hand tightly as they started into the crowd. Their bodies were jostled repeatedly as people passed by, and even Jeanie's usually calm nerves became raw with irritation. She could only imagine how sensitive Eleanor must be to it, and she glanced repeatedly in her direction to see if she was okay. Toward the middle of the bridge, Eleanor stopped walking and tugged Jeanie with her away from the center to a spot where there was no crowd.

"Elle, are you okay? Is it a panic attack?" Jeanie studied her face in alarm.

"No. I just can't talk with so many people bumping into me."

"Why do you need to talk?"

"Because you asked me what my wish was!"

Her stomach clenched. "And you're going to tell me?"

Eleanor nodded. "I was going to wait until tomorrow to talk about this, since that's what we'd agreed, but I think it's probably safe to do it now." She swallowed roughly, looking nervous. "Jeanie, I know we said no strings attached, but I can't imagine not seeing—"

Yes! Jeanie's heart was racing, the blood pulsing so loudly in her ears that she couldn't hear the rest of what Eleanor said. It didn't really matter, since she'd gotten the most important part already. *Eleanor wants to be with me!* Knowing that, anything seemed possible—the job, moving to Vienna, building a life together—all of her wishes might come true! Suddenly, Jeanie realized that Eleanor was staring at her, waiting for a response.

"I want you to move to Vienna with me!" She gasped and clasped her hand over her mouth, but it was too late. The words tumbled out in a rush before Jeanie could stop them. That wasn't what she'd meant to say. Not yet.

Eleanor's pale face looked whiter than usual, and she appeared to be in shock. "What did you say?"

Jeanie groaned. She'd gone about this in the worst possible way. "While we were in Vienna, I got a lead on a job. And I've just heard back this morning and—"

"You got a *job*? In *Vienna*?" Eleanor looked stricken. "Why didn't you mention it before?"

"I only just found out. And officially it's just an interview, but I think I have a shot at it. But Elle, I can't imagine not seeing you. I love… spending time with you." She'd nearly said *I love you*, but Eleanor had already had enough of a shock for one day and Jeanie decided to spare her further distress. "Working in a museum, living in Europe. It's what I've always wanted, but I was thinking…" *you could move there, too.* Her voice trailed off before she finished, too disheartened by the look on Eleanor's face to finish.

"Jeanie, I live in New York. So do you, which is why this thing we started might actually have any chance of going anywhere once we get home. I think it does, or I wouldn't have suggested giving it a try. But that doesn't change the fact that we just met."

"But, you said yourself that your client wants to hire you. And you've been trying to be more spontaneous, you just said so the other day. There's no reason not to give it a try, even just temporarily. Right?"

Eleanor's jaw dropped. "No reason? Jeanie, there are a million reasons: my job, my house, my sister. There's way too much risk!"

"You've said yourself that you were starting to see the benefit of risk."

"This isn't risk, Jeanie. It's recklessness!" Eleanor's breath quickened to short pants and she looked like she was struggling to maintain her focus. The crowd around them had once again grown thick. "Oh, God. I can't breathe. I've got to get off this thing!" Her eyes darted furtively around the bridge, then she slipped into an opening in the crowd and disappeared from Jeanie's view.

"Wait, Elle!"

Alone on the bridge, Jeanie shook as she stared at the spot where Eleanor had been. *What did I just do?* She'd been so close to having what she wanted, and she'd ruined it! She'd planned to break the news gently, explain it all slowly so Eleanor could see how exciting the opportunity could be. Instead, her inability to reign in her impulses may have cost her Eleanor for good.

JEANIE STRETCHED her hand across the bed, seeking the warmth of Eleanor's body. She came away empty. Disoriented, she bolted upright with heart pounding. She'd fallen asleep, fully dressed atop the covers, waiting for Eleanor to return. The sun had set and shadows shrouded the bedroom. The only light came from the streetlamps outside. Jeanie trudged into the living room to see if Eleanor was there, but the suite was empty.

With the snap of a switch the bedroom filled with light, and Jeanie cringed to see the pile of crumpled tissues that covered the bed. Her tablet was there, too, the black screen spotted from the shower of tears it had endured when she'd used it to call her mom. Hearing her mother's voice after several days had given her some joy, but apart from that, the conversation had yielded little comfort. Her mother had only confirmed what Jeanie knew: Her impulsiveness was destined to be her downfall. And it's not like words existed that could ease the pain of watching Eleanor walk away. She still hadn't returned, and Jeanie felt a prick of fear that she never would. She leaned her head against the window, looking at the bridge as fresh tears escaped and trickled down her cheeks.

A metallic click echoed in the silent room as the knob on the front door turned. *Elle!* Not bothering to stop to dab her wet face, Jeanie raced toward the door and flung her arms around Eleanor the moment she entered the room. Eleanor's frame, stiff at first, yielded to her touch as she covered her head with desperate kisses. As Eleanor's body softened against her, Jeanie's lips claimed her mouth, communicating with passion what words had failed to express. But as Jeanie's hands snaked beneath Eleanor's top, she pulled away.

"Jeanie, stop. Don't you think we need to talk about today?"

"Talking's what got me into trouble. I think I was having much better luck getting my point across just now. Elle, I was so worried. I didn't know what to think!"

Eleanor's shoulders slumped. "Jeanie, I'm sorry for running off. I was starting to panic in the crowd."

"I know. But when I couldn't find you and you didn't come back to the room, I guess I thought you'd had enough of me and left. I was afraid I wouldn't see you again." Jeanie's voice cracked as she remembered the darkness of the afternoon.

"I needed some time alone." Eleanor walked into the living room and sat down on the sofa, placing a pillow on her lap like a barrier. Taking it as a hint, Jeanie settled a safe distance away on the far end of the couch.

"Elle, I'm so sorry about this afternoon. I didn't

mean for any of that to come out the way it did. I was just excited."

"I know, and I love that about you. I love that you get excited, and that you're willing to dive headfirst after what you want, no matter what the risk. I'm not like that."

"But you could be!" Jeanie's eyes sparkled, pleading. "Look at the fun we had together at the German castle, once you set aside your anxiety and took a chance. Trust me, Elle, Vienna could be *such* an adventure."

"It's not who I am, Jeanie. It's not about trust, or learning to take chances, or not worrying so much over things. Fundamentally, I'm someone who needs to analyze and plan. And you're someone who needs to leap first and ask questions later."

Tears welled in Jeanie's eyes, turning Eleanor into a soft blur. "I don't have to. Just tell me what I need to do. Give me directions. You know I love it when you take charge." Though Eleanor smiled at her words, somehow it made her face look even more sad, and Jeanie felt her heart begin to break. "Please, Elle. I'll analyze and plan, day and night, if that's what you need me to do."

Eleanor sighed, her own eyes filling with tears. "I don't want you to change. I love you exactly the way you are, impulsive and daring. It's thrilling to me to know that someone like you exists. Someone who makes wishes and follows dreams."

Slowly, Jeanie let out the breath that she's been holding since the moment that those three important words had left Eleanor's lips. "Did you just say that you love me?"

Eleanor frowned, clearly thrown off by the question. "Of course I love you."

Jeanie grinned. "But, I love you too! Isn't that all we really need?"

"No." The quiet certainty of Eleanor's response dealt the final blow, shattering Jeanie's heart to bits. "I have a job to get back to in New York. You have a job to start in Vienna."

"Just an interview," Jeanie corrected. "It's not a sure thing. There's every chance that when the new semester starts, I'll be back in Poughkeepsie. And if I am, would you give me a chance then?"

Eleanor massaged her temples, her interior struggle evident on her face. "I can't make that promise, Jeanie. I just can't. If I say yes, then how do I know you won't pass up the job on impulse to be with me?"

"How can I spontaneously pass up a job I applied for on impulse?"

"Knowing you, you'd find a way." She put up her hand as Jeanie opened her mouth to argue. "Please, can we talk about this in the morning? I'm too tired to think."

Jeanie choked back her words in frustration, but as she studied Eleanor's face, she could feel the fatigue.

"Let's go to bed." She held out her hand, but Eleanor shook her head.

"You go ahead. I'll sleep here. If I follow you in there, either one of us might agree to anything by the end of the night. This is too important to settle with sex. We'll talk more in the morning."

Jeanie retreated to the bedroom in dismay. Eleanor claimed they would talk about it more, but Jeanie knew her mind was already made up. There was no chance for them now. Whether she took the job in Vienna or not, the result would be the same. They might agree in the morning to still be friends, but Jeanie knew that Eleanor was stubborn. Once they renegotiated the terms of their relationship to the status of friends-only, there would be no going back again.

The certainty of this outcome set Jeanie tossing and turning until dawn. She dreaded the finality that morning would bring. She could see it all as if it had already happened. Her final attempt at persuasion, which Eleanor would rebuff. Agreeing to remain friends. Knowing it would be impossible. An awkward goodbye kiss, or worse yet, a cordial handshake. She couldn't do it. Jeanie tossed off the covers and threw on her clothes. If she wasn't there when morning came, she wouldn't have to live through the experience of watching the one thing she'd wished for slip away.

Jeanie grabbed her two new suitcases, the ones Eleanor had bought for her to replace her broken bag, and rolled them behind her to the door. Their smaller size made them easy to handle, with sturdy wheels that allowed them to glide effortlessly along. Jeanie offered a prayer of thanks that Eleanor continued to sleep even as her quiet new bags rolled past. Her heart was as shredded as her old, discarded bag, but she'd managed to leave with some small measure of her dignity intact. That was a generous gift.

TWENTY-FIVE

IT WAS WELL after six on a Friday evening at the end of September, but Eleanor remained at her desk, her office light the only one still burning on her department's floor. There was no reason for her to be there. All the pressing work for the week was done and the nearest deadlines were distant on the horizon. She certainly wasn't there for her own enjoyment. In the two months since she'd returned home from the cruise, she'd finally come to realize what people had been hinting at for years. Her job was painfully dull. It served a vital business function and earned her an impressive yearly salary, but that was all.

Yet I chose it over her. In some alternate universe, Eleanor would have left the office hours ago to meet Jeanie at Penn Station. They might have gone from there to a club, or back to Eleanor's apartment with a bag of Chinese take-out. She would have gotten more satisfaction out of a few hours with Jeanie than a week at work. Or they could have moved together to Vienna, where, in addition to being with Jeanie, Eleanor could have taken on a leadership role with a promising new company. Instead, she'd stuck with a job where she no longer felt challenged, and where the opportunity to be promoted to a role she'd find more fulfilling was decades away. She'd been too afraid to take a risk, and now she was paying the price in every possible way.

With a heavy heart, Eleanor switched off her computer and gathered her things. She was just preparing to walk out the door when her phone buzzed with a text from Miriam. Eleanor's breath caught when she saw it. Miriam had used their code word. A million terrible possibilities presented themselves to her brain for inspection. *Don't let it be the baby!*

Of all the awful choices, that one scared her the most. Miriam had broken the news of her pregnancy almost as soon as Eleanor had arrived home from Prague. The prospect of being an auntie was one of the few things that had gotten her through the worst of her heartbreak over Jeanie. Miriam had just finished her first trimester, by far the riskiest time in a pregnancy, but it didn't mean she was in the clear. Eleanor held her breath as she waited for her sister to pick up the phone.

"Mimi! What's the matter? What's wrong?" she demanded breathlessly as soon as she heard her sister's voice.

"Elle?" Miriam's voice became muffled, as if she held a hand over the phone. "Mark! Never mind about calling the police. False alarm!"

"The police?" Eleanor's heart raced. "Mimi, what's going on?"

"Funny, that's what I was hoping you would tell me. I've left you three messages this week, Elle. Three! I told Mark if you didn't get back to me within fifteen minutes of my text, I wanted him to call the police and report a missing person."

Eleanor thought back to the messages she had ignored and felt a stab of guilt at how she'd repeatedly pushed them aside. "I'm sorry, Mimi. I should have called sooner. But you're sure everything's okay with you, Mark, and the baby?"

"Okay is a relative term. We're fine, but Mark's mother is driving me up a wall with all this baby stuff. I had lunch with her a few weeks ago and she made the server take the lunch meat off my sandwich and microwave it because she'd read somewhere it could be bad for the baby."

Eleanor had read a similar article recently and couldn't see the harm in being cautious. "Well..."

"Don't you dare! That was completely beyond normal risk management, Elle. You've gotta save me from her."

"Save you? What, do you want me to pull together a pregnancy risk analysis for her?"

"God, no! She'd find a way to use it against me. I'd never be allowed to leave my house. No, what I need is for you to run interference for me on Rosh Hashanah. We've been invited to their house to celebrate, and I need you to come, too."

"You want me to go all the way to the Upper West Side on Sunday to protect you from your mother-in-law?" She could only assume this was her sister's pregnancy hormones talking.

"And stay overnight. If you don't mind. They have an extra room."

"Fine, you win. If it's really that important to you." Her first instinct had been to say no, but a visit with Miriam would be nice, and it's not like she had anything better to do.

"Really? You're serious? You haven't accepted a single holiday invitation from me, or mom, in years! You'll really come?"

"Yes, I said I'd come, didn't I? What time's dinner?"

"Well, services start at six o'clock, so if you could get here by four."

Eleanor cringed at the mention of services. That's where she drew the line. "Hold on, Mimi. You're on your own for that. I'll come for dinner and even stay over, but that's it."

"But Elle, that's when I need you most! The only thing worse than Mark's mother is his mother plus all of her old lady friends. They'll eat me alive!"

"Even if I were inclined to go, which I'm not, it's only two days away. You know it's all reserved seating for the High Holidays. There's no way I could get a ticket at this point."

"You can have mom's. She and dad are still members. Even though they're in Florida now she hated to give it up."

Eleanor groaned. "You and mom are in on this together, aren't you." There was no doubt in her mind. For all she knew, her mother had convinced Mark's mother to drive Miriam crazy as part of the plot.

"You shouldn't be alone for the holidays, Elle. Not the way you've been feeling since you got home from Prague."

The concern in her sister's voice touched her, and for a moment when she closed her eyes, she could feel the peacefulness inside her that she'd experienced on her visit to the Old-New Synagogue. It was the first time she's been inside a synagogue in years, and the last place she'd truly felt happy. Before her panic attack on Charles Bridge, and arguing with Jeanie, then waking to find she'd disappeared in the night. *Before all the joy was sucked out my existence*. Recapturing some of that peace might not be the worst thing.

"You're shameless meddlers, both of you. I'll see you at four." She chuckled as her sister's delighted squeal reverberated in her ear. "You might as well hang up now and call mom so she knows the plan worked. Tell her I love her, while you're at it."

As Eleanor slid her phone into her purse, her fingers brushed across a rough lump of hardened clay. *Jeanie's Golem*. By now it had become as familiar an item in her bag as her wallet or keys. She'd taken it for safekeeping on their last walk together, and she'd never had the chance to give it back. It went with her everywhere. Given how things had played out, she held the tiny statue's protective abilities in serious doubt, but she carried it with her just the same. After over two months without contact, it was her only tangible link to Jeanie and the life that she wished could have been.

THE SUN WAS SETTING on a Friday evening in late September as Jeanie sat at the kitchen table in her apartment and graded the quizzes from that afternoon's freshman history class. The scores were abysmal. If she hadn't already decided it would be her last year teaching before the semester began, this probably would have pushed her to quit. It's not that her students were a bad bunch, but teaching had never been her first choice, and any remaining passion she'd had for it had withered away in the weeks since she'd returned home.

Perhaps the biggest surprise was that she was back in New York at all. On the morning she'd departed Prague, and left what remained of her heart in that hotel room overlooking Charles Bridge, she'd been certain her future was in Vienna. As it turned out, even though Eleanor had rejected her, the woman's analytical personality had influenced Jeanie in ways she'd never guessed. That was why, instead of accepting it on the spot when the job in Vienna had been offered to her, she'd surprised herself by insisting on taking time to think it over. And then, as if channeling Eleanor's essence, she'd gone a step further and conducted her own research.

Once she'd returned to the States, she'd taken the train to meet with one of her former professors at City University in New York. She'd doubted that he would even remember her after ten years, but that had been far from the case. He'd recalled with great enthusiasm the preliminary work she'd done on her thesis, and she was shocked to discover that if she wished to return, since it had been just under ten years since she'd left, the department would welcome her back to complete her degree. With her graduate degree and her classroom teaching experience, her professor had been confident that half a dozen opportunities would arise that were even better than what Vienna had to offer.

If only I'd realized that in July, things might have been so different. The thought made her insides ache. She closed her eyes, but all she could see was Eleanor standing on the bridge in Prague, just a fraction of a second before Jeanie blurted out her half-baked idea about Vienna and kicked off the downward spiral toward their end. If only she'd kept quiet and thought things through!

There'd been at least a thousand times since returning home that Jeanie had nearly picked up the phone and called, but each time she'd hesitated. Just the idea of it now made Jeanie's stomach tighten in a way that gave her some small insight into how Eleanor felt when her anxiety started to take hold. She couldn't do it, couldn't bring herself to take the risk. Now that she'd started thinking about the risks and consequences, she was too afraid to make the move and have to live through the pain of Eleanor rejecting her again.

There was a knock at the door and, pushing her grading aside, Jeanie rose and looked out the window above the kitchen sink. She smiled when she saw her mother standing outside, Since her return home, her mother had been a constant source of companionship and strength. As she opened the door, she smiled wider. She knew her mother worried about her melancholy moods, and she didn't want her to be concerned.

"Hi, baby girl," her mother said, greeting her with an energetic squeeze. "You ready for a three-day weekend?"

"Sure." Like many districts in the state, Jeanie's school would be closed on Monday for Rosh Hashanah. She'd given little thought as to how she would spend the time. She wondered if Eleanor would be celebrating with family, and sighed heavily, despite her resolve not to worry her mother.

"Jeanie, you need to get out of the house more. All you do is work and study for those art classes of yours." Her mother clicked her tongue, disapproving.

"It's art history, Mama." Jeanie spoke in measured tones, explaining once more what she'd explained before. "And I told you, if I finally finish my degree, I'll have a real shot at doing what I've always wanted to do. The offer I got in Vienna should be enough to convince you that I'm not wasting my time."

"Well, I still think you need to get out, which is why I brought you this."

"What's this?" Jeanie frowned at the sheet of colored paper her mother had handed her, printed with pictures of dancing couples.

"A big swing dancing festival in Central Park on Monday. One of the organizers came by to see if they could post this in the window at the store, so I asked for an extra one for you."

"Thanks, Mama. But I'm not sure if I'll have the time."

"Just think about it. You never know, maybe you'll meet someone there." Her mother enveloped her in another bear hug and then went on her way.

Jeanie studied the poster, biting her lip. Perhaps her mom was right. Not about meeting someone new, as Jeanie felt certain she wouldn't be ready for that again for quite some time. But she had been cooped up inside for far too long with grading and studying. Resolved not to make one of her typical knee-jerk decisions without gathering more information first, she sat down at her computer and pulled up the social media page for the swing dancing festival. It looked promising, so she even went so far as to add the event to her calendar and set a reminder, in case she felt up to it when the day came.

TWENTY-SIX

AFTER A RAUCOUS DINNER with Miriam's in-laws and at least a dozen invited guests crowded around the table, Eleanor sought out the privacy of the tiny study that was set up as a guest room for the night. Her whole body buzzed from the evening's steady onslaught of over stimulation. Attending services had turned out to be more pleasant than she'd anticipated, but at least three elderly women who remembered her as a teenager had honest-to-God pinched her cheeks when they saw her. Eleanor hadn't realized that could happen when you were thirty-eight years old.

Then had come the pressure of socializing at dinner, with the added concern of steering Mark's mother's conversation away from Miriam's pregnancy when her interest threatened to become too intense. Eleanor found it all exhausting, a reminder of why she was better off on her own. She stretched out on the couch that had been prepared and had been made up with blankets and pillows, and shut her eyes. The only thing she could see against her closed lids was Jeanie. She felt a tear roll down her cheek. There was a fine line between alone and lonely.

"Elle, are you okay?"

Eleanor sat up and tried to wipe her eyes, but it was too late. She'd been caught. "Mimi. I didn't know you were there."

Her sister shot her a sardonic look. "Clearly." Miriam sat down beside Eleanor and draped her arm around her shoulder. "You can't go on like this, Elle. It's been over two months."

Eleanor nodded. "But what am I supposed to do?"

"You could call her."

The suggestion filled her with dread. "I can't. Not after the way things ended between us. She was so eager to get away from me that she didn't even stick around to talk it through."

"You keep saying that, Elle, but it doesn't make sense to me. Are you positive that's why she left the way she did? Tell me exactly what happened that day."

Eleanor shut her eyes, the last day in Prague vivid in her mind. "We were on the bridge and it was so crowded. Jeanie told me she'd gotten a job offer in Vienna. I was upset, and then the crowd felt like it was pressing in on me and I had to get away. I wandered the city for hours, trying to calm down. Then I came back to the room," Eleanor swallowed roughly, remembering how Jeanie had run to her and kissed her so passionately. It had been their last kiss. "I said we'd talk about it more in the morning, but when I woke up on the couch the next day, she was gone. I think my anxiety finally just got to be too much for her, like usual. If I hadn't panicked and bolted the way I did, maybe she wouldn't have left."

"Your anxiety, huh? You stayed out late, and then you slept on the couch?" She ticked them off on her fingers as she went. "I bet you said something like 'we need to talk,' too, didn't you?"

Eleanor bristled. "We did need to talk."

"You really don't have the first clue about women sometimes, Elle."

Eleanor rolled her eyes. "I am a woman, Mimi."

"Which is why it's so puzzling when you fail to see the obvious." Miriam paused until Eleanor was paying complete attention. "Did it ever occur to you that Jeanie thought you were breaking up with her? That maybe she left to avoid being crushed by the inevitable 'we can still be friends' talk?"

Eleanor's brow wrinkled. "I don't think that was it."

Miriam gave her the look reserved for adorable children who are not very bright. "You should call her."

Eleanor shook her head vehemently. "It's too late for that now."

"Fine, Elle." Her scolding tone warned that Miriam's patience was running thin. "If it's really too late, then you need to get over it. Start fresh. If you're not willing to try to fix this, then I'm not going to let you wallow in misery forever."

"I'd really like to know how you propose I get this fresh start."

"I thought you'd never ask!" Miriam grinned. "Remember when we were kids and we'd walk to the river on Rosh Hashanah and throw breadcrumbs into the water?"

Eleanor nodded, a vague recollection in her head, though why it was important she couldn't begin to guess. "I'm not sure what feeding the birds has to do with anything."

"Feeding the—is that what you thought we were doing?" Miriam cocked her head and stared at her sister in bewilderment. "What kind of Jew are you?"

"I don't know, but I have a feeling you're going to tell me."

"First of all, what you thought was feeding birds is called tashlikh. It's a ritual of sorts, for wiping the slate clean in the new year. The breadcrumbs are all your sins and regrets, and the water carries them away." She shook her head. "Feeding the birds. Jesus, Elle."

"What?" She felt her cheeks burn with embarrassment. "All I remember is we used to walk to the Hudson River with the Abramsons who, you may or may not recall, had a daughter named Becky who was a cheerleader. It's possible I wasn't paying close attention to any of the other details."

"Fair excuse, I guess. The point is, that's what we're going to do tomorrow, you and me."

Eleanor sighed. "It's a nice symbol, Mimi, but I'm not sure it will help."

Her sister reached out and patted her hand. "It can't hurt. Now get some sleep. We'll go tomorrow after breakfast."

MIRIAM STOOD on the sidewalk outside her in-laws' building, holding a bag of stale bread and bouncing impatiently on the balls of her feet as Eleanor came down the stairs. Eleanor cradled a hot coffee in one hand as she held the iron railing with the other. "Sorry it took me so long. I was waiting for the coffee to brew."

Miriam groaned. "Don't talk to me about coffee! Mark's mother wouldn't even let me have a cup of decaf this morning, just in case one stray molecule of caffeine irreparably damages her grandchild." She started walking east, toward Central Park, and Eleanor followed, a confused frown tugging on her lips.

"Um, Mimi? I'm pretty sure giving up coffee has damaged your brain. The river's the other direction."

"I know that," Miriam said with a laugh. "I thought we'd go along the Loch Path instead. Riverside Park gets so crowded."

"Whichever you prefer," Eleanor replied. She'd

never noticed much difference between the two locations. It was New York. Every place was crowded. "Far be it from me to argue with a pregnant lady suffering from caffeine withdrawal."

They'd reached the edge of the park when Miriam suddenly stopped and slapped a hand to her head in almost comic exaggeration. "I left my phone back at the house." She shoved the bag of bread into Eleanor's free hand. "Here take this and head toward the path. I'm just going to run back for it."

"Seriously? Do you really want to walk all that way just for that? I have mine." It was obvious to Eleanor that growing a baby had caused Miriam to go completely loopy in the head.

"I'd feel better having it with me." Miriam wagged her finger at Eleanor. "Don't argue with the pregnant lady, remember? Go find a nice spot at the stream, maybe by one of the waterfalls, and I'll meet you there." She started back toward the crosswalk, then turned with a final thought. "Oh, Elle? Take a picture and text it to me so I know which one you're at, okay?"

Eleanor shook her head with a laugh, thankful that she was unlikely to ever experience this type of hormonal craziness on top of her pre-existing quirks. "Whatever you say. I've promised not to argue."

She entered the park and walked along the path to the first waterfall, but it was surrounded by a group of tourists taking selfies. Eleanor rolled her eyes. Miriam's insistence that this location would be less crowded didn't seem to have much basis in fact. She continued on to the next cascade and was pleasantly surprised to find the rustic wooden footbridge above the falls deserted. Perhaps Miriam's choice had been loosely grounded in reality after all. Eleanor grabbed her camera and clicked a picture, dutifully sending it to her sister, before settling herself on one of the large boulders along the stream to wait.

The minutes ticked by as Eleanor listened to the gurgling of the water as it splashed against the rocks on its journey to the shimmering pool below. A light breeze rustled the tree leaves, whose edges were tinged with the golden hues of early autumn. This, along with the coolness of the air, made it clear that summer was over. Eleanor opened the plastic bag and broke off a bit of the round loaf of challah bread left over from dinner the night before. She closed her eyes and saw Jeanie's face, the same as she did every time she closed her eyes. Time to let go of the past and make a fresh start. She lobbed the chunk of bread into the water and watched it slip over the edge of the cascade.

"That doesn't seem fair to the birds," said a voice coming from behind her. A sudden shot of adrenalin sent Eleanor's pulse racing. *I know that voice.* "If you're going to feed the birds," the voice continued, "shouldn't you throw the crumbs into the pool so they don't have to brave the waterfall for them?"

Eleanor spun around and stared, slack-jawed, at the

vision of Jeanie Louise Brooks, in a vintage navy blue and white polka-dot dress and fire-engine-red lipstick, leaning against the log railing of the footbridge. "Jeanie?"

"Hi, Elle." She picked her way cautiously along the uneven path, tottering in a pair of pumps that matched her handbag like something out of a 1940s' magazine ad.

"Just out for a nature stroll?" Eleanor couldn't help but laugh, an action that greatly helped to dispel the anxiousness in her belly that had begun its slithering the moment she'd realized that Jeanie stood just a few feet away.

"I'm on my way to a swing dancing festival at Bethesda Fountain." Jeanie smoothed her dress around her legs as she sat beside Eleanor on the boulder. Eleanor attempted not to stare as she did so, and failed miserably.

"Bethesda Fountain's on the other end of the park. You're in the wrong place."

"Am I?" It sounded like a challenge. Eleanor's heart thudded so loudly in her ears that she was certain Jeanie could hear it, too.

"Jeanie, what are you doing here? I assumed you'd be in Vienna by now." Eleanor tried not to wince at the hurt that showed through in her words. She attempted a softer tone. "I'm sorry, did you not get the job?"

"Funny thing about that. They actually did offer me the job, but I turned it down." She laughed as

Eleanor's eyebrows shot up. "It surprised me, too. But I kept hearing this voice in my head telling me I shouldn't rush into anything before weighing all the consequences and thinking it through."

"Did it sound like a nagging Jewish woman from New York?" Eleanor looked at her sheepishly.

"Uncannily so. Only maybe less nagging and more sultry." Jeanie grinned impishly as Eleanor's cheeks blushed scarlet. "Anyway, when I really thought about it, I realized I had better options here in New York." Their eyes locked and Eleanor shivered delightfully at this revelation, then Jeanie looked away. "Job options, that is," she clarified, looking disconcerted.

Eleanor studied Jeanie's face in wonder, still not completely believing that she was here. "And then our paths just happened to cross in Central Park."

"Our paths never just happen to cross. Didn't we figure that out before? As an analytical genius, you must know that running into each other here would be like finding a needle in a haystack." She paused a moment as if waiting for a response, but Eleanor just frowned, stumped. "Your sister saw that I had added an event in Central Park for today to my calendar. She sent me a message last night and told me where you would be if I wanted to see you. She even sent me a picture a few minutes ago so I wouldn't get lost."

Eleanor thought of the photo she'd been ordered to take and groaned. "Miriam never could resist meddling." Far from having her addled wits, it appeared her sister had transformed into a matchmaking mastermind. "I guess now I know why she insists on staying friends with all my exes." A sharp stab of regret struck her at the word choice, and she thought she saw a corresponding flash of pain on Jeanie's face. She squirmed at the sudden awkwardness. "What time does that festival start? I don't want you to be late on my account."

"Soon. But being on time's more your thing."

"Still." She realized too late that her shift in the topic of conversation made it sound like she was eager for Jeanie to leave. Panic grew within her at the prospect of watching Jeanie walk away. "Why don't I walk with you?" She offered, holding out a hand to help Jeanie back to the path before she had a chance to argue.

As they headed along the path, Eleanor reached inside her purse to stow the leftover breadcrumbs. As she did, her fingers brushed against a familiar, rough clay surface. On impulse, she pulled out the little statue and held it out to Jeanie. "You left this in Prague."

"The Golem! I can't believe you still have this." Jeanie took the figurine, a questioning look in her eyes.

"You left before I had the chance to give it back." She blinked rapidly, determined to keep back the tears. "I've had it with me ever since."

Jeanie stared fixedly at the ground, as if gathering

courage to speak. "I should have at least stayed to hear you out, even when I knew I wouldn't like what I was going to hear. That was wrong of me."

"You mean you didn't leave because my panic attacks started up again?"

"Of course not! I left because I couldn't face hearing you say that you'd rather stick with our original arrangement of a holiday fling."

"Damn. My sister was right! I truly think this baby of hers is giving her some sort of relationship superpowers."

"I don't understand."

"Jeanie, I'm not sure exactly what I would have said in the morning if you'd still been in that hotel room when I woke up, but it wouldn't have been that. What we had was never just a fling." Eleanor could see a crowd gathered at Bethesda Fountain several yards ahead. As she searched Jeanie's face for the answer, big band music started to play. They were running out of time, but the thought of saying good bye again broke Eleanor's heart.

Jeanie looked out across the crowd, where couples had started pairing off to dance. Her body swayed unconsciously to the rhythm, like a woman who was born to dance. "Elle, I was wondering something."

Eleanor's breath caught in her throat. Is she going to ask me to dance? She wasn't certain that she could.

"I know I'm impulsive. And we couldn't be more different. And you're probably not the slightest bit interested anymore, but just in case," Jeanie's voice had grown increasingly shaky. "I just thought that maybe..."

Eleanor felt her own body tremble like one of the leaves falling from the trees around them as she realized that Jeanie wasn't asking for a dance, but a second chance. "We need to talk. And I don't mean that as the standard relationship brush-off, if that's what you were thinking. We both seem to have a lot of feelings, and I'm not always good with those. I think it would help to try to put them into words, but I don't think I'm ready to do that just yet." With enough time in a quiet place, just maybe they could get this right. Eleanor needed to prepare. She couldn't afford to mess it it up, and she prayed that Jeanie understood. "So, can we talk over dinner tonight?"

"That sounds both promising and daunting." Jeanie's eyes crinkled as she considered the offer. "Will there be wine?"

"Without a doubt."

"Then yes, I'll have dinner with you. Even though you know I'm impatient and the wait might kill me. If you need to take your time, I understand."

As Jeanie said the words, Eleanor realized just how true they were. This woman understood her in a way that no one had before, maybe better than she understood herself. It was clear how desperately Jeanie wanted to put everything out in the open immediately in her usual haphazard way, but she was sincere in her willingness to wait, if that's what Eleanor needed from her. It's what made Jeanie unlike anyone she'd ever known.

The realization of how much she loved this woman struck Eleanor like lightning from a clear blue sky. She'd thought she'd been in love before, but she'd been wrong. She'd thought if she could analyze and quantify her feelings that she could understand them, but her relationship with Jeanie defied logic. How they fit together so perfectly when they were opposites in every way was an anomaly, a mystery that she might never fully comprehend. She was shocked to realize that she wouldn't want it any other way.

"So, you're really sure we can't talk about it now?" Jeanie offered a hopeful smile.

Accommodating as she was to Eleanor's needs, sometimes it was too easy to forget that Jeanie had needs of her own. If there was one way that she'd failed in the past, Eleanor knew that this was it. To be a worthy partner, there were things she'd need to learn to be better at, and things she'd need to be willing to do. One such thing was staring her in the face at this moment. Screwing up her courage, Eleanor vowed that she wouldn't let the opportunity slip away.

"Positive. Because right now, I'd rather dance with you."

Eleanor folded her arms around Jeanie as they melted into one another, erasing the distance of the past ten weeks. When at last they were able to pull themselves apart enough to move, Eleanor took Jeanie's hand and led her into the throng of dancers. Their bodies swirled in time to the music against the backdrop of the New York City skyline, thousands of miles from where their adventure had started, and exactly where they belonged.

A MESSAGE FROM MIRANDA

Dear Reader,

 I love to travel, but like so many people, I just can't find the time or money to go everywhere I'd like to go. That's why I started the Americans Abroad series, stand alone novels where American women find love abroad in the most humorous and unexpected of ways. And we get to go along for the ride—no passport required!

 Waltzing on the Danube is the first book of the series. I hope you'll decide to read the rest for more wonderful couples and fantastic adventures that you can enjoy from the comfort of your favorite reading chair.

 Best Wishes,
Miranda

Printed in Great Britain
by Amazon